One
Last
Summer

ALSO BY VICTORIA CONNELLY

One Last Summer

VICTORIA CONNELLY

LAKE UNION
PUBLISHING

Published by Lake Union Publishing, Seattle

www.apub.com

Amazon, the Amazon logo, and Lake Union Publishing are trademarks of Amazon.com, Inc., or its affiliates.

ISBN-13: 9781542041744
ISBN-10: 1542041740

Cover design by bürosüd° München, www.buerosued.de

Printed in the United States of America

In memory of my much-loved friend Anne.
Your passion for life and your fearless spirit were an
inspiration to us all.

Prologue

The priory stood at the end of the peninsula like a great stone guardian watching over the land and sea, its thirteenth-century tower thrusting up into the blue sky. Built by the Benedictine monks and worshipped in for centuries, it had fallen under the reign of Henry VIII and had later become a farmhouse, a large Georgian wing being added to its west side as the rest of the building had been left to decay.

It wasn't until the mid-twentieth century, after another period of abandonment, that a successful businessman bought it, throwing all his wealth at its crumbling walls and collapsed fan vaulting and flying buttresses. For a while, it flourished. It was the kind of building that needed people in it and a little bit of chaos, perhaps, and the businessman gave it exactly what it wanted, filling it with an enormous family and hosting parties in its cavernous rooms.

It was on his death that it came into the hands of a trust which preserved old buildings and let them out as holiday rentals. And that's how Harriet Greenleaf found it. She'd been looking for something special for her holiday, something that would take her breath away and make her heart soar. She'd attended an open day to view it, wandering around its cool corridors, admiring how many arches there were and how their express purpose seemed to be to frame yet more arches.

She trod carefully up its spiral staircases, loving how very like the inner workings of a shell they were, and her hand flew out to touch each wonderful wooden door with its metal studs and wrought-iron handles.

The furniture in each of the rooms was substantial – traditional, no-nonsense pieces in dark English oak – and the curtains and cushions were pretty but not overly so. There were pictures on the walls – old-fashioned prints and portraits of people from the past in frilly collars and funny hats – and large mirrors reflected back the light from the enormous windows, filling the rooms with a silvery quality.

There was a long refectory table in the kitchen, flanked by two benches. It could easily sit a dozen people, Harrie thought. And, all around the priory, there were endless secret places to just sit: squashy sofas where one might curl up and read a book or wide windowsills to perch on and gaze out into the gardens.

Then there was the oldest part of the building, part cloister, part tower. How often did one get to live within such ancient walls? And how many people could boast sharing their holiday home with gargoyles?

The garden was stunning. The borders were full of late tulips and early roses and there were great terracotta pots full of flowering rosemary and chives. Through an old wooden gate, the garden opened into a little meadow yellow with buttercups, and beyond that was an orchard full of fruit trees and a stream whose borders were laced with cow parsley. There was even a modest-sized swimming pool in the south garden, its winter cover pulled back to reveal aquamarine depths.

Harrie sighed in wonder and delight, but worried, just for a moment, if she could justify spending so much money on hiring such a place. But she batted the thought away as soon as it entered her head. If not now, then when? The answer was never, she knew that.

No, she deserved this treat, she told herself. This was the very thing that made life worth living.

She found a bench to sit on in the orchard and marvelled at how enclosed the place felt, surrounded as it was by the trees. It was a world of its own, cut off from the outside. She liked that. The priory was a little piece of paradise. More than that – there was a special kind of quietness that seemed to seep out of the stones. This place, this very special place, was just what she needed. Of course, she'd known that the moment she'd seen the photo of it online and made the booking earlier that year, but walking through its ancient corridors and inhaling the scent of wisteria in the garden made her absolutely certain that this was the place she wanted to be for her very last holiday.

Chapter 1

Harrie could have sent an email. It would have been easier and instant. But how many people really give emails the attention they deserve, she asked herself? Today's inboxes were always so full, flooded with rubbish and with so many things sent to the spam folder. She couldn't risk her message getting lost and so she sent letters by recorded delivery – two handwritten letters to her two oldest and dearest friends, written in blue ink with her favourite fountain pen, which was shocked out of its retirement into gainful employment. And, oh, how very satisfying it was to see the letters forming on the creamy pages on her kitchen table, her thoughts forced to slow down so her pen could keep up.

She posted them on the second of January, during the post-Christmas slump when thoughts were longing to reach towards summer. Seven months' notice would be enough, wouldn't it? She hoped so. She wasn't sure what she'd do if they said no or made some excuse not to come because the last thing she wanted to do was bribe her friends into coming by telling them the truth. She wasn't ready to let them know the truth. Not yet. But, luckily, both Audrey and Lisa had said yes. Admittedly, Audrey had been reluctant to commit to the whole of the summer holidays but Harrie had been very persuasive, sending her pictures of the priory and reminding her that they hadn't had a proper girls' get-together in over six years. There'd been a few rushed dinners and weekend shopping trips, but it was a full six summers since their last girls' holiday to Lanzarote to celebrate the year of their fortieth birthdays. They'd hired that funny little place on the hillside, Harrie remembered, with the dodgy balcony and the lizard that freaked Lisa out every time she went in the bathroom.

Six years, she thought. Where had that time gone? Well, she'd divorced Charles for one thing. They'd met at her first teaching job. He was the head of the maths department and she'd told him that she'd always hated figures and he'd made some wisecrack about liking hers. He'd then looked mortified in case she reported him to the headmaster and she'd left him to dangle in his own discomfort for a moment before laughing. He'd insisted on buying her a drink and that drink had led to dinner and, less than two years later, a wedding and a baby girl called Honor. But, somehow, at some time, they had fallen out of love and had merely been co-habiting. When they'd both come to the realisation, there were no arguments, no recriminations – just a polite packing of boxes and a rather sad goodbye. They'd managed to remain friends too, which pleased Harrie because Honor was close to her father.

Her friend Lisa, on the other hand, never stayed friends with any of her exes. She'd fallen in and out of love during the past six years more times than Harrie could count. She and Audrey had long since stopped trying to remember the names of all Lisa's beaus.

Audrey was the steady one out of the three of them. She'd been married to Mike for nineteen years and had a wonderful son called Jack. Harrie still remembered all those years ago when Mike had made that phone call to say that Audrey had gone into labour, and she and Lisa had rushed across the country to welcome Audrey's son into the world. What a moment that had been. Audrey had a good strong marriage, although Harrie knew that her friend regularly tested her husband's patience. Mike was always worrying about her, especially since she'd started up her own small school teaching English to foreign students. Audrey simply overdid things, she always had, and Mike was the one who carried the burden of constant anxiety.

But, perhaps the biggest thing to happen during those six years was Harrie's diagnosis. D-Day, she called it, and now her life seemed to be divided between everything that had happened before D-Day and everything that had happened after.

As she drove her car down the single-track Somerset road that led to Melbury Priory, she thought back to that awful day four years ago, blinking back the tears as she remembered the look on her daughter's face. It was the word that paralysed everyone with fear, wasn't it? Cancer.

At first, it was a small lump. She hadn't told anyone at that stage. But, when a double mastectomy was advised, she'd had no choice but to tell Honor. Chemotherapy and months of feeling as if she'd come to the very end of her days followed. But then there'd been a blissful period of remission. She'd been able to go back to work, to rejoin her dance class, and do all the normal things that made her the person she was, and she felt good, *really* good. She'd beaten it, hadn't she? She'd changed her diet and exercised, she'd stopped drinking alcohol and had bidden adieu to processed foods and sugar. She'd even eaten spirulina, for heaven's sake. If anyone deserved to survive, it was Harrie.

But, last October, it had returned and, this time, they couldn't operate. Time was suddenly running out. She'd been told that in no uncertain terms. She'd looked into alternative treatments, but there was nothing that could touch what she had and she'd made her peace with that.

'And I'm here now,' she said out loud as she caught that first beautiful glimpse of the priory from across the green fields. She wasn't going anywhere. Not until after the summer. That had been given to her as a wonderful gift and she was determined to enjoy every single minute of it with the women she loved best in the world.

Perhaps the hardest thing for Harrie had been telling her mother. Her father had left when she was very small and she had no memories of him, but she was close to her mother and she'd never forget that look of pure fear in her mother's face when she'd told her the news.

When Harrie had said that she was going to spend the summer with her friends, her mother had protested. But Harrie had promised that the rest of the time she had would be theirs.

But summer first, she told herself.

She'd decided to arrive at the priory a full day before her friends were due – not to grab the best of the four bedrooms, although she took the one which suited her best with a view over the garden and out towards the orchard – but because she wanted to make sure that everything was absolutely perfect. She'd filled the fridge, freezer and cupboards. She aired the bedrooms and straightened things that really didn't need straightening and, when evening began to fall, turned on all the lamps and wandered through the ancient building. She needed these long, cool corridors and simply furnished rooms. A place without clocks, TV or Wi-Fi. It was as if the building still had echoes of the holy life that had, at one time, filled its rooms. The monks had definitely been on to something, Harrie thought. An uncluttered room led to an uncluttered mind.

She opened the great wooden door set in a large stone wall and stepped into the garden. The July sky was turning from blue to pink and the heat of the day was now just a memory. Once she'd reached the orchard, she looked back towards the priory. Red valerian grew out of the walls surrounding the garden and half a dozen gargoyles gazed down from the tower. A pair of swifts screeched in the air above her and a large moth danced before her eyes. It was so quiet. There was no traffic here, no neighbours to disturb her peace as there were in the busy Wiltshire market town she lived in. Here, it was just her and a few winged friends. And her thoughts.

It was all too easy to fall prey to negative thoughts when she was alone, but she was absolutely determined not to. She had to stay strong – for herself, for her daughter, and her friends. Anything else would be totally unacceptable.

She walked back towards the priory. The swifts had vanished from the sky and there were more moths now, pale ambassadors of the night. Lisa didn't like moths. Harrie would have to make sure she'd closed all the windows and checked the room she'd set aside for her friend.

Once she was back inside, Harrie locked the door with the iron key that was the length of her hand and bolted both the top and bottom. Suddenly, she wished she'd asked Honor to join her for that first evening, but then reminded herself that she needed this time alone to gather her thoughts and still her mind.

She walked through to the living room. There was an enormous stone fireplace with huge mullioned windows on either side. A large wooden door led out into the walled garden and a small, round table sat by the window. Having already turned on the lamps, she drew the curtains and picked up the paperback novel she'd placed on a coffee table earlier. Novels had been her salvation over the course of her treatment, shutting out the real world and opening up another – a world of safety and security where happy endings were guaranteed. But, that evening, her eyes skimmed over the words and she found she couldn't concentrate. She was restless, wanting her friends to arrive so they could start their holiday.

And what will you tell them? a little voice whispered.

The truth.

But when?

I don't know.

You can't hide it forever. No matter how much you want to.

I know.

Her eyes misted with tears, but she blinked them back. This was going to be a happy holiday. She'd make sure of that if it was the last thing she did.

Which it probably will be, the little voice whispered.

She swallowed hard and chose to ignore it.

Chapter 2

Audrey was the first to arrive, as Harrie had predicted. Punctual to a fault, she drove up at precisely the time she'd said she would and Harrie was at the front door to meet her.

'Harrie!' her friend screamed as she caught sight of her, running across the garden and enveloping her in a hug. Harrie was instantly lost in a cloud of dark hair and expensive perfume.

'It's so good to see you,' Harrie told her, blinking back the tears before they could be seen.

'It's been too long. Way too long,' Audrey said as she stood back. 'How've you been?'

'Good,' Harrie said. She was getting better at lying these days and there was nothing wrong with that. Lies, she'd learned, protected people, including herself. 'Really good.'

'You look tired,' Audrey said, placing her hands on Harrie's shoulders and studying her closer.

'Maybe a little,' Harrie conceded, squirming slightly under the scrutiny, afraid that her friend might be able to see the truth in an instant.

'Are you okay?'

'Yes, of course!' Harrie assured her. 'It's just – well – I never sleep properly the first night in a new place.'

'But it's comfy here? I mean the beds. My back won't take a bad bed these days.'

'Oh, it's comfortable. Good firm mattresses. Come and see your room.'

'I'll just get a few things from the car.'

Harrie went to give her a hand and smiled at the BMW Audrey drove. It was immaculate, just like Audrey. Not like the beaten-up old Ford Harrie drove. She hoped Audrey hadn't noticed it.

Predictably, Audrey had turned up not only with a suitcase but with a laptop and a briefcase.

'Please don't tell me there's work in there,' Harrie said.

Audrey looked as if she might try to deny it for a moment but then nodded. 'Just a little.'

'But this is a holiday.'

'It won't take me long. I can do a little every day and it won't seem like much at all.'

'Oh, Aud! You can't.'

'It's fine.'

'No, it isn't. Really.'

Audrey frowned. 'Has Mike rung you?'

Harrie didn't reply.

'He has, hasn't he?'

Harrie sighed. There was no point trying to fool Audrey. 'He might have texted me yesterday. He knew you'd probably bring a heap of work with you and he was right.'

Audrey looked annoyed. 'He shouldn't have done that.'

'He cares about you, that's all,' Harrie said, taking the briefcase from her. 'Come on. Let me show you your room. You're going to love it.'

They entered the priory through the kitchen and made their way up the spiral staircase, stopping at a first-floor landing and turning right into a spacious double bedroom with a large stone fireplace and a window which looked out over the courtyard garden.

'I thought you'd like this room.' Harrie placed the briefcase on the floor. 'There's plenty of light.'

Audrey dropped her suitcase and laptop and took a moment before speaking.

'You're crazy,' she said at last.

'What do you mean?'

'I mean hiring an ancient priory for the summer. What on earth made you do it?'

Harrie shrugged. 'I thought we deserved an adventure and I didn't fancy traipsing through a jungle or backpacking in the Himalayas.'

Audrey nodded in understanding and began to unpack a few of her things. 'No, Somerset's much more you, isn't it?'

'You think?'

'You always were the homely one,' Audrey said. 'I mean out of the three of us.'

'I suppose.'

'Lisa's always jetting off to yogic retreats on distant shores and I . . .' Audrey paused.

'What?'

'I was going to say that I like nice hot holidays in the Med, but I've just realised that I haven't had a holiday in years. Not really. Mike managed to get me to go on a couple of weekend city breaks, but I've told him I've been too busy setting up the new business to go away for any longer than that.'

'But you love your holidays,' Harrie said.

'I know,' Audrey agreed, 'which is why I'm here now.'

They smiled at each other.

'I'm so happy you could make it,' Harrie told her.

'Me too.' Audrey stepped forward and hugged Harrie again, her hair tickling her face. 'And you're okay?' she asked a moment later. 'You look so pale.'

'I do?' Harrie said. 'Oh, I just haven't had a chance to catch the sun yet.' She could feel the full weight of Audrey's gaze upon her. Her friend was a shrewd one but, if she suspected anything now, she didn't say, and Harrie breathed a sigh of relief when Audrey's attention was caught by the view from the window. The two of them looked down onto the courtyard garden, taking in the paths lined with huge lavender bushes and the neat knot garden in its centre, which was full of herbs.

'It's so quiet here,' Audrey observed. 'This is just what I need at the moment.'

'Me too,' Harrie said.

'Yoohooooo!' a voice called from downstairs.

'Spoke too soon,' Audrey said with a laugh, and the two of them went down to the kitchen.

Lisa was standing by the kitchen table with a yellow suitcase on one side of her and a pink yoga mat on the other.

'Oh, my god! Look at you two!' she screamed, her chestnut hair flying out behind her as she launched herself at them. The three of them embraced, laughing and leaping around each other to the chorus of 'Too long! Too long!' When they finally broke apart, Lisa took a good look at Harrie.

'Your hair's shorter.'

You have no idea, Harrie thought to herself, remembering the horror of losing her hair completely during chemotherapy.

'Yes,' she said, her hand flying to touch the fair locks which were now chin-length rather than shoulder-length. 'I fancied a change.'

'You look good,' Lisa said.

'So do you – as ever!' Harrie said. 'I like this – what *do* you call this look?' Harrie asked, examining Lisa's black leggings, the flat ballet pumps and the tiny pink vest top which looked two sizes too tight.

'Yoga chic,' Audrey supplied.

'Is that right?' Harrie asked.

'You're making that up,' Lisa said. 'This just happens to be what I'm comfortable in. Like your business-tycoon chic.'

'Ha ha,' Audrey laughed.

Lisa and Harrie gave Audrey's neat conservative skirt and blouse the once-over. She did look as if she might be going into a boardroom meeting, Harrie had to admit.

'As long as you're comfortable,' Lisa added.

'Ladies!' Harrie said. 'Let's start as we mean to go on.'

'This *is* how I mean to go on,' Lisa said. 'I miss our banter.'

'Well, let's keep it civil.'

Lisa grinned and then looked around the kitchen.

'This place is amazing, Harrie! I couldn't believe this was really it until I saw your cars. How on earth are you paying for it?'

'With my life savings.'

Lisa laughed. 'And you don't want us to chip in?'

'Not necessary.'

'Well, it's very generous of you,' Lisa said. 'I was facing the summer in my horrible flat and there's a new neighbour who blasts music every weekend. The landlord refuses to do anything about it. I have to sit with earplugs in.'

'And is that place rented or have you bought it?' Audrey asked.

'It's rented,' Lisa said defensively. 'I've told you, I don't want to buy until I have enough for my dream home.'

'But to throw all that money away on rent – for all these years,' Audrey went on.

'It's not throwing it away. I'm experiencing life in many different locations.'

'But you're not a student anymore, Lisa. Are you at least saving for a deposit?'

Lisa's eyes widened. 'Not all of us want to be tied to one place and one man our entire lives.'

Audrey's face reddened. 'And what's wrong with that? Mike and I are very happy and we love our home.'

'I've told you before that buying isn't convenient for me at the moment. I need to be able to move around and go where the work is.'

'I know,' Audrey said. 'I just worry about you—'

'Well, you don't need to!'

'Let's not fight – please,' Harrie said.

'I'm not the one who's fighting. It's Audrey who's pulling my life apart.'

Audrey sighed. 'I'm sorry, Lisa. I didn't mean to. It's just that I worry about you.'

'Yeah? Well, you don't need to. I can take care of myself.'

'I know you can.'

There was a moment's silence.

'Are we all okay?' Harrie dared to ask.

'Come here!' Lisa said, opening her arms up and flinging herself at Audrey. 'We'll hug it out like we used to do.'

'Don't I get a hug?' Harrie asked.

'But we weren't fighting with you,' Audrey pointed out.

'All the same, I don't want to be left out,' she said, and the two of them opened their arms so she could join in.

Lisa seemed in better spirits after the hug. 'How is everyone?' she asked. 'How's Mike and Jack?'

'They're good,' Audrey said. 'Both working hard.'

'I love those photos you emailed us of you all by the Thames,' Harrie said.

'Yes, I can't believe Jack's so grown up now,' Lisa told her.

Audrey beamed a proud smile.

'Right,' Harrie said a moment later, 'come and see your room – you're going to love it.'

They walked through the kitchen and went up the spiral staircase to the first floor. Harrie opened the door into the room she'd set aside for Lisa.

'It's got its own fireplace,' Lisa observed, dropping her suitcase and yoga mat.

'All the bedrooms have,' Harrie told her.

'Look at the size of this place!'

The room was large and airy with wooden floorboards and two red-patterned rugs. The bed was a robust one with a great wooden headboard.

'You've got an en suite,' Harrie said, and Lisa went through the adjoining door.

'Come and see this!' she cried. 'Am I really meant to use this?'

'Use what?' Audrey asked as she and Harrie entered the bathroom.

'This – this *thing*!' Lisa said, pointing to the bath.

'The bath?' Harrie said.

'It is rather huge,' Audrey observed.

'Huge – it's brutal!' Lisa said.

The three of them looked at the ancient bathtub with its massive taps.

'What's your room like, Aud?' Lisa asked, and Harrie detected a hint of suspicion in her old friend's voice which was all too familiar. In any given situation, Lisa liked to have the best, the prettiest, the most expensive – it was just the way she was.

'I'm not swapping,' Audrey said.

'Who said anything about swapping? I just want to see it.'

They left Lisa's room and crossed the landing and went up two steps to enter Audrey's.

'It looks like an office in here!' Lisa observed.

Sure enough, as Harrie looked around the room, she noted the stack of files and papers, the laptop and the fact that Audrey's mobile was vibrating and she was obviously itching to answer it.

'Mike would be very disappointed,' Harrie whispered.

'Don't say that,' Audrey said. '*Please* don't say that.'

Lisa looked from one to the other. 'What's going on?'

'Mike's worried about Aud. She's working too hard.'

'So what's new?'

'Exactly,' Audrey agreed. 'I'm used to it. It's my natural setting. I'd probably die of boredom if I didn't work so hard.'

'But you could die of a heart attack if you do,' Harrie pointed out.

'Nonsense! I'm in my prime. I *thrive* on work!'

'But this is your holiday,' Harrie reminded her.

'I know, and I have every intention of enjoying it. I just need to tidy a few things up first, that's all.'

'What's your en suite like?' Lisa asked, nodding towards a door at the far end of the room.

'I'm not swapping rooms, Lisa.'

But Lisa had crossed the room already and was in the bathroom.

'Oh, you have a darling little shower!' she said.

'Do I? I haven't seen it yet.'

Lisa gave a little sniff and Harrie cleared her throat.

'How about drinks in the garden?'

Lisa took one last look around Audrey's en suite and then came back out into the bedroom.

'Yes, a drink would be great,' she said.

'Good! I'll let you both freshen up and meet you outside, okay? There's a picnic table in the garden through the first arch as you come out of the front door.'

Harrie made a hasty retreat. Only Lisa could complain about staying in a luxurious medieval priory.

Half an hour later, the three of them were sitting sipping their wine, the sun setting low in the sky, leaving a luminous pink trail behind it.

'Six years?' Audrey said. 'It can't be.'

'It is,' Harrie said. 'At least when all three of us were together. I had that flying visit to London for a conference a couple of years ago, remember?'

'Of course I do!' Audrey said. 'It was when you sneaked out in the afternoon and we had tea and cake at Fortnum and Masons.' She laughed.

'But it's hard to get us all together, isn't it?' Harrie went on. 'With you in London, me in Wiltshire and Lisa up in Yorkshire.'

'But was it really six years ago?' Lisa asked.

'It was the year of our fortieth birthdays, remember?'

'How could we forget? That was some holiday,' Audrey said. 'I still miss that little beach we found.'

'The one near the restaurant with the waiter that fancied Lisa?' Harrie said.

'He did not fancy me!'

'Funny how you always got bigger portions,' Harrie teased.

Lisa grinned at the memory. 'That seems like an age ago now and I still haven't got used to being in my forties,' she said, shaking her hair back from her face.

'I sometimes feel like I'm in my sixties,' Audrey said, 'never mind my forties.'

'You work too hard,' Harrie told her.

'Yeah, yeah. You've said that already.'

'Well, it's true.'

'But you wouldn't want to go back, would you?' Audrey asked.

'What do you mean?' Harrie said.

'You wouldn't want to be young again and have to go through all we went through to get to where we are today. I mean, all those awful jobs we've had to do.'

'And teacher training!' Lisa said.

'Exactly!' Audrey said. 'Who'd want to go back to that horrible school with the head of English with the whistling nose?'

Lisa snorted at the memory. 'Oh, god! I'd forgotten about him! He used to lean over my shoulder to look at my lesson plan when I was in front of the class and I had to will myself not to laugh. I think all the pupils were just waiting for me to crack up.'

'Or waiting for you to thump him,' Harrie said. 'I nearly did once. He just got a little bit *too* close for comfort.'

Audrey shook her head. 'No, I wouldn't want to go back.'

'But there were fun times too! Don't forget those,' Harrie said. 'Being able to stay up all night if we wanted to, hiding bottles of wine under the bed for secret parties.'

'*Cheap* wine!' Lisa said with a laugh.

'Of course – that's a rite of passage. But we've got the good stuff now.' Harrie took a sip from her glass.

'Getting to spend three whole years reading books,' Audrey said. 'Now, *that's* a joy no longer afforded to us.'

'Well, we've got a few weeks here to make up for it,' Harrie said. 'I hope you've bought a stack of books with you.'

Audrey sighed. 'When I look back, I can't help thinking of all those long years trying to get things right – professionally *and* personally.'

'I'm still trying,' Lisa said.

Harrie looked at her. 'You haven't given up, have you?'

'About being an actress?' Lisa said.

'Yes.'

'I'll never give that dream up. I had an audition last week.'

'What for?'

'A commercial,' Lisa said.

'Really?' Harrie said.

'What was it selling?' Audrey asked.

Lisa suddenly became interested in the rim of her wine glass. 'I don't remember.'

'Nonsense!' Audrey said. 'Come on – out with it.'

Lisa grimaced. 'It was for – it was for those pads for women. For little leakages.'

Audrey guffawed and Harrie couldn't help giggling.

'The market is getting a lot younger!' Lisa said. 'They were obviously looking for someone glamorous.'

'But you didn't get the job?'

'No, I didn't.'

'Never mind. Something else will come along.' Harrie leaned forward and squeezed her hand.

Lisa sighed. 'I wonder when. It's years since my soap opera. Nobody recognises me anymore.'

Harrie gave her a sympathetic smile. She remembered when Lisa had first heard she'd be leaving the prime-time soap. Harrie had immediately called Audrey and the two of them had spent time with their friend when she'd needed them the most. There'd been a lot of tears and a lot of wine, she recalled.

'Even my agent has trouble remembering who I am,' Lisa went on now. 'All I'm getting thrown my way are rubbishy commercials.'

'But that's keeping you in the public eye, isn't it?' Audrey asked.

'Did you see the latest one?'

'The one for that multi-purpose mop?' Harrie asked. 'You looked gorgeous, Lisa!'

'Thanks, but dancing around a kitchen with a mop isn't exactly where my aspirations lie.'

'Poor Lisa,' Harrie said, thinking about the brief time their friend had been on prime-time television and had graced the pages of the TV guides for a few months. It had ended badly. The producers had mercilessly killed her character off in a gruesome building-site accident and Lisa had had to go back into teaching. She'd never got over her disappointment.

'I hate teaching,' Lisa announced.

'Do you?' Harrie asked in surprise.

'I mean, not *teaching* teaching. I love that whole sharing of knowledge bit, but some of the schools I go to – they're a bit trying. It's not teaching at all at places like that. It's more crowd control.'

Harrie knew that, for the last few years, Lisa had been working as a supply teacher because the freedom allowed her to audition whenever she needed to. The downside was that she had struggled in the more challenging schools.

'I'm telling you, drama is *not* the best subject for a supply teacher. You get thrown into sports halls which are far too big and echoey, and the kids just run riot. It's a nightmare.'

'Poor Lisa,' Harrie said again. 'I don't envy you. I feel so lucky to have found my school.'

Lisa laughed. 'A girls' school in a nice market town. I can only imagine what that must be like.'

'Well, why don't you do something else?' Audrey said. 'I did.'

Lisa took a sip of her wine. 'Like what?'

'I don't know – something with your yoga. You've been on enough retreats, you're a good teacher and—'

'Pardon?' Lisa said, cupping her ear.

Audrey grinned. 'You heard me.'

'Did you just pay me a compliment and say I was a good teacher?'

'I don't know, I can't remember,' Audrey said, her grin still in place.

'She did. I witnessed it!' Harrie laughed.

'But you should do something. If you're not happy. Life's too short.'

Harrie nodded. 'Yes.'

Lisa groaned. 'I sometimes wonder if I've messed up. If I've just been wasting my time with this acting lark.'

'Don't say that,' Harrie told her. 'You're a wonderful actress. You just need a lucky break.'

Lisa smiled at her. 'You're so sweet, Harrie. You've always been so supportive, but I often think I'm just fooling myself. I mean, what if I've missed my life? What if I took a wrong turn somewhere – made a wrong decision – and somebody else is leading the life that was meant for me with the perfect job and the perfect man?'

Her friends looked back at her blankly.

'Don't you ever think about things like that?'

'I don't,' Audrey said. 'I'm happy with all my decisions.'

'All of them?' Lisa asked sceptically.

Audrey looked thoughtful for a moment. 'I'm kind of regretting buying these shoes,' she said, looking down at her feet. 'They're a bit on the tight side.'

Harrie laughed again. 'Why don't you take them off? Go barefoot. The grass feels so good.'

Audrey looked under the table and Harrie wiggled her bare toes at her. Audrey kicked her shoes off and breathed a sigh of relief.

'Wine and bare feet. It's the antidote to most things,' Harrie revealed. 'Actually, we could all walk around naked here and nobody would see us. Erm, except there's a gardener twice a week and some guy coming to do restoration work.' She'd thought that would get Lisa's attention, but she was still looking serious.

'Lisa?' Audrey said, also noticing the sad expression on her face.

'Do you think I've messed my life up?'

'Of course not!' Audrey said.

'But you've always thought I've just drifted through it, haven't you?'

'No, I—'

'Don't lie to me. You think I've wasted my time with this acting business, don't you? You think I should have focused on my teaching and been a head of department by now.'

'I've never said that. I might have worried about you, but I'd never dictate your life. You have to make your own decisions about what you want.'

'But what if I've made the wrong ones?'

'Then make new ones,' Audrey said. 'That's what I did. When I'd finally had enough of the classroom, I set out to start up my own school. It's a lot of work, but it's so rewarding. I've discovered so many things about myself. You could do that too. It's not too late, is it? I mean, it isn't as if we're done yet. Look at us all – in the prime of our lives.'

'Oh, she's gone all Miss Jean Brodie on us,' Lisa joked.

'I mean it,' Audrey said. 'They say life begins at forty and we're all still young and gorgeous and ambitious, aren't we? There's plenty to look forward to. We're only just getting going. I really believe that.'

Harrie downed the last of her wine and stood up.

'Where are you going?' Audrey asked.

Harrie looked at her friend, trying to control her emotions and formulate a response.

'To get more wine, I hope,' Lisa said with a laugh. 'That's right, isn't it?'

Harrie nodded and smiled in relief. 'That's *exactly* right.'

Chapter 3

Harrie didn't sleep well that night. Thoughts of their conversation kept going round in her mind, and Audrey's assertion that they all still had so much ahead of them to look forward to had hurt her deeply. Harrie had cried silent tears into her pillow. The thoughts that ran through her mind had visited her before, of course. They tortured her on a regular basis and it took all her willpower to bury them. But who in her situation wouldn't think about all the things that they were going to miss in the future? There were the big events like seeing her daughter get married and settle down. Harrie was quite sure that Honor was the marrying kind and it pained her that she wouldn't be there for that special day. Children would follow. Harrie's grandchildren. Little people that would carry her genes and yet never know her. What would they look like? What would their names be? What jobs would they grow up to do? The future tormented her with such questions.

Then there were the little things which seemed to sting just as much. The knowledge that she would most likely never see another Christmas, never reach up into the dusty loft to take down the boxes of decorations. There was the agony of knowing that she had seen her last spring – that she might not be there to greet the first snowdrops of January or see that marvellous row of cherry trees blossom in her neighbour's garden. There was also the hugely annoying fact that the latest US TV drama she'd become addicted to would go on without her and she'd never know if the hero and heroine would get together. She suspected that they would, but when and how? She'd given some serious thought to writing to the producers and asking them if they could give her a little insight, and she laughed now at the letter she had penned in her head.

There were so many things she would miss. Her job, her pupils, her friends and family; all would go on without her, leading good and happy lives, she hoped. She didn't begrudge them but, in her darkest moments, she wondered how often those people would think of her. Would they stop in their daily routines and pause for a moment, to recapture her face or to recall something she had said? Could she hope to still live in the memory of those she had known?

And then there was Audrey and Lisa – her dearest friends. Seeing them again and enjoying their company once more made her realise just how very precious they were to her and she berated herself for not having spent more time with them recently. That was something that being ill made you so aware of – how you had chosen to spend your time in the past. When time started to run out, you really began to question every single second that passed.

She closed her eyes as she recalled the dreadful day of her last diagnosis. It was all so clear in her mind and she couldn't help playing it again like a film she had become obsessed with.

Honor had been with her in the hospital – her dear daughter had never missed an appointment – and they'd waited patiently for over an hour. Harrie had wanted to rail against that. Sick people shouldn't be made to wait – not when they didn't know how much time they had left. When life was suddenly running out, the last place you wanted to spend it was in some dreary hospital corridor.

Finally, their time had come and they'd been ushered into a room where Harrie's doctor had given her the news in a slow and even voice, her eyes soft and apologetic as if she herself was to blame.

Harrie hadn't been able to speak, but had sat with her lips parted as if a silent scream was trying to exit, but Honor had been anything but dumbstruck.

'I don't understand,' she'd told the doctor, her eyes flaming. 'What's going on? My mum's been well for years now. *Years*. She's full of energy. We've just been walking in the Peak District, for god's sake! She was fine then so it *can't* have come back, can it? Things can't change that quickly. You've made a mistake.'

Harrie's heart had swelled with love for her fierce little warrior daughter and she'd quietly reached across the space between them and taken Honor's hand, noticing how hot it was in her cold one. She could almost still feel it now, she thought, as she swung her legs out of bed and got into the shower, hoping that the water would wash away some of those appalling memories. She really wasn't sure how she would have coped without her daughter. Honor had been so strong for her. There'd been tears too – of course there'd been. So many nights had seen them sitting on the sofa together at Harrie's, crying until they'd felt completely hollow.

Harrie thought back to one of those nights now after the last diagnosis. They'd been watching one of their favourite films together – a lovely old black-and-white one with a young Judy Garland called *The Clock*. They'd laughed once again at the long-beloved scenes and their eyes had misted with tears at all the usual places and, by the end of it, when the camera slowly zoomed out and Judy Garland was swallowed up in the New York crowd, Harrie and Honor were bawling.

'I don't want to lose you,' Honor had cried, and Harrie hadn't been able to say anything. What *did* you say to something like that? And so she'd held Honor oh-so-tightly until the tears had stopped.

Harrie blinked her own tears away now as she switched off the memory. She combed her hair and chose a turquoise shirt dress in a soft linen. It was already hot and it wasn't even eight o'clock. Going down the stairs, her hand outstretched as she was still unused to the spiral steps, she decided to walk through the cloisters. It would be cool there.

It was as she was crossing the courtyard that she spotted the van in the driveway and frowned. It seemed early for somebody to be there, and then she remembered. When she'd booked the priory for the summer, she'd been told that there was a discount – not because she'd booked it for six straight weeks, but because during that time there'd be a man working on the tower. Important restoration work, she'd been told, which might occasionally mean a little noise. Was that okay? Harrie had said yes. After all, there was plenty of space both inside and out. Surely there'd be a quiet corner they could escape to. Besides, restoration work had always fascinated her and she'd felt sure it would add to the interest of staying in an old building.

The van door was open and she could just make out the back of a man. He was tall with broad shoulders and hair the colour of dark sand and, as he turned to face her, she saw that his skin was dark as if he spent a lot of time outdoors.

'Did I disturb you?' he asked as he approached her.

'No, not at all.'

'There will be some noise, I'm afraid.'

'That's okay. I mean, I was told when I booked the place.'

'Good.' He gave a curt little nod and moved on. Harrie followed him.

'Can I watch?' she asked.

'Watch what?'

'What you do.'

He looked confused.

'I'm interested,' she went on.

'I generally don't have an audience.'

'I'll be very quiet. You won't know I'm there. I promise.'

He didn't look convinced and ran a hand through his hair. 'I'm not sure.'

'I can provide tea.'

'I bring a flask.'

'Oh.' She waited for him to say something else. An apology at his abruptness, perhaps. But none was forthcoming. 'I'll – erm – leave you to it, then.'

He nodded and walked towards the tower.

Harrie watched him for a moment, disappointed that her dream of seeing an interesting restoration over the course of her summer had been scuppered by this very rude man.

Well, *he* might not want her to make him a cup of tea, but she could jolly well make herself one, she thought, going to the kitchen and putting the kettle on. She looked at the great trestle table with its two long benches either side. It was an extravagance, booking such a huge place for just the three of them. They could have easily managed with a modest cottage somewhere. But where was the fun with modest, she thought? Modest was for amateurs.

Or people with more time.

No, she had wanted to be outrageous – to book something so spectacular that her friends would never forget it.

Or ever forget her.

Once again, her fears surfaced and it was that one – that fear of being forgotten – that affected her the most. She didn't want to leave behind a life with no meaning. She wanted – no, she *needed* – to be remembered.

An overwhelming sense of grief threatened to obliterate her, but she refused to allow it.

'Tea,' she said to herself. Tea was good. Tea made things better.

She was just sitting down at the trestle table with her cup of peppermint tea in hands which had finally stopped shaking when there was a gentle knock on the kitchen door and a sandy head popped round a moment later. It was the rude restorer.

Her mouth dropped open, but she closed it again. She wasn't going to say anything to him, she decided. She wouldn't let him rebuff her again.

He looked at her and she thought she detected something approaching an apology in his expression.

'I – erm . . .' he began hesitantly.

'What?' Harrie prompted when she was quite sure he wouldn't continue without a tiny bit of encouragement.

'I forgot my flask.'

Audrey never slept in. She didn't have the luxury of lie-ins, not when she was the boss of a new company. Even at weekends, she was up and working by eight o'clock at the very latest. But that first morning at the priory, she'd woken with a start and had stared at her bedside clock in horror. It was ten to nine. Ten to nine! Never before had she slept so late. Never had she not set her alarm clock, but a tiny rebellious streak had overtaken her the night before and she'd switched it off, knowing full well that she'd wake up at her regular time. How could she not? It was ingrained. Only she hadn't woken up then. She'd overslept. Horribly.

Her instinct was to get up as fast as she could and make amends but, instead, she wondered what it would be like to *not* get up for once in her life, but to luxuriate in a lie-in – to deliberately crawl back under the covers, sink her head into the pillow and close her eyes again.

No, she couldn't! It went against everything she held dear and yet the temptation was there all the same.

You're on holiday, a voice whispered.

Well, she kind of was, only she had a heap of work to get through. But surely ten extra minutes wouldn't do any harm. Although she couldn't quite silence the nagging voice that told her that it was all the little groups of ten wasted minutes that made a difference to getting ahead.

She settled back down onto her pillow and experimented. The bed was certainly comfortable. She'd slept exceedingly well. The room had been cool but not cold and it was so peaceful. The curtains could have benefitted from being a tad thicker, but she quite liked the way that the morning light was slipping into the room, colouring her vision even though her eyes were resolutely closed.

But it was no good. With a sigh of exasperation, she sat up in bed, pushed her hair out of her face and took a deep breath. She'd left one of the windows open overnight and the clean Somerset air smelled glorious to her suburban nose. They couldn't leave the window open in their London home because of the noise. She lived in a terraced house from where she could see at least fifty other houses and, at any given time, there was noise coming from at least ten per cent of them. To save her sanity and preserve her sleep, Audrey had taken to wearing wax earplugs. She also wore an eye mask because of the intrusive beams from neighbours' security lights which would pierce right through their bedroom curtains.

But here at the priory, she had slept with her ears and eyes unencumbered and she felt all the more refreshed for it. Now she could see why Mike was always trying to persuade her to move to the country. He'd been brought up in rural Norfolk and was always singing the praises of village life.

'It's quiet in the country,' he'd tell her when a neighbour's noise was getting her down.

'I'd be unemployed,' she'd rebuff.

'You'd find something,' he'd tell her.

'But my business is here,' she'd say. She'd worked long hours to get her new school up and running. They might only have thirty-two pupils on their books, but it was a start. She'd secured a suitable building which was handy for a tube station, had signed on two other teachers and hoped to see a healthy profit very soon. Which reminded her, she needed to check some spreadsheets.

She got out of bed and, before even allowing time for a quick wash, she'd switched her laptop on. The familiar whirr and flash of light felt out of place in the pale serenity of the priory bedroom. She couldn't help wondering if the ghost of a long-departed monk who may have slept in this very room was frowning down upon her from heaven, shaking his head in despair at her addiction to modern technology. Still, the pull was too great to ignore.

She grabbed her mobile phone and plugged it into the nearest socket to recharge, checking her messages and responding to half a dozen quickly, and then she made a start on the spreadsheets. She had surprised herself at how good she was with figures and she'd found that she enjoyed the challenge of running her own business and making all the decisions. It certainly beat being a humble team player in a school. She didn't miss that at all.

If only she didn't get so tired. Her long hours were catching up with her, she thought as she rubbed her eyes. She seemed to have a constant headache, permanent backache and regular eye-strain. Perhaps she needed new glasses and a decent office chair. That would be it. Then she could work even longer hours and really get ahead.

As was always the way when she turned her laptop on, she got sucked into her work. It wasn't until her belly rumbled that she realised she could do with some breakfast. Audrey sighed. If they'd invented a pill one could eat to replace meals, she would be a happy woman. Still, eating with her friends would be fun and, with that in mind, she closed her laptop and took a quick shower, pulling out a summer dress which she thought was pretty, but which Lisa would probably still think of as office-worthy.

Leaving her room, she headed towards Harrie's. The door was open, but it was obvious Harrie wasn't in there. Audrey smiled as she saw a photo frame standing on the bedside table. Instinctively, she walked towards it. It was of Harrie and her daughter Honor. How grown up she was now. Like her own son, Jack. Smiling, she thought back to the first time she'd met Harrie at university. They'd bumped into each other in a corridor, desperately trying to find their way around one of the enormous buildings. They'd struck up a conversation and had been part of each other's lives ever since. And now they both had grown-up children who'd flown the nest. How on earth had that happened? Sometimes, Audrey still felt like that inhibited student, wandering lost through the corridors.

She looked around the room and caught sight of a row of bottles on a dressing table. Nosiness got the better of her and she went to see what they were. Harrie, it would seem, had turned into a health freak. They were all vitamins and supplements, but there was something else too. She didn't recognise the name when she picked up the bottle. How on earth could anyone be bothered to take so many pills each day? Audrey just didn't have the time for anything like that. She replaced the bottle, thinking no more of it, and decided to head downstairs in search of her friends.

In the kitchen, Harrie was reboiling the kettle.

'How do you like your tea?' she asked the rude restorer.

'Black, no sugar,' he said.

'Or would you like herbal? I have all sorts with me. Peppermint, camomile, ginger—'

'No, thanks.'

Harrie smiled. She had yet to meet a man who enjoyed herbal tea.

'You haven't yet told me your name,' she said, turning to face him.

'You haven't told me yours.'

'True.'

'Haverstock,' he said.

'That's . . . unusual.'

'Samson,' he added.

'Haverstock Samson?'

'Samson Haverstock.'

'Right.' She bit her lip, trying not to laugh.

'What?' he asked.

'Nothing.'

'You're laughing.'

'I'm not laughing.'

'Yes you are.'

'Okay, yes I am,' she said.

'My name isn't funny.'

'Well, it is just a bit.'

He frowned at her and she grinned. He was very easy to rib.

'Here,' she said, handing him his tea. 'I'm sorry. I've just never met a Samson before. Or a Haverstock.'

'What's your name, then?'

'Greenleaf,' she said with a grin. 'That's my surname and Harriet is my first name, but I prefer Harrie.'

'But that's a man's name.'

'It's with an *ie*.'

'Still sounds like a man's name. I've never met a woman called Harrie.'

'Well, now you have and I've met a Samson Haverstock.'

He drained his cup of tea and took it to the sink and washed it.

'So,' he said, clearing his throat, 'you want to see what I'll be working on?'

'Yes, please,' she said.

'I don't like chatter,' he told her.

'I don't do chatter.'

'Good. Or questions.'

'Ah,' Harrie said. 'I *do* do questions.'

He frowned at her.

'What? I can't help it. I'm a teacher; I'm curious by nature.'

'Well, try not to be curious while I'm working.'

33

Again, Harrie desperately tried to hold her laughter in. She'd never met anybody like this man before with his gruff manner. But, as much as he irked her, she had to admit that there was something she liked about him. Perhaps it was his honesty. He didn't mess around with being polite. Harrie liked that, she realised. Not enough people were like that, were they? Most people slyly danced around the truth, wasting time with one another, and Harrie didn't have any time to waste these days so it was quite refreshing to be told the truth from the beginning. It saved time.

'Can I ask questions at the end?'

'At the end of what?'

'When you've finished your day's work?'

He shrugged. 'If you must.'

'I think I must.'

He nodded.

She followed him out of the kitchen and towards the tower, the oldest part of the priory. A couple of jackdaws had found their way inside and cawed in alarm at being disturbed, flying out of the windows, which no longer had glass in them. Harrie marvelled at being able to see the clear blue sky through the tracery. It was the most beautiful building she had ever seen and she once again felt truly privileged to be staying there.

Turning her attention back to Samson, she noticed that his work tools were already laid out.

'How long have you been doing this?' Harrie began.

'I'm working now,' he said, his eyebrows raised.

'Oh, sorry,' Harrie said, her hand over her mouth in horror at having already managed to disturb him. 'I'll sit over here. I won't bother you here, will I?' she asked, pointing to a stone step.

He was glaring at her and part of her wanted to laugh again. He was so very earnest. But she didn't get a chance to laugh because she heard someone calling her name.

'Audrey?' Harrie turned around to see her friend approaching. 'Good morning.'

'I wondered where you were.' She stopped, looking across to Samson.

'He's the restorer. He'll be working here over the summer,' Harrie explained.

'Hello,' Audrey said.

Samson nodded.

'He's called Samson and he only speaks when he wants a cup of tea.'

Audrey looked perplexed and Harrie laughed.

'Have you seen Lisa?' Audrey asked.

'No. Isn't she still in bed?'

'I checked her room and she wasn't there.'

'I suppose we'd better go and find her,' Harrie said, getting up from the step she'd been sitting on and brushing her hands over her bottom. 'I'll see you later,' she told Samson. He gave a half-nod, but didn't say anything.

'He's an odd sort,' Audrey said, once they were out of earshot.

'I kind of like him.'

'You do?'

'For some strange reason, he brings out the perverse in me,' Harrie admitted.

'What do you mean?'

'His reluctance to talk makes me want to keep bothering him until he does. Is that awful?'

'It's probably awful for him,' Audrey told her.

'But fun for me.'

They entered the courtyard garden, but there was no sign of Lisa.

'Where do you think she is?'

'Let me see,' Harrie said. 'The sun will have risen over there, right?'

'Erm, I guess.'

'Then that's where we'll find her.'

'How do you know that?'

'Her yoga.'

They found Lisa a moment later in the herb garden. She was seated on her pink yoga mat, her legs folded and her hands resting on her knees, palms facing the sky, a look of total serenity on her face.

'Is she meditating?' Audrey asked.

'No, she's probably just sleeping.'

'I can hear you!' Lisa told them, and they both giggled.

'I was worried. You weren't in your room,' Audrey said.

'I've been up for hours.' Lisa stretched her arms above her head as she slowly blinked her eyes open. 'Well, at least one hour.'

'Meditating?' Harrie asked.

'Greeting the morning,' she revealed. 'It's glorious here. The perfect place for a sun salutation.'

'I had a pillow salutation,' Audrey said.

'A what?' Lisa asked.

'A lie-in!'

'Audrey Wells had a lie-in?' Harrie cried. 'Are you *sure*?'

'And I'll carry the guilt for the rest of the summer,' she said.

'You mustn't do that,' Harrie said quickly. 'This place – our time here – isn't for regrets. It's for living life to its fullest.'

Audrey smiled at her. 'I'll try and remember that.'

'Good.'

Lisa stood up and began to roll up her yoga mat.

'Oh, I should warn you, there's a guy doing work on the tower today,' Harrie said.

'There's a man here?' Lisa asked.

'The restorer,' Harrie explained. 'Samson.'

'What's he like?'

'Sullen, abrupt and very odd.'

'Good-looking?' Lisa prompted.

'I think so.'

'I'll go and take a look.'

'He doesn't like being disturbed,' Harrie warned her. 'So I wouldn't if I was you.'

'Oh,' Lisa said, crestfallen.

'What about some breakfast?' Harrie said. 'Anyone had any?'

'Only a glass of warm water to get my digestion moving,' Lisa said.

'Blimey, I hope we're not going to hear about that all summer,' Audrey said.

'People tend to overlook their digestion,' Lisa went on, 'but nothing else will function properly if you don't pay it attention.'

Audrey grimaced and the three of them walked through the garden. The morning light was a clear silver and there was a slight breeze now that was refreshing.

'I'm going to make a smoothie,' Harrie said. 'Anyone want one?'

'They have a blender here?' Lisa asked as Harrie plugged one in.

'No,' Harrie laughed. 'I brought it with me.'

'You brought a blender on holiday?' Audrey asked in surprise.

'What can I say? I like my smoothies.'

'That's a bit obsessive, isn't it?'

'Not when we're going to be here for six weeks. It's important to start your day well and a freshly made smoothie is just the thing. I put all sorts of wonders in mine: fruit, oats, spinach—'

'Spinach?' Audrey said, wrinkling her nose.

'You don't taste it. It just turns it a bit green, that's all.'

'You're not really selling the idea to me,' Audrey confessed.

'Let me make you one,' Harrie said, addressing both of them. 'I bought a heap of bananas and the freezer's full of frozen fruit and you both look like you could do with one.'

'What do you mean?' Lisa said, ever mindful of her looks.

'I don't mean anything.' Harrie bit her lip. Perhaps she'd gone too far trying to push her healthy-eating regime onto them so early. 'I just want to take care of you.'

'Ever the mother,' Audrey said.

'I'm good with my coffee,' Lisa said.

'But that's so bad for you,' Harrie said. 'All that caffeine and dairy.'

'Don't forget the sugar,' Lisa said.

'You shouldn't put all that into your body.'

Audrey placed her hands on her hips. 'Are you having a mid-life crisis or something?'

'What do you mean?'

'I mean this sudden interest in diet.'

'It isn't sudden.'

'No?'

'I changed my diet a while ago.'

'Well, you've certainly lost weight, that's for sure,' Lisa observed. 'Your dress is hanging off you.'

Harrie's hands immediately flew to her waist. She was conscious of the fact that she'd lost weight, but she'd been happy with that, believing that she'd found a more natural way to live since her diagnosis. It was funny but her illness had actually made her healthier. If she'd never got cancer, she might easily have overloaded her body with all sorts of sugars, fats and chemicals and got diabetes. She truly believed that. Her new diet had saved her in so many ways and had allowed her to have a certain amount of control over her body. It was a positive focus on the good that she could do herself. So much of having cancer was out of your control, but her diet was something she alone was in charge of and she'd embraced her new regime with a vigour she didn't know she had. It might not save her life, but it was at least going part way to saving her sanity.

'I'm not sure I'll be able to cope for six weeks with a health freak to my left and a meditating Buddhist on my right,' Audrey said.

'I'm not a Buddhist,' Lisa insisted. 'I'm just a very spiritual person.'

'You're making fun of Harrie for bringing her blender, but you've got your yoga mat and singing bowl.'

'It was *you* who was making fun of her blender!'

'I hope you're not going to stink the priory out with your incense sticks like you used to in your room at uni,' Audrey went on.

'Well, *I* hope *you're* not going to keep sloping off to your room to work like a boring person.'

'Ladies!' Harrie said. 'I thought we weren't going to argue.'

'Talking of being boring,' Audrey said, 'this six weeks is a long time.'

'It'll fly by,' Harrie said.

'Yes, I know, but I do think we should organise things.'

'Like what?' Harrie asked as she loaded her blender with frozen fruit.

'Like chores. I mean, we're going to be here for the entire summer – we need to decide on things like cooking and washing-up. A rota, perhaps.'

'I can't believe you just said that,' Lisa groaned. 'A *rota*! We're on holiday!'

'Yes, but it won't remain a holiday-like atmosphere if we're knee-deep in dirty dishes before this week is out.'

Harrie shook her head. 'Don't worry,' she said. 'It's all taken care of.'

'What do you mean?' Audrey asked.

'I've hired someone. Mrs Ryder. She'll be coming in three times a week to sort us out. She'll be cooking a few meals, bringing a bit of shopping and generally tidying up after us.'

Audrey's mouth had fallen open. 'Isn't that expensive?'

Harrie shrugged. 'Yes.'

'I hope you're not expecting me to chip in,' Lisa said, 'because I'm broke after the last retreat I went on. You've no idea how much those places charge.'

Harrie grinned. 'I didn't want us to be bothered by dull things like household chores. This time's about us. No chores. No TV. No work. Just *us*.'

Lisa looked as if she'd been punched in the face. 'What do you mean, *no TV*?'

'There's no TV here. It's part of the ethos of the trust that owns this place. There's no TV and no clocks. You knew that, didn't you? I did tell you. Don't you remember?'

'But I can't go without TV for the whole summer!' Lisa cried. 'There's a great new series everyone's talking about and I want to catch up.'

'Charming!' Audrey said. 'And here was I thinking I was riveting company.'

'But just remember those days when we weren't glued to the TV or our mobile phones,' Harrie said.

Lisa shook her head. 'Nope. Can't remember them.'

'There are shelves of books to read and footpaths to explore . . .'

'You'll be telling us that there's no electricity next and that we'll have to bake our own bread by candlelight,' Lisa said.

'There's electricity,' Harrie told her. 'I thought you'd be used to all that sort of thing with you going away on retreats.'

'They're different.'

Harrie finished adding her ingredients to the blender and switched it on.

'Blimey, that thing's noisy,' Lisa said.

'I could feel my chakras vibrating.' Audrey's hand moved over her chest. Lisa threw her a dirty look and Audrey winked at her.

'Hey, who's that man?' Lisa asked as she looked out of the window.

'Samson Haverstock. The restorer I was telling you about. I wonder what he's up to,' Harrie said.

'Where are you going?' Lisa asked.

'Just to see.'

Harrie left the kitchen.

'Hey,' she called after Samson. He slowed his pace, but he didn't stop. 'Everything okay?'

He nodded.

'You haven't finished for the day, have you?'

He shook his head. 'Got to get a special tool from the van.'

They walked towards the vehicle and he opened the doors at the back.

It was then that Harrie saw it and, by the look on his face, Samson knew that she'd seen it although she didn't say anything. She didn't need to, did she?

It was Samson's flask.

Chapter 4

Harrie hadn't said anything, of course, and neither had Samson. He'd merely cleared his throat, reached into the van for the tool he needed, closed the door and returned to the tower. Harrie had left him to it, smiling secretly to herself. He was an odd one, she thought, but she couldn't help liking him.

If she were honest with herself, Harrie couldn't remember the last time she'd even attempted to flirt with a man. It seemed like an age ago. Another lifetime; another Harrie. Since divorcing Charles, there'd been other men in her life, but nobody serious and no one at all since her diagnosis. Not only had her working life stopped, but her love life had too and it wasn't just because she'd felt so ill for so long, but because she'd felt so insecure. Even when she'd felt well during her remission, the thought of dating had appalled her. She'd heard that was normal for a woman who had undergone a mastectomy. Intimacy could be a scary thing and the mere thought of trying to explain what she had gone through to a man was a problem she decided she could live without.

But, oh, how she missed men! It had been yet another thing cancer had taken away from her: not just her breasts but her confidence. That was it, she thought. She'd lost a little bit of the old Harrie – the naughty flirt who loved male companionship.

But now here was Samson. Was the world trying to tell her something? Might a summer flirtation be a good idea? She took a deep breath, sighed and reminded herself that this summer was about her friends.

When she returned to the kitchen, Audrey and Lisa had gone but she soon spied them out of the window, sipping their drinks on a bench in the sunny courtyard, a plate of croissants beside them. She took a moment to watch them, feeling blessed they were here with her. It had been too long since they'd all shared some special time together and she was excited at the prospect of the long summer ahead.

She was just about to join them when she heard a knock on the front door.

'Hello?' Harrie said a moment later as she was greeted by a short, stocky woman with ruddy cheeks and a rather severe perm. She was wearing an old-fashioned gingham dress with a crisp white apron tied around her large waist and no-nonsense plimsolls. Harrie guessed her to be in her late fifties.

'Good morning,' the woman said with a little nod.

'Mrs Ryder?' Harrie asked, guessing that this must surely be the housekeeper.

'Yes. That's me.' She extended a large, plump hand, shaking Harrie's slender one.

'Very pleased to meet you,' Harrie said.

Mrs Ryder nodded, her eyes sliding down Harrie as if in appraisal. 'You're too thin.'

'Excuse me?'

'Are you one of these modern women who spend all their time working and not enough time eating properly?' Mrs Ryder asked.

'No,' Harrie said.

'I'll soon sort that out, don't you worry.'

Harrie almost did a comedy double-take at the woman's forthright manner. 'Erm, my diet doesn't need sorting out.'

'I had a look at the meal plans you sent through.'

'Good,' Harrie said.

'They won't do.'

'What do you mean?'

'All kale and broccoli. You need to get some meat down you.'

'I don't eat meat.'

Mrs Ryder frowned. '*Don't eat meat?*'

'I'm a vegan.'

She tutted and shook her head. 'Bad. Very bad.'

'I'm on a very strict diet,' Harrie stressed. 'I thought I'd explained that in my letter.'

'I don't look at letters; I look at the people I'm cooking for.'

'Well, if you don't want the job, I guess I'll have to find somebody else,' Harrie said, deciding that she'd had enough of this outspoken woman. Harrie was employing her to make life easier – not to antagonise her and make her feel like a naughty child.

'Now, now, wait a minute,' Mrs Ryder said, pursing her lips. 'No need to be so hasty. I'm sure we can come to some arrangement.'

Harrie saw a slight softening in the woman's demeanour.

'I do hope so,' she said, 'because I hate wasting time.'

Mrs Ryder nodded. 'My job, you see, is to take care of people and, well, one look at you tells me that you need taking care of.' Her eyes fastened on Harrie again, making her feel decidedly uncomfortable. 'I didn't mean to upset you.'

Harrie accepted the apology. 'All right then, let's begin again, shall we?'

They moved into the kitchen.

'I've familiarised myself with the place,' Mrs Ryder said.

'You have?'

'Always do before a job.'

Harrie was impressed. 'I don't need to give you a tour then?'

'No, no. I can find my way around just fine.'

'And you're okay for three days a week?' Harrie checked.

She nodded. 'No more? It's a big place to take care of.'

'I know.' Harrie had thought of this, anxious that hiring a medieval priory would just mean a lot of work all summer. She decided to be honest. 'The thing is, we don't want people coming and going all the time. This is a holiday, you see. A chance to unwind.' And we've already got a grumpy restorer to contend with, Harrie privately thought.

'Of course,' Mrs Ryder said. 'Well, if you change your mind—'

'We'll let you know.'

Mrs Ryder had been carrying a large handbag and she placed it on one of the benches by the trestle table now, opening it up and pulling out a sheet of paper. 'This is the letter you sent via the agency.'

'About the food, yes,' Harrie said, recognising it. 'We'd like everything to be organic, locally grown and in season.'

'And no meat?'

'That's right.'

'So your companions are vegan too?' Mrs Ryder asked, nodding to the two ladies outside.

'No, they're not,' Harrie informed her. 'But you don't need to buy any meat for us. We'll be catering for ourselves too so I guess they'll have what they want then.'

'This is quite a list,' Mrs Ryder stated.

Harrie couldn't help but agree, but she didn't think it was unreasonable. It was just, well, healthy.

'I trust you'll be able to cope?' Harrie said.

Mrs Ryder looked at her again. 'I could make you the best shepherd's pie you've ever eaten,' she told her.

'I don't want shepherd's pie.'

'Sirloin steak's a speciality of mine.'

'No, thank you.'

'Or a nice pork chop?'

'Not happening.'

She shook her head and folded the piece of paper, putting it back in her bag. 'I'll see what I can do with these leafy greens and nuts then.'

'Good.'

Mrs Ryder picked up her bag. 'I'd better go shopping.'

'That sounds like a good idea,' Harrie said. 'Let me give you a key so you can come and go without having to wait for one of us to open the door.' She went to the key hook and pulled down one of the smaller keys. 'This will let you in through the door from the courtyard.'

Mrs Ryder took it. 'Thank you. I'll be back to make you lunch.'

'I'm looking forward to it.'

Harrie watched as she went, her thick legs thumping down the path through the garden, her handbag looped in the crook of her arm. Harrie hoped she hadn't made a dreadful mistake in hiring her. The last thing she wanted was to be fighting with somebody all summer. Still, it was early days. She'd see how lunch went before she started to worry.

Returning to the kitchen and pouring herself a glass of water, she joined her friends in the courtyard garden.

'Who was that?' Audrey asked her. 'We saw someone in the kitchen with you.'

'It was Mrs Ryder, the cook and housekeeper.'

'Blimey,' Lisa said. 'She looks like a right battleaxe.'

'Yes, she was a bit,' Harrie said, 'but I think I've put her in her place. If I haven't, we can always get rid of her.'

Audrey shielded her eyes from the sun as she looked at Harrie. 'I'm impressed,' she said. 'You're normally so polite and obliging.'

'Not this summer. I don't want to have to cope with anyone difficult.'

'Hear hear!' Lisa said. 'Have a croissant.'

'No, thank you.'

'You're on holiday but you don't want a croissant?' Lisa asked, bemused.

'I'm good,' she told Lisa, secretly acknowledging to herself that the croissant Lisa was now slicing in half looked very good indeed. She did often wonder why she was still depriving herself of some of her favourite things. If the doctors were to be believed and her cancer was terminal, was her plant-based, low-sugar diet really doing her any good?

'You're skinny,' Lisa pointed out. 'Skinnier than me, and I've always been the skinniest out of us all.'

'It was time I lost a bit,' Harrie said. 'It's important to stay healthy.'

'I think I've kind of put health on the backburner since starting my own business,' Audrey admitted.

'You mustn't do that,' Harrie said. 'We've got plenty of time this summer. We can go for nice long walks together. Get things moving again.'

'And is that how you got so skinny?' Lisa asked.

Harrie paused before answering. 'I just watch what I eat these days.'

'Well, that's very disciplined of you,' Lisa said. 'Personally, I can't resist a muffin or a chocolate-chip cookie and, if there are crisps in the house, then heaven help my waistline!'

'Mike said he'd love me even if I was double the size I am now,' Audrey confessed. 'That's not a very good incentive, is it?'

'*Not* helpful to a woman!' Lisa nodded.

'I think you're both in really good shape,' Harrie said honestly.

'That's because you've not seen me in my bikini yet,' Audrey said. 'Actually, I've got a swimsuit these days which helps hold the tummy in.'

'I've got knickers like that,' Lisa confessed. 'Horrible things. You wouldn't want to be seen in them, if you know what I mean, but they do their job.'

Harrie couldn't help but laugh.

'It's all right for you!' Lisa said. 'You're a skinny stick with no boobs.'

Harrie stopped laughing and pulled her light cardigan around her body in a self-conscious manner.

'Yes,' Audrey said. 'You'll have to give us some tips. Other than green juices, that is.'

There was a part of Harrie that wanted to cry out, 'Try a double mastectomy,' but she wasn't quite ready for that revelation yet and so she simply smiled and nodded.

'Getting older sucks, though, doesn't it?' Lisa said.

'But there's a positive way to look at it,' Harrie stated.

'What's that?' Audrey asked.

'It's a privilege denied many people,' Harrie said. 'That's how I look at it. It doesn't make me feel grateful every time I see a new grey hair or a wrinkle, but I can't help thinking about all the people that haven't even made it this far. I lost a cousin when she was only twenty-five. She was just getting going, you know? Her career, her relationships. Sometimes, I think of all the incredible things I would have missed out on if my life had ended at her age – all that unfulfilled potential, all those moments I wouldn't have enjoyed. That's why I think we have to be grateful for every minute and if that means bemoaning a few aches and pains and grey hairs then it's worth it because we're still here.'

Audrey and Lisa didn't say anything for a moment, but sat staring at Harrie as if absorbing every single word she'd said.

'Yeah, but you forget all that as soon as you see a grey hair,' Lisa pointed out. 'Well, I do anyway.'

Audrey grinned. 'I'm afraid we're always so wrapped up in our own little microcosms, aren't we? Nothing ever seems as important as our own worries and fears.'

'Isn't this all getting a bit too heavy for the first day of our holiday?' Lisa asked.

'I agree!' Harrie said, shaking off her thoughtful mood. 'Let's do something wonderful. Mrs Ryder's going to be making lunch today so that's something we don't have to worry about. We've got the whole morning stretching out in front of us.'

'A whole morning with nothing to do?' Audrey said. 'I might have a panic attack. I've forgotten how to do nothing!'

'We could go for a walk,' Harrie suggested.

'Walk off these croissants, you mean?' Audrey said with a chuckle.

'And work up an appetite for our lunch,' Harrie said.

'As long as it's a nice gentle stroll and not a mountain hike,' Audrey said. 'I'm really not in shape, you know.'

'I'll need to change,' Lisa said.

'Me too,' Harrie said. 'Meet you back down here in five?'

The women went up to their bedrooms and Harrie closed the door to her own, careful to lock it behind her while she got changed. She chose a loose T-shirt in a soft cotton that would allow plenty of movement and wouldn't cling in awkward places. She was wearing a lot of baggy clothing these days, so conscious was she of her breast form prosthesis. How strange it had been to be given those. She still remembered her surprise at how heavy they'd felt. Apparently, it was a normal reaction. Women simply didn't realise the weight they carried around in front of them. But, as alien as the prostheses had seemed, the thought of not having them had seemed even stranger.

For a moment, Harrie looked at her reflection as she stood in the middle of the room in her bra. She was still so self-conscious about wearing them, but you really couldn't tell, could you? There'd been a slightly dodgy moment downstairs when they'd all embraced and Harrie had felt her left prosthesis move upwards at an alarming angle. She'd wondered if Lisa had noticed, but it was probably all in her head.

'You ready in there?' Audrey shouted from the landing, and then she rattled the door handle.

'Just a minute!' Harrie called, quickly pulling her T-shirt over her head.

'Why did you lock the door, Harrie?' Audrey asked as soon as it was open.

Harrie hesitated. 'Habit, I guess. Living on your own makes you a tad nervy.'

'Really?'

Harrie nodded. 'Come on – let's get out into that sun.'

A few minutes later, having put on appropriate footwear, the three friends met at the front door and left the priory through the little gate which led into a meadow.

'There's a public footpath from here,' Harrie announced, looking down at a map she'd brought with her. 'Here we are.'

A stile over a low wall took them out onto the footpath and they walked down an unsurfaced lane lined with trees. Harrie glanced back at the priory, its tower dominating the landscape.

'Can you believe we're here?' she said.

'When I woke up this morning, it took me a while to realise that I wasn't in the centre of Leeds,' Lisa confessed. 'I couldn't understand where all the traffic had gone.'

'I panicked because I'd never overslept,' Audrey told them.

'You are going to *love* oversleeping,' Harrie said. 'I think I should take your alarm clock off you just to make sure you don't set it.'

'How do you know I've got my alarm clock with me?'

Harrie laughed. 'You're kidding, right? You're Audrey. Of *course* you've got your alarm clock with you.'

'Yes, but I didn't set it last night.'

Lisa gasped in mock horror. 'Audrey Wells not setting her alarm clock for the first day of her holiday?'

'Very funny!'

'Seriously, you really should let me have your clock,' Harrie insisted.

'She'd only just go and set the clock on her phone or her laptop or something,' Lisa pointed out.

'You wouldn't, would you?' Harrie asked.

'I won't, I promise. I'm going to make a real effort here.'

'Yes, she's going to work really hard to relax. She's got a spreadsheet and a mission statement on how to go about it too,' Lisa teased.

Audrey shook her head. 'I'll go home right now if you're going to do nothing but tease me.'

'Sorry!' Lisa said, linking her arm through Audrey's. 'You know you're my favourite person to tease in the whole world!'

'How lucky am I?'

The three women came to a crossroads in the path.

'This way,' Harrie said, nodding straight ahead.

For a few moments, they walked in silence, their legs slicing through the long summer grasses of the lush Somerset countryside. It was a gentle landscape of rolling hills and wooded valleys, but there was something extra special about it, a magical quality about the air which told of its close proximity to the sea.

The footpath suddenly became stony as it led through the trees, following a hill upwards between twisted hawthorns.

'I thought you said this was going to be a gentle walk?' Audrey complained from the back after a few minutes of hard walking.

'Sorry!' Harrie called back. 'I didn't read these contours properly on the map.'

'Still, the view should be good if we ever get out of these trees,' Lisa said. 'And if it isn't, we'll dunk you in the pool later, okay?'

'We'll see about that!' Harrie retorted.

The three of them continued to march, too focused on the effort to talk much now. The strip of sky above them become narrower and narrower as the trees thickened, but then everything opened up and they found themselves at the top of a grassy hill. On one side was the sea, the pearly-blue water stretching out for miles, and on the other were the fields they had just walked through and the landscape far beyond.

'Wow! That's pretty spectacular,' Audrey said, taking a swig of water from the bottle she was carrying and passing it around.

'Told you!' Harrie said.

'No, you didn't,' Lisa said. 'You've no idea what you're doing with that map, do you?'

'Not really,' Harrie admitted.

'Don't put an English teacher in charge of geography,' she said, bending forward and resting her hands on her knees. She suddenly felt light-headed.

'Are you all right, Harrie? You look a bit red,' Lisa said.

She took a moment before answering. 'I'm just hot, that's all,' she said at last. 'I didn't realise it was such a climb.'

'Sit down for a minute. Catch your breath.' Audrey placed a hand on her shoulder and peered at her in that disconcerting way she had that seemed to see everything. 'Heaven only knows, *I* need to sit down. I haven't had a workout like that in yonks.'

'I told you to have a croissant.' Lisa joined the two of them on the grass. 'You can't live on smoothies alone.'

'I'm not.'

'You didn't have much of a breakfast as far as I could see.'

'I eat enough.'

'Yeah, well, I'm not so sure about that.'

'Hey, quit with the diet advice, okay?'

Lisa looked a little taken aback. 'Sorry,' she said.

Of course, her immediate apology made Harrie feel guilty for having snapped.

'No, I'm sorry, Lisa.'

Lisa held her hands up. 'It's not my business what you choose to eat. Or don't.'

Harrie sighed. 'That's right.'

'Hey – you're treading on my toes, Harrie. I thought it was *me* and Lisa who did the fighting around here,' Audrey said.

Harrie gave a little smile. 'Let's just enjoy this moment, shall we?' She lay back on the grass and closed her eyes against the brilliant blue of the sky, listening to the mournful sound of gulls in the distance and feeling the wind playing across her face. She'd felt anxious back there when that wave of exhaustion had hit her. She had to remember that she couldn't race around anymore. Life had to be at a more sedate pace these days, thanks to the medication she was on. The look on Audrey's face had worried her. Honestly, her friend's laser-like gaze unnerved her at times. She'd have to be careful around her or the truth would be out in no time.

She took in a deep breath and sighed it out, instantly feeling better. Nobody spoke for a while. Companionable silence, Harrie thought. It was nice to experience this again. She'd missed it. Living on her own, it was mainly just silence she experienced, but this felt good. She liked having her friends there even if there was the occasional spat between them.

Her mind drifted back over the years and the fun they'd had together. Lisa the livewire and Audrey the efficient. And Harrie. Who had she been to them? How did they see her? She was always the one in the middle. The peacemaker. The person behind the scenes keeping them all together. The ideas person. The instigator.

The one who would be leaving the party first.

There it was again – that negativity. Lying comfortably on a beautiful hill high above the sea, her two best friends in the world beside her, and still she couldn't completely shut out the pain. Maybe it was because everything was so perfect that the negative thoughts crept in. She often found that in life – you could be in the middle of a completely happy moment and, the very next second, be totally aware of your own mortality. Did that make the moment even sweeter, she wondered?

As she felt the tears rise, she did her best to will them away, refusing to open her eyes until she had recovered her composure. Just take a moment, she told herself. It will pass. Think of something else: something silly. That often worked. She used to do that while waiting for hospital appointments. All those dark dreary hours hanging around in corridors. She'd read her way through so many books and magazines and had gone through her whole life, mining it for all the silly moments, recalling them and reliving them over again, like the time she'd walked into her first classroom as a newly qualified teacher and had tripped over her own feet and flown across the room. It hadn't been funny at the time and certainly hadn't created the impression she'd wanted on her first day, but she could imagine how she'd looked to her pupils. Their first flying teacher. They'd called her Mary Poppins after that, but she'd soon managed to nip that in the bud.

Slowly, trusting herself now, she blinked her eyes open. She could blame any stray tears on the brightness of the sun and sky, she decided as she sat up. Lisa was still lying down, but Audrey was staring out to sea, her long dark hair blowing behind her.

'A penny for them,' Harrie said.

'They're not worth that much.'

'They are to me.'

Audrey turned around and smiled. 'I was just thinking about the first time we were all together.'

'Wasn't it in that dreadful student bar?' Lisa said, pushing herself up from the grass.

'You were flirting with the barman,' Audrey said.

'Lisa's always flirting,' Harrie added.

'And Harrie walked in looking like she was about to cry,' Audrey remembered.

'I did not!'

'You did a bit,' Lisa agreed.

'I probably did too,' Audrey said. 'It was the first time I'd been away from home and I was as nervous as hell.'

'Me too,' Harrie admitted. 'I remember unpacking my suitcase and thinking that I'd give it to the end of the week and, if I didn't like it, I'd leave.'

'Well, I'm glad you stayed!' Lisa said. 'It wouldn't have been the same without you.'

'Oh, I don't know,' Audrey said with a shrug. 'We'd have probably hooked up with that Tania girl. She would have been a good Harrie replacement.'

'I hope you're joking!' Harrie cried.

'Yes!' Lisa gasped. 'She was *awful*!'

'Remember when your earrings went missing?' Harrie said to Audrey. 'You said she'd been in your room asking to borrow a book or something.'

'That's right,' Audrey said, 'and it was after that when I noticed they were gone. They'd been my grandma's. I suppose it was silly to take them to university, but I didn't expect anyone to steal them.'

'But you got them back, didn't you?' Lisa asked.

'Yes, they mysteriously turned up in a place I'd already looked at least a dozen times. I think Tania realised how much they meant to me and felt bad about it and sneakily returned them.'

'Weirdo,' Harrie said. 'It's a good job I didn't leave. Heaven only knows what would've happened to you two if you'd been friends with her instead of me.'

Audrey laughed.

'It was so lovely that we all found each other,' Lisa said.

'Friends forever,' Audrey said, looking at Harrie and winking.

Harrie nodded. 'Absolutely.'

'Even when we don't see each other for years at a time.'

'But that's the true test of friendship, isn't it?' Harrie pointed out. 'I mean, don't you just love that we can pick up exactly where we left off? There's no awkwardness. We're just back to being us three.'

Audrey and Lisa nodded and the three of them sat for a few moments, gazing out to sea, the sun on their faces and the wind in their hair. Suddenly, Harrie giggled.

'What is it?' Lisa asked.

'Remember Dr Bulmer?'

'Oh, my god! *Yes*!' Lisa said. 'He fancied himself as an actor, didn't he? He was always reading things out loud and getting into character. *So* embarrassing.'

'Remember the time he was reading from *Far from the Madding Crowd* and started doing all the sound effects of Captain Troy's sword-play?' Audrey said.

Harrie started laughing. 'How could anyone forget that? I think I turned red trying to hold all the laughter in!'

'You did. I remember,' Lisa told her. 'I've never read so much in my life as that first year at university. I was horrified at the time when we were sent that reading list and the first book on it was *Vanity Fair*. I thought I was never going to make it through the term, but I really miss those days now. We had such a wonderful excuse for doing nothing but curling up with a book.'

'I remember skimming *David Copperfield* and then having to fudge my way through a seminar,' Audrey confessed. 'I'm sure the lecturer knew if you hadn't read it properly.'

'Wait a minute,' Lisa said. 'Audrey didn't do her homework properly?'

Audrey shook her head. 'I don't know why you think I'm Mrs Perfect all the time.'

Lisa laughed at Audrey's obvious discomfort. 'Yes, I don't know where I got that impression from!'

Audrey sighed. 'I have to say I was so relieved when that first term was over.'

The three of them fell silent and Harrie looked at Lisa, remembering that it had been at the end of that first term when Lisa's mother had fallen ill. Mrs Coulson had picked Lisa up from university because she couldn't bear the thought of her daughter having to catch 'a grubby train', she said, and she'd treated the three girls to a slap-up lunch in town. The odd thing was, she hadn't eaten much herself. Lisa had asked her mother if she was all right and Harrie had remembered the look on Mrs Coulson's face.

'Of course I'm all right!' she'd declared with a smile, but Harrie had noticed something behind that too-bright smile and had guessed she was hiding something. Lisa broke the news to them when she came back after that first holiday. She'd been pale and fragile and totally dependent on Harrie and Audrey to keep her going. The cancer had been cruel in its swiftness, taking Mrs Coulson in a matter of months. Lisa's father hadn't coped well and his sister, Lisa's aunt, had stepped in. Having no children herself, Aunt Katharine had fussed over Lisa as if she was her own daughter. Lisa had told her friends that she could look after herself, but they'd seen only too well the support she needed. She'd let her work slide and her lecturers had given her endless extensions for her essays and had even allowed her to go home mid-term during one particularly difficult patch.

Harrie still remembered those dark days. They were one of the reasons why she'd delayed telling her friends about her own cancer. They'd been through so much with Lisa's mother and Harrie had felt so protective of her dear friend and hadn't wanted to put her through any more than she needed to. She was absolutely dreading telling Lisa her news.

Harrie looked at Lisa now. The sun was full on her face and a happy smile danced across it. What would happen when she told her, she wondered? How would Lisa react? Harrie could feel the butterflies rising in her stomach at the mere thought of the scene that lay ahead.

But not today, she told herself.

'Shouldn't we be thinking about getting back?' Audrey asked, looking at her phone at last.

'Gordon Bennett, Aud! Don't you ever do anything that's not on the clock?' Lisa cried.

'I'm just thinking of what's-her-name and the lunch she's preparing us.'

'Mrs Ryder,' Harrie said.

'She won't want us to be late,' Audrey told them.

'I'm not having my holiday ruled by some tyrant in the kitchen,' Lisa said.

'Still, we shouldn't keep the poor woman waiting if she's gone to a lot of effort,' Audrey pointed out.

'And I can't believe you've brought your phone out here,' Lisa said. 'I thought you were going to make an effort to relax.'

'I am,' Audrey insisted. 'I didn't bring my watch – look! I've got a great white mark where it usually is.' She pointed to her arm and, sure enough, there was a slim band of pale skin. 'But I can't relax without having a phone for emergencies. Imagine if one of us twisted our ankle.'

'We'd manage,' Lisa said.

'Or went over the cliff,' Audrey added.

'It would be too late for a phone then.' Harrie got up from the grass.

Audrey and Lisa followed, making their way down the hill through the trees.

'Ah! How wonderful it is to go downhill,' Audrey declared.

'But the view is from the top,' Harrie said.

'Ever the philosopher!' Lisa teased.

'Just an observer of life.'

As soon as they were out of the trees, the priory came into view.

'Isn't it magnificent?' Harrie said.

Lisa pursed her lips. 'I think it looks slightly spooky. It took me ages to fall asleep last night. I kept expecting to see a hooded monk shuffling about in the shadows.'

'Don't say that! I'll never sleep now!' Audrey cried.

'I've never stayed in such an old building before,' Harrie said. 'I'm so used to modern places. I think I've been missing out. I've always thought I wouldn't like them. Too many bumpy walls and uneven floorboards with squeaks in them.'

'And mice and spiders,' Audrey added.

'And moths and monks,' Lisa said.

They all laughed.

'But I'm really loving it. I love all the funny little idiosyncrasies – you don't get those in a newbuild. You might have perfectly straight walls with everything at right angles, but it's somehow soulless, don't you think?'

'I wouldn't swap my modern flat,' Lisa stated.

'Aren't these old buildings notoriously difficult to heat?' Audrey asked. 'I like my double-glazed windows. Those Georgian sash windows might look lovely, but I wouldn't want to be sitting next to one on a winter's evening.'

Harrie smiled. 'I don't think it would be so bad.'

'Oh, no!' Lisa cried. 'You're not thinking of taking on some dreadful old project, are you? You've got that dreamy, ambitious look about you.'

'No, nothing like that. But I can't help thinking that I've missed out.' She paused, feeling that she'd said too much. 'I mean, it's a young person's job, isn't it? Renovating.'

'It doesn't have to be,' Lisa said.

'What did you have in mind?' Audrey asked.

'Nothing,' Harrie said honestly. 'I just wondered what it would be like to live in a really old place. A place that was filled with the stories of its previous residents. I guess that's why I booked the priory. There's something so romantic about an ancient place.'

'Not if you read Dodie Smith's *I Capture the Castle*,' Audrey pointed out. 'Wasn't it always damp and full of rats?'

'There is nothing romantic about sharing your home with rats,' Lisa agreed.

Harrie smiled again. 'We have so many choices, don't we? Choices we completely overlook. Like where and how to live? A flat or a bungalow, a cottage or a castle . . .'

'I don't think everyone has a choice,' Lisa said. 'I can't afford anything more than my tiny flat.'

'But imagine if you *did* have a choice,' Harrie pressed. 'What would you choose?'

Audrey took in a deep breath. 'I've never really thought about it.'

'You're always working too hard,' Harrie told her. 'You need to relax more, dream more. It's important.'

Audrey seemed to be contemplating this. 'Well, I've always liked the idea of an eco-house,' she confessed. 'Maybe near the sea.'

'You want to live near the sea but you live in London?' Harrie said.

'I know where I live,' Audrey told her. 'You're the one who told me to dream.'

'It just seems a shame that, well, so many people have dreams but their real lives are so different.'

'So what's your dream home, Lisa?' Audrey asked.

'Something big and posh with a sweeping *Gone with the Wind* staircase and a beautiful studio where I can do my yoga without listening to a neighbour's music blaring. And I want thick soft carpets,' Lisa said, 'so I can walk around barefoot and not be cold. There's this horrible piece of sticky linoleum in the kitchen in my flat. It never comes clean no matter how hard I scrub it.'

Harrie and Audrey both made commiserating noises.

'What about you, Harrie?' Audrey asked. 'What would your dream home be like?'

'You're looking at it,' she said, nodding to the priory.

'Really? You'd want to *live* here?' Lisa said.

'Why not?'

'Well, it's a bit *big*, isn't it?'

'More room to dream in,' Harrie said.

They'd reached the meadow now and walked through the grasses and flowers, their legs and feet sending up clouds of butterflies into the air.

Reaching the garden of the priory, they crossed the lawn and entered through the great wooden door.

'Something smells good,' Lisa said as they walked into the kitchen. She gasped when she saw the table. It had been laid for three with crockery, cutlery and glasses and looked wonderfully inviting.

'I think we'd better wash our hands,' Audrey said. 'I suddenly feel like I'm a child again.'

A few minutes later, the three women met back in the kitchen and settled down to lunch. Harrie had to admit that Mrs Ryder's first attempt looked surprisingly good. She had filled a big bowl with crisp green salad leaves and had left roasted peppers stuffed with wild rice in the oven for them.

She came into the kitchen as they were halfway through.

'I hope this will do for you,' she said.

'It's splendid,' Audrey said.

'No need to fire you then,' Harrie said.

Mrs Ryder's eyes widened at this comment.

'I think she's teasing you,' Audrey quickly added, shooting a look of disapproval across the table at Harrie.

'There's no meat,' Mrs Ryder told them. 'Not anywhere, although I daresay you would benefit from a bit of bacon.'

'Oh, yes!' Lisa said. 'Is there some?'

'No,' Harrie told her.

'I've made an egg-free, dairy-free quiche which I've put in the fridge for your dinner.' She shook her head as if in disapproval.

'Thank you,' Harrie said.

'And I've made your beds up and, well, had a bit of a tidy round.'

Audrey looked slightly alarmed by this. 'You haven't moved any of my files, have you?'

Mrs Ryder turned her attention to her. 'So you're the one with the files, are you? Odd thing to bring on a holiday.'

Harrie bit back a smile. 'Tell her off, Mrs Ryder.'

'It's not my job to tell anybody off – only to point out right from wrong when I see it.'

'It isn't wrong to want to keep my business afloat,' Audrey said through gritted teeth.

'It is in the middle of a summer holiday,' Mrs Ryder said. 'All them spreadsheets and things.' She shook her head, tutting like a disappointed parent.

'We told her,' Lisa piped up.

'Everybody's told her,' Harrie added.

'Hey! What is this? Some kind of intervention?' Audrey cried.

'Seems like it!' Harrie said, highly amused.

'Just shred the spreadsheets and have done with it,' Lisa said with a laugh.

'I'm not shredding them. They're important.'

'So's taking a break,' Harrie told her.

'I know!' Audrey said. 'Why else do you think I've given you the *whole* of my summer?'

Silence greeted Audrey's question, but then Mrs Ryder tutted again.

'You career women – you've got your heads down so often that you've forgotten there's a sky above you.'

The three of them watched as Mrs Ryder picked up her handbag from a nearby chair and collected the large canvas bag full of her tricks of the trade. 'I'll see you in a couple of days.'

'Thank you, Mrs Ryder!' Harrie called after her.

They waited until the large front door had closed behind her.

'Rude woman!' Audrey declared.

'I like her!' Lisa said. 'She's kind of like a scary headmistress that you want to please.'

'I like her too,' Harrie said.

'Well, I'm happy to be in the minority on this occasion,' Audrey said, 'and if she so much as touches one of my spreadsheets, I'm out of here!'

Chapter 5

That first week at the priory was a happy time as the three women gently fell into a new routine with one another, with Mrs Ryder and with the extraordinary rhythms of the old building and its gardens. They read together, reminisced about their student days, dozed off in deckchairs, cooked on the days Mrs Ryder wasn't there and had the sort of easy, drifting conversations that only happen amongst true friends. Harrie couldn't have been happier. Well, she could.

There was, she recognised, still progress to be made on the Samson Haverstock front. She'd given him a bit of breathing space since the flask encounter, watching him come and go with his tools and, if she ever managed to catch his eye, he'd give a curt little nod.

Lisa had clapped eyes on him properly for the first time a couple of days ago.

'Wow! He's cute!'

'I wouldn't bother,' Harrie warned her. 'He's only interested in stone.'

'You've got to be kidding me. He's gorgeous. Look at those arms. I bet he could pick up that trestle table in the kitchen and walk a hundred miles without breaking into a sweat.'

'Well, I bet he'd break into a sweat if you so much as said *boo* to him,' Harrie said.

'Maybe I should try that sometime.'

Lisa hadn't gone through with her threat, but it was only a matter of time. The truth was, Lisa liked men and Harrie couldn't imagine that she'd spend the whole summer living like a nun, even though they were in a priory.

It was on a hot sunny morning when Lisa and Audrey had gone for a dip in the pool that Harrie decided to go and see the surly stonemason again. She was as genuinely curious about his job as she was about the man.

Scaffolding had been set up in the tower before Harrie had arrived and Samson was somewhere up there as she approached. She heard him before she saw him – the light sound of his chisel on the ancient stone.

'Good morning!' she called.

He paused in his work, but he didn't turn around. Perhaps it was his profession which made him so unfriendly, Harrie thought. Spending most of your life with your back to the world wasn't exactly conducive to conversation, was it?

'My friends are in the pool, but I didn't fancy it,' she told him, undeterred by his lack of interest in engaging with her. 'I wanted to see how you were getting on.'

'Don't stand there!' he called down.

'Why not?'

'You'll get covered in dust.'

'Oh!' Harrie leapt back and discovered she could see him better from that vantage point anyway. She couldn't make out exactly what he was doing and wondered, for a brief moment, if she should climb the ladder up the scaffolding, but it was probably best to be invited first.

She looked around and spied Samson's denim jacket neatly folded on an old wooden chair, and there was a large toolbox and his flask. She sighed. So, he didn't have plans to bother her for more tea then. That was a shame. She'd have liked him to bother her again. Still, she could try another tactic.

'I'm going to make a cup of tea. Would you like one?' she called up to him.

'I've got my flask.'

'Yes, I can see that, but I think tea tastes better out of a china cup, doesn't it?'

He stopped banging for a moment.

'Shall I take that as a yes?' she asked, peering up. She still couldn't see him properly.

'Only if you're making one.'

'I said I was.'

He started banging again and Harrie left to make the tea.

While waiting for the kettle to boil, she ruminated on what it was that made a personality. Why, for example, was Lisa naturally exuberant? And why was Audrey's default setting anxious? They say you should never judge a person by first impressions, but Harrie had to admit that these were often a very good indicator. Many times, she'd taken just one look at someone and decided that they were either going to feature in her life or that she wanted nothing to do with them. You could so often tell by the way a person's features were set in their face. It wasn't anything physical. Beauty counted for very little when it came to personality, but there would often be an expression in the eyes or something in the way the mouth was set which would mark somebody out as either friendly or not.

Harrie believed that you could tell immediately if a person was kind. Kindness. That was the trait she'd come to value most in recent years. You realised that as soon as you became ill. Kindness trumped absolutely everything else. You couldn't live without it or, at least, it wouldn't be an existence worth very much at all. And, even though Samson hadn't shown any kindness in his manner, she truly believed there was kindness behind the gruff exterior. She'd seen it in his eyes, she was sure of it.

Having made the tea, she took the cups through to the tower on a tray, a packet of cookies on it too. He was still banging away. She smiled. He probably wouldn't appreciate his carefully skilled restoration work being referred to as *banging away*.

'I've got the tea!' she called up to him from the bottom of the scaffolding. The banging stopped and she watched as he slowly climbed down the ladder, returning to earth once more with a gentle thump of his steel-capped boots. She'd forgotten how tall he was and felt practically dwarfed standing next to him, especially as she was wearing the flattest of sandals.

He nodded, taking a cup and a cookie. She smiled at that. She had found a weakness.

'So, what exactly are you doing up there?' she asked, genuinely interested.

He craned his head back to look up at the wall he'd been working on. 'Mostly repointing. Replacing the old cement with new.'

Harrie nodded.

'There's a whole section of wall that needs attention, but then I can move on to the fun part.'

'What's that?'

'The angel.'

'There's an angel up there? Can I see it?'

'Not yet. Too dangerous.'

'Oh.' Harrie couldn't help but be disappointed. She took a sip of her tea. 'Are you working on anything else besides our tower?'

'I'm working on a few projects, yes.'

'Anywhere interesting?'

'Wells.'

Harrie frowned. 'The cathedral?'

Samson nodded.

'How wonderful! That's one of the most beautiful buildings in England,' Harrie said. 'So tell me about it. I mean, what's it like holding your chisel so close to something so ancient and wielding that kind of power?'

He shrugged. 'Pretty good, I guess.'

Harrie laughed. 'You don't give much away, do you?'

'Should I be? Is this some kind of interview?'

'No, just a conversation. I'm interested in what you do. Tell me a bit about it. What's your favourite part of the job?'

He paused before answering. 'I don't know. There are lots. I like handling the tools. A stonemason's tools are like an extension of himself.'

Harrie smiled. She liked that. She liked the way he talked too – it was slow and careful, as if he were measuring each word.

'Go on,' she encouraged when he paused.

He took a sip of his tea.

'I like the stone I work with – the colours, the different weights and textures. I like seeing all the thousands of fossils in the limestone we get to work with, and spotting the stonemasons' marks from centuries ago, knowing that somebody else from a different time was here before me. And I like the finished job – when you revisit a place you've worked on and all the scaffolding's gone and people are coming and going and have no idea that a stonemason lived high above their heads for months at a time to restore the place they love.'

Harrie listened, spellbound. It was the most Samson had said to her and she was enraptured by the beauty of his words and his obvious passion for his work.

She was just about to ask him more when he drained his cup.

'I've got to get back to work.'

Before she could say anything, he was climbing the ladder back through the scaffolding and the light sound of his chisel was heard a moment later.

After her morning swim, Lisa showered and then grabbed her yoga mat. It was a real treat for her to be at the priory and it was an even greater treat to be able to practise her yoga there. In the cramped space of her Leeds flat, she was forced to move her sofa and chairs in order to make room. Even then, her fingers would occasionally hit the horrible plastic chandelier that hung from the middle of the ceiling and, more often than not, she would just get herself comfortable and then some awful noise would start up, like roadworks or a neighbour's music.

As she made her way outside, she couldn't help thinking of what Audrey had said. Her friend was right, of course. She shouldn't still be renting – not at her age.

Somewhere, something had gone horribly wrong with her life and she couldn't help but cast her mind back to the heady days ten years ago when she'd starred in the successful daytime soap opera. She'd been dating Kyle Hanson, her co-star, and they'd sizzled both on the screen and off.

What a whirlwind it had been. They'd been the golden couple, beloved by the tabloids and followed everywhere by hungry photographers and eager fans. They'd even talked about moving in together, but the relationship never got that far. Her character, the vibrant Suzie, had exited the show as dramatically as she'd entered it, killed off in a horrific accident. There'd been no coming back from that, Lisa thought, and Kyle soon lost interest in her when she was no longer grabbing the headlines. He'd gone on to fall in love with his new co-star. They were married now with two children and there was a little bit of Lisa that couldn't help thinking that it should have been her.

Who are you kidding? she asked now. You – a *mother*? The role would not have suited her. That's what she told herself anyway. She had far more than enough children in her life in her role as a teacher. Then there'd always been that doubt residing deep inside telling her that she could never be as good a mother as her own had been. Losing her mother had, perhaps, meant that Lisa remembered her with the sort of golden glow that reality might not have lived up to had she survived, but Lisa wasn't going to take any chances. She simply had never wanted to be a mother herself. She was married to her career as an actress, such as it was these days.

Her grandmother, who was a very robust eighty-nine years old, still had all her press clippings and regularly got them out for visiting relatives and friends. It was highly embarrassing because, if Lisa happened to be there, they would naturally question what she was doing now.

'Oh, she's just a teacher now,' her grandmother would say, her face unable to hide its disappointment.

So, here she was, a forty-six-year-old out-of-work actress and sometime supply teacher living in rented accommodation with only a yoga mat and a singing bowl to call her own.

Count your blessings, she told herself. Focus on the positive. Meditate. But how hard it was to shut out all the noise. It was no mean task to ignore all those insecurities. Audrey seemed to have got it right. Everything she did seemed to work out. She was such a natural when it came to business and success. She could set herself any task and win through.

Lisa shook her head. Jealousy was not a good way to begin one's meditation, she told herself. Comparing oneself to others was a sure way to madness. One should glory in the success of others, she knew that. Hadn't she wanted Audrey to be pleased with her when she'd had her moment in the spotlight? And she was genuinely thrilled now that Audrey was doing so well with her business. Still, one couldn't help measuring one's own mediocrity against another's success. It seemed to be human nature.

But I'm going shut all that out now, she told herself as she unrolled her mat. She had found a very special space in the herb garden which was glorious in the morning when the first rays of sunlight would find their way there. It was still sunny there now after her morning swim and she got herself comfortable, crossing her legs, lengthening through her spine and resting her palms facing upwards on her knees.

She closed her eyes, seeking that moment of stillness and clarity which came from emptying the mind of its worries. She took a few deep breaths, in through the nose and out through the mouth, feeling the natural rhythms of the body that one so often forgot in the daily rush of life. It was so important sometimes simply to breathe, to remember that vital link between the mind and the body which could make all the difference. Breathe.

Slowly, Lisa felt her body relax and her mind began to drift.

She frowned. The drifting had been interrupted by an appalling noise.

Reluctantly, furiously, she opened her eyes, momentarily dazzled by the light as she tried to identify the noise. It was a strimmer – there was no question about it.

'You have got to be kidding me!' she said through gritted teeth as she stood up from her yoga mat and left the herb garden.

As she walked across the lawn, the noise became louder. She could feel the peace she had been reaching for quickly drain away to be replaced by anger.

As she rounded the corner, she saw him. The man with the strimmer. His back was to her and he obviously didn't know that she was standing behind him, her hands on her hips, ready to erupt.

'Hey!' she shouted, trying to make herself heard above the horrendous noise. 'I said—'

He turned around and almost jumped out of his skin as he saw her.

Finally, thankfully, the machine was switched off and she found herself looking at a man in his early twenties with dark curly hair and piercing blue eyes. As handsome as he might be, he had still disturbed her peace.

'Can I help you?' he asked her.

'You can help me by not making such a bloody awful noise,' she said, the words spilling out of her before she could stop them.

His mouth dropped open and he looked sincerely sorry. 'My noise disturbed you?'

'I was trying to meditate.'

'Meditate?'

'Yes,' she said. 'This is my holiday. I've come here for some peace and quiet. Is that too much to ask?'

'Of course not. I'm sorry.'

Lisa nodded, feeling as though she'd got through to the man. 'Well, good.' She turned to leave.

'The thing is,' the man continued, 'I'm being paid to take care of this place and that means keeping on top of the grass. It won't take me long.'

She turned back to look at him, willing herself to be patient.

'I'm Alfie,' he added, taking a step forward and extending a hand.

'Lisa,' she said, shaking it.

'I promise I'll be as quick as I can,' he told her.

'Right,' she said.

He nodded then turned his back on her and began strimming once again. Lisa watched him for a moment longer. How annoying he was. And how very handsome.

Audrey looked out of her bedroom window onto the garden below. They had been there a whole week now and she'd made a real effort to relax and not work, she really had, but her fingers were itching to hit her keyboard. She turned around and looked at the laptop sleeping on a chair in the corner of the room. Harrie had told her she would change her password and lock her out if she caught her working on it and Audrey believed her.

Dear Harrie. She meant well and Audrey really appreciated her care, but she simply didn't know the pressure she was under. Starting a new business from scratch was no mean feat. Taking on staff, being responsible for thirty-two pupils, paying the exorbitant London rates on a building, organising lessons, and the myriad other jobs that went with it, all could sometimes take their toll. Some months, Audrey didn't even know if they would make the payroll.

Mike had repeatedly told her that she'd taken on too much, but this was something Audrey felt she had to do. She smiled at that, remembering a conversation she'd once had with a colleague at her school.

'Middle-child syndrome,' her colleague had told her. 'You *are* a middle child, aren't you?'

Audrey had nodded.

'I thought I'd remembered that right. You see, you weren't the firstborn – you never carried that accolade – and you weren't the youngest – the one who was mollycoddled, the baby of the family. You were the one in the middle, the forgotten one, and middle children often go on to be overachievers. They push themselves for recognition.'

Audrey had dismissed her colleague's summation of her life as psychobabble, but she'd never forgotten it and it was true that she had always striven to do better and to always be moving forward. Perhaps that's why she was so tired now.

Harrie was looking tired too, Audrey noticed. They were none of them as young as they once had been and the long years of teaching had certainly done them no favours in the health department. She could hardly believe that it was twenty-seven years since they'd met at university for their teacher training degree. How young they'd all been: so full of energy and enthusiasm. They'd all been going to make a difference in the world. And here they were, burnt out with exhaustion. Well, she was anyway. Harrie still seemed so full of that same enthusiasm for life and Lisa certainly hadn't given up on her dreams.

Mike had been right. Audrey needed this holiday and, although it went against all her principles to do nothing for a long period of time, she realised that she needed a break.

Walking across the room, she took a look at her reflection in the dark silver mirror, which was spotted with age and wonderfully flattering. Forty-six, she thought. There were a few lines around her eyes and mouth which couldn't be ignored any longer. Laughter lines, weren't they? And a few grey hairs at the parting in between trips to the hairdresser's. Mike still told her she was beautiful. He was sweet like that – always paying her compliments and buying her flowers and little gifts. She couldn't remember the last time she'd told him how much she appreciated these gestures. Wasn't that an awful thing to admit to? But her work was so all-consuming these days that there seemed to be little time for anything else. Mike understood that.

She still couldn't believe Mike had rung Harrie ahead of the holiday. Well, she could. He was that kind of husband and he'd been on Audrey's case for some time now about working too hard. It had taken all her powers of subterfuge to sneak her laptop, briefcase and box of files out of the house and into her car.

But this place. It was something else. It demanded that you slowed down a bit and took time for yourself and your friends. She'd been enjoying taking a walk before breakfast. She couldn't remember the last time she'd gone for a walk from home. Working had taken over from walking. Sometimes, she didn't get into bed before one in the morning, her eyes red from staring at a computer screen as she tried to balance the books.

It would all be worth it, though, that's what she told herself, and then everyone would clap her on the back and tell her how clever she was. Maybe there was something in that middle child syndrome after all. She really did have this need for approval. Perhaps it was because she'd always been in the background, whether in her family home or the classroom or the workplace. She was always the quiet, invisible one

– the pupil overlooked by her teachers, the teacher overlooked by the head of department. Her achievements were never recognised because they were rarely big or brash, they were simply consistent and that didn't seem to count for very much.

But she kept going. That was her strength. Others might make a bigger noise and a bigger splash but, very often, they would fall by the wayside, leaving Audrey to chug on past. She was good at that and Harrie and Lisa had always admired her success, telling her what a good job she was doing. But they only saw the glossy surface, didn't they? Lisa did anyway. She had seen the envy in her friend's face when she told her about the new business. Well, perhaps *envy* was too strong a word. But there'd been something there – some little vein of jealousy perhaps. The irony of it was that Lisa didn't see the struggle that went on behind the scenes. She probably thought it was a twenty-four-hour joy to be the head of a new company but, more often than not, Audrey was left feeling depleted and insecure, wondering why she was putting herself through it all. What was it that made her such a workaholic? Who was she trying to prove herself to? Surely she wasn't still trying to win the approbation of those around her?

She took a deep breath, catching sight of her briefcase beside the wardrobe. The sun was shining and it was tempting to reach for a book and lie back on one of the sun loungers in the garden, but she had to do a little bit of work first.

Chapter 6

The second week at Melbury Priory was blessed with sunshine which turned the garden into a golden glory where the scent of lavender, roses and herbs filled the air. For the three women, it meant hours spent by the swimming pool – Lisa with a book in her hand, Harrie with iced water and Audrey with a cup of tea.

'Who fancies a dip in the pool?' Audrey suddenly asked. 'Harrie?'

A shot of cold fear ran down Harrie's spine. 'I'm good here, thanks,' she said quickly.

'Come on! You've hired this amazing place with a pool and I've not even seen you in it yet.'

'I had a swim the other night.'

'Did you?'

She nodded. She had sneaked out in the quiet of the midnight garden when she was quite sure Audrey and Lisa were asleep.

'Well, let's get you in there now,' Audrey said, on her feet and shedding her light dress, underneath which she had on a pretty blue-and-gold swimsuit. She leaned forward, taking hold of Harrie's left hand.

Harrie could feel her heart hammering in her chest. 'Audrey, please don't!'

'Come *on!*'

'No, really. Maybe later, okay?'

'Oh, Harrie!'

'Really – I . . .' Before she could protest any further, Audrey had hauled her out of her sun lounger.

'You'll love it once you're in!'

'Go on, Harrie!' Lisa encouraged from the safety of her own sun lounger. She obviously had no intention of joining them.

'Audrey – *no!*' she screamed, surprising herself and her friend by the force of her command.

Audrey stopped trying to manoeuvre Harrie towards the pool, but she still had a hold of Harrie's arm and that's when she blanched and suddenly dropped it. Harrie saw the change in expression in Audrey's face. She'd seen it, hadn't she? The scar under her arm. Harrie instinctively hugged her arms to her chest, but it was too late to hide it.

'I thought you were going to throw her in there for a moment,' Lisa said with a laugh.

'No,' Audrey said. 'I wouldn't do that.' Her eyes never left Harrie's.

Turning away, Harrie sat back down on the sun lounger and, a moment later, Audrey jumped into the pool and swam to the far end. Harrie watched her as she returned and stopped, eyeing Harrie before swimming back.

'I'm going to get a drink,' Harrie said. 'You want anything, Lisa?'

'No, thanks.'

Harrie got up and walked the short distance across the lawn to the priory. Her feet were bare and, after the warmth of the grass on her skin, the flagstone floors of the kitchen felt so cold that it was as if she'd plunged her feet into an icy stream.

What she needed was a cup of tea. A good strong one. None of this herbal rubbish. She wanted thick brown builder's tea.

Reaching into the cupboard, she took out a mug and a spoon from the drawer.

'Harrie?'

Harrie had known Audrey would probably follow her into the priory, but she'd been hoping she wouldn't.

'Yes?' Harrie said innocently, her back to her friend as she filled the kettle. She could see that her hands were shaking and willed them to stop. She had to be in control.

'What was it I saw out there?'

'What do you mean?'

'You know what I mean.'

Harrie paused with the kettle. 'What did you see?'

'Your scar.'

Harrie pursed her lips as she tried to deal with her thoughts.

'Harrie – look at me. You're hiding something and it's freaking me out.'

After switching the kettle on, Harrie turned to face Audrey. She had a large white towel wrapped around her body and her hair was wet from her swim, the long tendrils dripping water over her shoulders.

'There's nothing to worry about.'

'No? Then what's the scar? You sure didn't have it when we were in Lanzarote.'

'No,' Harrie said, trying to remain calm and in control. 'I've had a little procedure since then – that's all – and it was all fine.'

'A procedure? What sort of a procedure?'

'Just a small biopsy.'

Audrey frowned. 'A *small* biopsy? There's no such thing as a *small* biopsy!'

'Yes, there is,' Harrie assured her. 'It was very simple really. I found a lump. It was removed. Everything was fine.'

Audrey swore. 'Oh, my god, Harrie! A lump! Why didn't you say something?'

'Because there wasn't anything to say.'

'So you're okay?'

'Everything's good.'

Audrey didn't look convinced.

'Honestly,' Harrie said. 'It couldn't have been simpler.'

'But I – we – could have helped, surely?'

'I didn't want to worry anyone, really.'

'God, Harrie – you shouldn't have to go through something like that on your own. Remember when I dragged you to the dentist's with me when I had root-canal work done?'

Harrie smiled. 'Nobody should go through root canal on their own.'

'And nobody should go through a biopsy either,' Audrey said, placing her hands on Harrie's shoulders. 'Promise me you'll never hide something like that again.'

Harrie took a moment before answering. It had been one of the most painful decisions of her life not to tell her friends about her diagnosis and a part of her still felt she'd betrayed them by not telling them the truth from the outset.

'I promise,' she said at last.

'Good,' Audrey said, and then she looked around the room. 'So is that why you hired this place for the summer? You had a health scare and it's put everything into focus?' Her friend held her gaze.

Harrie took a deep breath. 'You've found me out.'

Audrey nodded. 'I did think it was a bit odd. I mean it's a *good* odd, don't get me wrong! But it seems a rather extravagant thing to do.'

'I know,' Harrie agreed, 'and it is. But it had to be done.'

Audrey smiled and then leaned forward to give her a hug and Harrie suddenly felt horribly exposed because she was wearing her swimsuit with the pockets for her breast form prosthesis. She wore them all the time without thinking now and had become quite used to them, but was still very aware of them when in close contact with people. Still, Audrey didn't seem to notice anything was out of the ordinary.

'You must have been so scared,' Audrey said.

'I was,' Harrie said. At least that wasn't a lie. She could still remember that chilling day in the shower when she'd discovered the lump. It was the kind of thing that most women imagined at some point in their lives. Perhaps they'd watched *Terms of Endearment* and thought, *What if that was me?* And one always did those checks that doctors were always reminding you to do but, until you actually felt a lump, you couldn't really imagine the depth of fear that was possible.

'And you didn't tell Lisa?' Audrey asked.

'No. Only Honor knows.'

'You mean Charles didn't know either?'

'Of course not,' Harrie said. 'We're just friends now.'

'But friends *share* things,' Audrey said.

'I know, I know. But – well – it's not like that between us now. Besides, he's married again. I can't go running back to him every time there's a bump in the road.'

'But this wasn't a bump – it was a *lump!*' Audrey said.

Harrie laughed.

'This isn't funny, Harrie!'

Harrie covered her mouth with her hands in order to try and control herself. 'I know. I'm sorry!'

'It could've been serious!'

'I know. I know.'

'Are you going to tell Lisa?' Audrey asked.

'No. She'll only panic.'

'You really should tell her, Harrie.'

Harrie glanced down at the floor and nodded. 'I will. But later, okay? I just don't want to remind her of what happened to her mum.'

'But her mum had cancer,' Audrey pointed out, 'and you're okay, aren't you?'

'Yes, of course I'm okay. I just don't want to remind her of all that when we're meant to be enjoying the summer together.'

'Yes, that was a bad time,' Audrey said, and Harrie acknowledged that the memory of it still had the power to leave her breathless. Witnessing her friend's enormous loss had never really left Harrie. She'd felt Lisa's pain so very deeply.

'I still have nightmares about it all,' Audrey confessed.

'You do?'

She nodded. 'Remember those nights we sat up with her while she cried and cried?'

'I'll never forget them.'

'We took it in turns to comfort her because we were both so knackered with it.'

'It was an awful time,' Harrie said, 'and it's one of the reasons I didn't want to tell Lisa about my little procedure. You won't mention it to her, will you?' Harrie asked now, and Audrey sighed.

'Well, okay, but I'm not happy about it.'

'I know you're not,' Harrie said. 'Now, I'm going to make that cup of tea. Want one?'

'No, thanks.' Audrey headed towards the fridge for a can of cola and Harrie watched as she left the kitchen. She felt absolutely awful for lying to Audrey, but she'd been caught off guard and really didn't want the big showdown so soon. It was still the beginning of the holiday and she wanted to enjoy her time with her friends as a regular person because she knew that that was bound to change once she told them the truth. That terrible thing which was growing inside her would get all the attention. Her friends wouldn't look at her in the same way. They would always see the cancer first and she couldn't bear to see the pity and fear in their eyes. It had happened at her workplace. She'd had to be honest there when she'd given her notice. She had thought about just sneaking away, but that would be so cruel to the colleagues she cared about. The colleagues at the school she'd worked in for so many years had become like a family and she felt that she owed them the truth. But how awful it had been afterwards. It had seemed to her that the disease had reached out and touched so many more people than just its host and that really didn't seem fair. So, after that, she'd tried to protect people from the truth for as long as possible.

And that's exactly what she was doing now, she reminded herself. She was protecting her dearest friends, buying them time, allowing them to live in blissful ignorance and be happy for a little while longer.

She *would* tell them, just not yet.

***

There was nothing quite like a day spent in the sunshine with a good book, Lisa thought as she crossed the grass towards the priory and entered the cool stone building. She hadn't felt this relaxed in months, even with her daily yoga practice. Truly, nothing beat quality time spent with friends.

After taking a bath in the monstrous tub in her en suite, which she was gradually becoming quite fond of, she slathered her skin in an expensive moisturiser she'd treated herself to for the holiday. If one couldn't treat oneself to the occasional luxurious beauty product, life really wouldn't be worth living. For a moment, she remembered the brief period of her life working in television when she had been on such a ridiculous salary that she'd been able to buy such items without thinking twice. But, now, on a part-time teaching salary, she usually couldn't justify it.

Slowly, luxuriously, she stroked the cream into her arms and into the backs of her hands. Those ugly brown marks had begun to march across her skin. Liver spots. Ageing spots. Whatever they were, they were most unwelcome. Of course, hours spent in the sunshine didn't help, but that was so good for the soul, wasn't it? And what was more important: the skin or the soul? It was the same dilemma with food, wasn't it? One was constantly weighing things up, trying to lead a balanced life where health and happiness went hand-in-hand.

But – oh – the ageing process was an unhappy one. Those little brown spots wielded such power over her psyche. They made her feel as if she was going mouldy, like an overripe pear. Then there were the lines around her eyes. Perhaps she smiled too much. Yes, she should definitely stop smiling. She smiled at that and then cursed herself for smiling again. If only one could freeze-frame life for a bit. It was all running away so quickly and she hated to look too far ahead and acknowledge the fact that the big five-o was looming in the not-too-distant future. Fifty! A woman should never have to hit fifty.

She looked at her reflection in the mirror. She didn't look nearly fifty, did she? Her agent used to tell her that she looked at least ten years younger than her age, only Lisa wasn't sure that was still the case. Still, whenever she moaned about ageing, she reminded herself of the painful fact that her mother had never had that privilege. She'd died of cancer at just thirty-nine. That was no age at all, was it? And how odd it had been for Lisa to reach that age and then to go beyond it, each year becoming older than her own mother.

Looking at herself again, she could clearly see her mother's image and, while there was comfort in that, there was a little pain too – a constant reminder of what she had lost.

Lisa yanked a rebellious grey hair from her parting. Her mother would have loved to have reached an age where grey hairs, ageing spots and laughter lines started to take over. And Lisa had to remember that whenever she thought she had the right to complain. Still, Lisa was trying to work in an industry where women were judged and measured by those very things. Youth ruled when it came to the world of television and Lisa guessed that her time was up unless a really good character role came in now. A soap-opera villain, perhaps? She'd like that. Or the mother of one of the latest hot actresses. A *young* mother, Lisa thought, pulling her face taut with her hands and wondering if she should try Botox or one of those face peels.

She checked her phone for messages. She rarely heard from her agent these days. Gone were the long, lazy lunches together in the corner of some fancy London restaurant. She didn't get invited to those anymore. She was no longer a part of that inner clique. It still stung even after all these years because she knew she was a good actress. She'd proved herself with that one brilliant role and yet that seemed to count for nothing in this industry. She was yesterday's news. So why was she still finding it so hard to accept? She really should have moved on with her life by now and settled into a full-time teaching job, but her heart just wasn't in it. She still felt restless with ambition. And there was only one thing to do when she was feeling restless: yoga.

Changing into her yoga pants and choosing an apple-green top, Lisa grabbed her mat and headed out into the garden. The sun was lower in the sky now, but it was still pleasantly warm and she made her way to her favourite corner, where the herbs grew.

After a few settling breaths, Lisa closed her eyes and focused on the world within, letting all the little cares and worries of life slip away. You couldn't see your laughter lines with your eyes closed, she thought, and then cursed herself for even having that thought. Then she cursed herself for cursing herself because one of the things she had learned through yoga was to acknowledge any thought that entered your head, not to judge yourself for having it but to simply let it pass through. And so she did her best to practise that, batting away all the silly thoughts that entered her mind, like had she brought her nail polish with her? She couldn't remember. And should she have texted her agent just to keep in touch?

How hard it was to just live in the moment, she thought. There were always so many distractions from just simply being. The mind was a constant source of prey for the demons of the past and the worries of the future.

Lisa worked through a series of stretches, easing out the kinks of her body and aligning everything with her breath. She loved losing herself in the practice of yoga, and it was a true joy to do it in such beautiful surroundings.

It wasn't until she'd finished her practice that she became aware that somebody was watching her. Turning around, she saw it was the handsome gardener with the piercing blue eyes. She frowned. He might well be handsome, but she didn't like the idea of somebody watching her like that.

She decided to say something.

'Get a kick out of spying on people, do you?'

He looked shocked. 'Oh, sorry! I wasn't. I mean, well, I kind of was, I suppose. Is that yoga you were doing?'

'Well, of course it's yoga. What did you think I was doing – weeding the garden at right angles?'

He smiled. He had a nice smile, she couldn't help noticing.

'It's just that I was told to do a bit of yoga. I had an injury last year and my physio recommended it,' he told her.

'But you haven't done any?' she asked him.

He shrugged and Lisa nodded knowingly.

'I see. You think you're too young for yoga, don't you? You think it's for middle-aged people like me.'

'No,' he protested. 'I just couldn't imagine myself . . .'

'What?'

'Bending like that.'

'It would probably do you good,' Lisa told him. 'What kind of injury was it?'

'Back. Rugby injury.'

Lisa winced. 'I think you should try a few stretches.'

'Oh, I stretch. My physio has given me plenty of those.'

'And do they work?'

'I don't think anything will work, short of a new back.'

'You should really try yoga. You don't have to have a pink mat, you know.'

He laughed. 'You offering to teach me some moves?'

'I wouldn't want to be responsible for inflicting injuries on you.'

'You wouldn't. It's just twinges now. I've been assured nothing's going to break. It's annoying, but I can live with it.'

'Should you be gardening if you're in pain with your back?'

'I'm meant to keep moving,' he told her. 'It's not as bad as it was.' He walked towards her, putting the trowel he'd been holding on top of a low wall. 'Go on – teach me some moves.'

Lisa observed him for a moment, trying to gauge if he was being sincere or if he was taking the mickey. He looked pretty earnest.

'Would a *please* help?' he asked.

'Shouldn't you be working?'

'Nah. I've finished for the day.'

Lisa looked around the garden as if she might discover a hidden camera or something because she wasn't totally sure that she trusted him.

'Hey – look – I didn't mean to put you in an awkward position,' he said with a shrug. 'I shouldn't have disturbed you. I'm sorry. I'll leave you to it.'

Lisa instantly felt guilty. 'No – wait!' she called as he turned to go. 'I've got time to show you a couple of nice stretches.'

'Yeah?'

'Yeah.'

He grinned. She really did wish he'd stop doing that.

'Shall I kick my boots off?'

Lisa nodded. 'You'll get a better grip with bare feet.'

He bent, untying his laces and taking off his boots and socks. It suddenly felt rather strange and very intimate to be standing next to this stranger with bare feet. But he didn't seem to notice Lisa's awkwardness.

She took him through a series of moves and stretches, finishing with him lying on his back with his knees bent in semi-supine.

'Bending the knees like this gives your lower back wonderful support if you have problems there,' she told him.

'It feels good.'

'Yeah?'

She guided him through some deep breaths and then he stood back up, stepping off her mat and putting on his socks and boots.

'Hey, you're a pretty good teacher,' he said.

'Thank you!'

'You do this for a living?'

'Goodness, no.'

'You should.'

She smiled.

'You know, you look kind of familiar,' he said.

She bent to roll up her yoga mat, doing her best to shield her face.

'Have you been on telly?'

She sighed. 'Once or twice.'

'Really? I thought so. Remind me.'

'It was a long time ago.' She placed her mat in its carrier and looped it over her shoulder.

'Go on – you've got to tell me now.'

'It was just a soap opera. Long before your time.'

Suddenly, Alfie's eyes widened. 'You were that Melinda Blake from *Gargrave Road*, weren't you?'

Lisa felt her face flush.

'I've got it, haven't I?'

She nodded and began heading back towards the priory.

'I used to watch it with my mum. She used to love it. Used to love *you*. She was furious when they killed you off.'

'Well, thank your mum for her support,' Lisa said, not slowing down and hoping he'd drop by the wayside at some point.

'So, what did you do after that? I mean, you kind of disappeared.'

'Yes, thank you for reminding me.'

'Oh! God. Sorry.'

'It's okay. I just don't like talking about it, that's all.'

'I didn't mean to put my foot in it.'

'It's okay, really. It's just, well, the work I'm getting these days isn't up to much.'

'But you were really good,' he added. 'That scene in the bar when you walked out on Barry after finding out he was having an affair. *Classic!*'

'Thanks.' She felt the stirrings of a smile.

'That was so cool.'

Lisa stopped and turned to face him. 'How do you remember all that? You must have been really young when that aired.'

He shrugged. 'I always remember a pretty face.'

Lisa's mouth fell open at that. She truly didn't know what to say and she was usually quite brilliant with the comeback quips, especially to a handsome man, and Alfie was more handsome than most. But she was also old enough to be his mother and that made him out of bounds as far as Lisa was concerned.

Anyway, it was the young Lisa he was fascinated with, she told herself.

'Well, ain't that something?' she told him and, turning her back on him, headed into the priory.

'I see you've introduced yourself to the gorgeous young gardener,' Harrie teased as Lisa walked into the kitchen.

'*He* introduced himself to *me* as a matter of fact,' Lisa said.

'So, when are you two going out, then?'

Lisa frowned. 'I take offence at that kind of question. Just because there's a man around, it doesn't mean that I'm going to hop into bed with him at the first opportunity!'

Harrie looked visibly shocked by Lisa's declaration.

'I just thought . . .'

'You know, why do you always assume that I'm going to go off with any bloke that just happens to come along?'

'I don't, Lisa!'

'No? Are you sure?'

'It's just that – well – you've always been the first to spot a hand-some man.'

Lisa realised that she was being unreasonable, but she couldn't help being defensive because she felt so vulnerable. She was forty-six years old and still living in rented accommodation with no proper career to speak of and no man in her life. Being at the priory this summer with her two friends had made her realise what a mess her life really was.

'Lisa? What's wrong?'

Lisa put her yoga mat down and sat herself on the bench by the trestle table.

'Sorry,' she whispered. 'I didn't mean to lash out at you like that.'

'It's okay.'

'No, it's not.'

Harrie took a seat opposite her and reached across the dark wood to hold Lisa's hands in hers.

'I'm just – oh, god – I don't even like talking about it.'

'What?'

'Feeling my age,' Lisa confessed at last.

Harrie smiled. 'Is that all?'

'Isn't that enough?'

'I suppose. But it's natural, isn't it?'

'I hate nature. And I hate this feeling of needing to measure up,' Lisa said.

'Then don't do that to yourself.'

'I don't know how to *not* do it.'

'You just ignore it and get on with each day as it comes, living it the best way you can.'

'Blimey, listen to you! You sound like a new-age guru.'

'Do I?'

'Yes! It should be *me* coming out with those sorts of lines. I've been practising yoga for so many years now and I meditate every single day, and yet I'm still an ungrateful sod. I'm always a little bit dissatisfied with something.' She shook her head. 'But isn't that part of being human – always to want more? To be forever pushing?'

'I suppose it can be,' Harrie said, 'but you can change that mindset if you really want to and stop always pushing and decide to be happy with being exactly where you are now.'

'Oh, I'm happy being here at the priory with you and Audrey. This is a real treat. But I know that the minute I get home that awful feeling of disappointment will settle over me again. That makes me sound so ungrateful, doesn't it?'

'No, it doesn't,' Harrie assured her. 'It just makes you honest.'

'I mean, I know how lucky I am in so many ways,' Lisa said. 'I was just thinking about my mum and how many more years I've had than she ever did.'

Harrie squeezed her hands. 'You see? You have so much to be grateful for even with just that.'

'And yet I can't help this feeling that I'm doing it all wrong. Maybe I'm having a mid-life crisis or something. I don't know. I've got all this time on my hands here and that's kind of made me turn inwards.'

'That's one of the reasons I wanted to come here,' Harrie told her. 'I think we all need to do that at some point, don't you?'

'Yes, but I'm not sure it's doing me any good. I just feel as if I'm brooding all the time.'

'You'll get through that stage.'

'Yeah? How do you know?'

'Because I'm going through it too.'

Lisa frowned. 'But you're so sweet all the time, Harrie, and I've done nothing but grouch.'

'That's not true! You've been so much fun to have around. I wouldn't have invited you if I'd thought you'd be a grouch.'

'Well, my apologies if I've been a bit down.'

'You don't need to apologise.'

'I'm just feeling sorry for myself, I guess,' Lisa confessed.

Harrie took a deep breath. 'You know what?'

'What?'

'I think what you need is a wonderful summer fling.'

'What?' Lisa all but screamed.

'I couldn't help noticing the way that young gardener was looking at you.'

'Don't be daft!'

'I think he has the hots for you, Lisa. I could definitely see it in his eyes.'

'No, no, no! He's way too young. Definitely off limits.'

'Says who?'

'Anyone with a conscience,' Lisa told her.

'You mean you're not tempted?'

'Nope!'

'Oh, well, if *you're* not, maybe I'll chat him up next time he's here.'

Lisa gasped. 'Don't you dare, Harriet Greenleaf! I saw him first!'

'So, you *do* like him?'

'Well, of course I do! You'd have to be crazy not to. But it's simply not going to happen, okay?' Lisa suddenly laughed. 'He used to watch me in *Gargrave Road with his mum*! Talk about ageing a person.'

'Some guys like older women,' Harrie pointed out. 'He obviously has very good taste.'

'I don't think he's interested in me. Maybe he's a little star struck, that's all. And he might want me to help him with some stretches. He's got a rugby injury.'

'Then help him stretch,' Harrie said, 'and who knows what could happen on that yoga mat!'

'Oh, don't!'

They giggled together and Lisa instantly felt better.

'You're such a good friend, Harrie,' she told her. 'I don't know what I'd do without you in my life. I know we sometimes go months and months without seeing each other, but I always know you're there if I need you.'

'I feel the same,' Harrie said.

'You'll always be there, won't you, Harrie?'

There was a pause before her friend answered. 'Of course I will be.'

Lisa breathed a sigh of relief and then stood up from the table. 'Right, I'm going to sneak into Audrey's room for a cold shower. All this talk of hot young rugby players on my yoga mat and I'm overheating!'

Harrie watched her friend leave the kitchen and then got up to make a cup of tea. Not for her – for Samson. She hadn't seen him for a few days and thought it was time to catch up with him. She was enjoying the slow progress of making friends with this man. Perhaps it was because he knew so very little about her and she didn't feel that weight of pressure at having to reveal her condition to him. The thought had occurred to her, briefly, but what would be the point? No, she liked this light summer relationship – this casual talk about stone over a cup of tea and the knowledge that she needn't divulge anything about herself that she wasn't totally comfortable with.

With cup of tea in hand, Harrie left the kitchen and walked through the cloisters to the tower. The oldest part of the priory still gave her goosebumps of delight whenever she ventured out there. You could almost smell the history. Well, you actually could when Samson was knocking centuries of dust about. But there was something timeless and magical about the very air in that part of the priory and walking there felt like a kind of time travel.

'Hello there!' she called as she walked towards the scaffolding. 'It's me, Harrie, with your cup of tea.'

He paused in his work momentarily and glanced down towards her, giving a little nod. 'I'll be down in a minute,' he said, his voice a little warmer today, she thought. Perhaps he was getting used to her.

'No rush, but I might take a sip if you take too long.'

Harrie walked across to the other side of the tower and perched on the ledge of a stone alcove. She could get a good view of Samson from there. He was wearing a blue-and-green checked shirt today and the sleeves were rolled up to expose his strong, tanned arms. He was also wearing goggles and a dust mask, which wasn't the best of looks, she had to confess. Still, with clouds of ancient dust and bits of sharp stone flying around, she suspected he didn't much care what he looked like when it came to protection.

She watched him work for a few moments and then he removed his goggles and mask and came down the ladder.

'I've just lied to one of my best friends,' she told him as she handed him the cup of tea.

His eyes widened perceptibly, but he didn't say anything.

'Actually, I've lied to both of them now. Is that awful of me?' She looked at him, awaiting a response, but he simply sipped his tea. She hadn't planned on telling him anything; it just kind of blurted out and she found that, once she started, she couldn't stop.

'I hate this subterfuge,' she went on. 'I wish I could just be open and honest with them, but I can't, you see? Not yet anyway. It's horrible, trying to keep the pain away from them.' She paused. She was saying too much, even though Samson wasn't really listening. Or maybe he was, in his own quiet, thoughtful way.

'Subterfuge is never a good thing,' he suddenly said.

Harrie started. So he *was* listening. She smiled and then sighed.

'Anyway,' she said, 'there it is. A problem that I'm not going to solve today.' She gave a little shrug and Samson held his empty cup towards her. She took it from him and wrapped her hands around it. It still felt warm. 'I'll leave you to it, then.'

He nodded and turned to go and she watched as he climbed back up the scaffolding.

'Thanks for the tea!' he called down, and she smiled.

He might not have said anything much, but it had sure felt good talking to him.

Chapter 7

It was a rather surprising fact that, even though she'd celebrated forty-six years on the planet, Harrie had never had a large birthday cake. Even as a child, she'd never been given one of those jaw-dropping beauties all smothered with icing and lit with candles. Her mother simply hadn't liked baking and she'd never thought to get a store-bought cake. Harrie wouldn't have minded that. In fact, she'd have loved one of those cakes she'd secretly spied in bakery windows, but there simply hadn't been the money for such frivolities and so they'd celebrate with a quarter of pick-and-mix instead.

'Sweets for my sweet,' her mother would say.

Of course, Harrie had gone on to spoil her own daughter, Honor, with beautiful, decadent cakes to mark each and every one of her birthdays. They'd had everything from girly creations smothered in pink icing to a cake in the shape of a Shetland pony when she'd been going through her horsey stage, and another which looked like a fairy-tale castle with fondant princesses dancing across it.

Perhaps Harrie was living her childhood again through her daughter and perhaps that was why she was doing what she was doing right now. Anyway, she wasn't going to overanalyse it. She wanted to do it and that was enough of a reason.

She'd arranged the cake weeks before their stay at the priory, choosing a small family-run company in the area and speaking to them on the phone after looking at their unique creations on their website. It was to be delivered at the end of the second week at the priory. Harrie had figured they'd have relaxed into a routine by then and they had, with Mrs Ryder taking the sting out of self-catering with her delicious meals and the occasional trip to a pub for lunch. It was time, she believed, for a wonderful surprise.

It was due to be delivered in the afternoon and Harrie had left instructions with Mrs Ryder to hide it in one of the cupboards.

'You don't want me to put it out on the table for you?' she'd asked.

'Oh, no!' Harrie had said. She wanted to do it all herself.

Harrie had arranged for them to visit a nearby town and they happily browsed the shops and an antiques centre with Audrey treating herself to a china cup and saucer and Lisa buying postcards for her father and housesitter.

Harrie could barely wait to get back to the priory. She was filled with a nervous kind of excitement that came from hiding a really delicious secret.

'Anyone for a cup of tea?' she asked as they entered the kitchen, picking up the kettle to fill with fresh water. She was desperate to check the cupboard for the cake, but it would be suspicious if tea wasn't offered after an outing.

'Please!' Audrey said. 'If I wash my lovely china cup and saucer, I'll have mine in that.'

'Good idea,' Harrie said.

'I'll just go and freshen myself up first.'

'Me too,' Lisa said, and the two of them went upstairs.

Harrie washed her hands in the downstairs cloakroom and, when she was quite sure she was alone, went to check the cupboards. It was in the second one she tried. Mrs Ryder had pushed aside some pans and there sat a great white square box tied with a fat red ribbon. Harrie reached out to touch it. Oh, the anticipation.

'That kettle boiled yet?' Audrey asked, waltzing into the room and unpacking her tea cup and saucer before washing it carefully at the sink.

Harrie quickly closed the cupboard door. Her sumptuous delight would have to wait a little while longer.

Later that evening, once the dishwasher had been loaded after dinner, Harrie cleared her throat.

'Would you two mind going into the living room?'

'Why?' Lisa asked.

'There's something I want to do in here,' Harrie told her. 'A surprise.'

'Oh, I love surprises,' Lisa said.

'A nice surprise, I hope,' Audrey said.

'Well, of course a nice surprise!' Harrie said with a laugh. 'You think I'd arrange a nasty one?'

'I'm just remembering the time Mike arranged a surprise party for me a few years ago and there were all these people from work I couldn't stand.'

'I promise there will be no awkward encounters with colleagues this evening,' Harrie assured her.

'Good to know,' Audrey said, leaving the room with Lisa.

Harrie made sure the door was closed after them and then went to the cupboard to get the cake. She could feel her heart thumping with excitement as she placed her hands carefully on either side of the box and slid it out, making sure she then supported it underneath as she carried it to the table. How pretty it looked just as it was, she thought. It seemed a shame to unwrap it. Quickly, she took a photo with her phone and then untied the red ribbon and lifted the lid, gasping as she saw the cake for the first time.

Harrie's brief had been 'An English summer garden' and she was delighted with the result. The round cake was covered in the palest green icing and it was festooned with hundreds of flowers in pretty pastel shades, with tiny bees and butterflies flitting amongst them. It was the prettiest thing she'd ever seen and tears filled her eyes as she gazed at it.

She'd wondered whether to go for two tiers, but had felt that was much too extravagant and she couldn't imagine it could possibly be any more fabulous than the creation in front of her now. There was no writing on the cake and Harrie was pleased about that decision now. Wishing herself happy birthday would have been a little bit bizarre and would also have made her uncomfortable because the likelihood was that she wasn't going to see her birthday. How strange a thought was that – to know that you have seen your last birthday? Those were the kind of thoughts that could darken a whole day if they entered Harrie's head and so she did her best to shut them out.

After taking more photographs of the cake from every angle imaginable, she went to find the candles she'd brought with her from home, taking them out of the little paper bag where they'd been hiding inside her handbag and placing them on the cake, careful to avoid breaking the delicate petals of the flowers or spiking a bee in the back.

Matches were next, again hidden in her handbag. She took one out and, with shaking hands, immediately snapped one. She tried again. This time, she was lucky, but she only managed to light half of the candles before the flame got too close to her fingers for comfort. One more match did the trick. A neat dozen. That was enough. One didn't want to overwhelm the beauty of the cake.

Harrie switched the kitchen lights off and walked back to the table, making sure it looked absolutely perfect, which, of course, it did. She took a moment on her own to take it all in. Her first big beautiful birthday cake. It was a shame that it would also be her last.

No, she told herself. This was going to be a perfect moment. There was no room for negative thoughts. With that in mind, she left the kitchen, mindful to close the door behind her, and walked through to the living room.

'Is that surprise of yours ready yet?' Lisa asked as soon as she entered the room.

Harrie beamed her a smile. 'You want to see it?'

'Of *course* we do!' Lisa was on her feet in an instant, closely followed by Audrey.

'Okay,' Harrie said a moment later as they reached the kitchen door. 'I want you both to close your eyes.'

'Oh, how exciting!' Lisa said.

'What's going on?' Audrey asked. 'I don't want to knock into anything.'

'Oh, ye of little faith!' Harrie said. 'Just keep your eyes closed and trust me!' Harrie led them into the kitchen, guiding them slowly and carefully.

'Let me guess,' Lisa said. 'You've organised some massage in the dark.'

'Not exactly,' she said, steering them towards the table. 'Okay, you can open your eyes now.'

They both did as they were told and gasped.

'What's this?' Audrey asked.

'Whose birthday is it?' Lisa asked.

'Mine, silly!' Harrie said.

'But it isn't your birthday until December,' Audrey pointed out.

Harrie sighed. She'd known she'd have some explaining to do when she came up with the idea and she'd hoped her friends wouldn't question her too closely, but would take it all in the spirit of fun.

'I do know when my birthday is,' she assured them, 'and I also know that we'll never get together for it, nor for yours in January, Aud, or Lisa's in May. But we are all here now so I thought we'd celebrate all the birthdays we've missed in the past and all those we'll no doubt miss in the future.'

Audrey was frowning, but then shrugged. 'I *suppose* that makes sense.'

'Well, I think it's a lovely idea and I've never been known to turn down cake,' Lisa said.

'Exactly,' Harrie said.

'So this is for all of us?' Audrey asked.

'Of course!' Harrie told her. 'But I'm going to blow out the candles.'

Harrie moved towards the table, her face soon feeling the heat from the flames.

'How many are there?' Audrey asked.

'A nice neat dozen,' Harrie said, 'which is more than enough, I think. I didn't want to spoil the cake.'

'Or admit to your age! *Our* ages!' Lisa joked.

'I thought you were avoiding sugar,' Audrey pointed out.

Harrie gave a little shrug. 'Well, I am *mainly* but, as I'll be the first one of us to hit forty-seven, I thought a little sugar might ease the journey.'

'Go on, then – blow them out,' Audrey said. 'I want to tuck in!'

'Let's all make a wish first!' Lisa said.

Harrie didn't need to be told twice and, bending over the cake, closed her eyes. One wish. What could she wish for? Peace? Happiness? Health? They were the top ones, weren't they? But could twelve supermarket candles really provide her with a miracle cure if she wished for one? Probably not. Best to be on the safe side.

I wish for quality time with my friends and family.

She blew. Hard.

Audrey and Lisa clapped their hands as Harrie turned the kitchen lights on.

'Happy birthday to you! Happy birthday to you!' Lisa sang.

'Oh, please don't!'

'Don't worry – I won't join in!' Audrey promised.

'Thank you. A true friend!'

'Happy birthday, dear Harriet! Happy birthday to you!'

Lisa flung her arms around Harrie and kissed her on the cheek.

Audrey joined in. 'Happy birthday for December, darling friend.'

Harrie closed her eyes as they both embraced her, willing herself not to cry. 'Come on!' she said at last. 'Let's eat!'

'It's so beautiful,' Lisa said. 'Almost too pretty to eat.'

'Yes, but only *almost*,' Harrie said.

'Let me take a photo before it's all gobbled up!' Audrey said, and Harrie smiled as both her friends went to find their phones.

Photographs taken, Harrie grabbed three plates from the dresser and a large knife.

'I'm actually shaking,' Harrie confessed.

'Want me to do it? I'm very good at cutting extra-big slices,' Lisa said.

But the knife was now hovering over the icing, ready to cut through its pristine beauty.

'Oh, look!' Lisa cried a moment later.

'Victoria sponge?' Audrey asked.

Harrie nodded. 'My favourite.'

'It looks fabulous,' Lisa said. 'You're just *full* of good ideas!'

'I hoped you'd like it and wouldn't think it was too weird.'

'Why would we ever think cake was weird?' Lisa asked.

'I mean celebrating my birthday so early.'

'It is a little bit weird, but I get it,' Audrey assured her.

Lisa suddenly giggled and nudged Harrie.

'What is it?' Harrie asked.

'I was just remembering Audrey's thirtieth when Mike hired that gorgeous cottage in the Cotswolds and we both turned up as a surprise!'

'Oh, that was so cool!' Harrie said.

'I did wonder why Mike had booked such a big place with so many bedrooms,' Audrey said. 'I thought he was just trying to spoil me.'

'That was so sweet of him to think of us,' Lisa said with a soppy smile.

'I think I still have the deflated helium balloon you bought for me,' Audrey told them. 'But the cake is long gone!'

'It was a lovely cake,' Harrie said. 'I'd never seen a cake in the shape of a windmill before.'

'It was a little reference to our last holiday in the Netherlands,' Audrey told them.

'So romantic!' Lisa said.

'I don't know how he kept it all a secret from me.'

'You sure did get lucky with Mike,' Lisa said.

They took their plates through to the living room, which was beautifully lit by lamplight. The thick curtains had been drawn now and the room felt cosy. Each of the women found a seat and there was blissful silence as cake was consumed. Harrie took her time, carefully angling her fork to slice through each perfect layer, admiring the lightness of the sponge and the jewel-bright jam. Lisa was going for it with her fingers and Harrie let out a little chuckle.

'What?' Lisa asked, her mouth crammed with cake. 'It's the only way to eat it. Like fish and chips. Utensils would be a travesty.'

Audrey shook her head. 'Can't take you anywhere.'

'There's nobody here to judge me,' Lisa said.

'*We're* here,' Audrey said.

'Yes, but old friends don't count. You expect the worst by now, surely.'

'And we don't mind,' Harrie said.

Lisa grinned and took another enormous bite. 'I hope we get seconds!'

'No way! This has got to last us,' Harrie told her. She looked down at her own empty plate. How had she eaten all that already? 'Well, maybe just a tiny second sliver.'

'That's more like it,' Lisa said, leaping up from the sofa and racing into the kitchen. Harrie and Audrey were quick to follow.

'Just a small slice!' Harrie cried.

'Yeah, yeah!' Lisa said. She'd already picked up the knife. 'Hey, have we got any wine? Or, even better, champagne? Shouldn't we have champagne for a birthday?'

'There's some wine in the fridge,' Audrey told them.

'I'll get some glasses,' Harrie said.

Once the wine was poured, they trooped into the living room with their cake.

'Hey, Lisa – have you had any more yoga sessions with that gardener?' Harrie asked.

'What's this?' Audrey asked.

'Lisa's been flirting with that young gardener.'

'I have not!'

'What's his name?'

'Alfie,' Lisa said, and then frowned. 'I don't know his last name.'

'How come I've not run into him?'

'Because you've had your nose in spreadsheets since you got here?' Harrie said.

'I have not!' Audrey cried. 'Or maybe just a little bit each day.'

'You are incapable of switching off,' Harrie told her.

'No, I'm not. I simply like things to be moving forward.'

'I'm amazed you're here at all,' Lisa said. 'I mean, that you agreed to the whole summer.'

Audrey's expression suddenly changed. 'Ah, well . . .'

'What does that mean?' Lisa said.

'Yes, I'm not liking the sound of this,' Harrie added.

'It's just – well – six weeks is a long time,' Audrey stated.

'Not if it's your only holiday for the last six years,' Harrie told her.

'I've had holidays.'

'Only the odd night here and there. That's not time to really relax,' Harrie said.

'Look, I'll only be gone for four or five nights at the most!'

'What?' Lisa screamed.

'Oh, Audrey! You're not really going, are you?' Harrie said.

'I'll be back before you know it. There's just a couple of things I've got to deal with, that's all. I told you, this is a new business venture for me and I've got to keep on top of things. I'm the boss. I can't simply walk away for weeks at a time.'

'But you promised!' Harrie felt as if she was losing control at a rapid pace.

'I know, and I'm here, aren't I?'

'Well, some of you is. I think your mind might still be stuck at work a lot of the time,' Harrie told her.

'But it'll be better when I return,' Audrey promised. 'I'll be able to relax more.'

'Until the next crisis?'

'You're not being fair, Harrie.'

Harrie shifted in her seat. 'This holiday was all about letting go of our real lives and relaxing together. I thought you understood that. I thought we'd all agreed.'

'I did agree. I don't know what the fuss is about. I'll only be gone for five, six nights maximum.'

'You see – you've just added a day,' Harrie pointed out. 'One minute, you say it's for five nights, and then you say it could be six. Before we know it, you won't be coming back at all!'

'Why are you getting so worked up about this?' Audrey asked.

'Because you made a promise, Aud! I thought friends kept their promises.'

'You're being spectacularly unfair. I *always* keep my promises. It's just that this is a really crazy time for me.'

'You think you're the only one who's having a crazy time?'

'No, of course not.'

'You think I'm being selfish and ridiculous wanting us all to spend this time together and that you can just up and leave whenever you want?'

'Harrie – no – I don't think that at all. What's got into you?'

'Nothing!' Harrie cried, suddenly aware that she might be causing more of a scene than she'd intended. 'I'm just really disappointed.'

'But it's only for a few days and then I'll be back for the rest of the summer.'

'Will you?' Harrie said. 'Are you sure you won't just swan off again as soon as the whim takes you?'

'Well, I might if I feel you're picking on me!'

'Hey, you two – let's take it easy, okay?' Lisa said.

'Look, I'm not going right away,' Audrey added.

'When are you going?' Lisa asked.

'In a couple of days.'

'And you've known from the start?' Harrie asked.

'I didn't plan it,' Audrey said, 'but I did kind of know that I'd have to go back at some point.' She sighed. 'You don't need me here for the whole summer anyway.'

'That's not the point, Aud. I very much *want* you here.'

'And we can always do this another time too, can't we? Now that we've got the ball rolling again, we can get together every summer,' Audrey said.

Harrie's fingers curled into the palms of her hands until her nails dug into the soft skin.

'Anyone for more wine?' Lisa asked.

'Yes,' Audrey said. 'Most definitely.'

'You know, I think I'll have an early night.' Harrie got up from the sofa.

'You're not going to have another glass with us?' Lisa asked.

'No, thanks.'

'Oh, Harrie, don't go like this,' Audrey said. 'You're making me feel horrible.'

Harrie turned to look at her friend. 'I don't mean to make you feel horrible. I'm sorry if I did.'

'And I'm sorry if you feel disappointed about me leaving, but I'll be straight back, I promise. As soon as I can.'

Harrie smiled. 'Well, you'd better be, otherwise we'll come to London and get you. Don't think we won't!'

Chapter 8

'She was pretty mad with you,' Lisa said as they browsed a rail of clothes in a small seaside boutique the next day.

'You don't need to tell me that. I was there,' Audrey replied.

Lisa's hand reached out to caress a silver-and-white T-shirt.

'Is this too young for me?' she asked Audrey.

'Definitely.'

Lisa frowned. 'You sure? It's really pretty and it's in the sale.'

'I'm sure.'

'Hmmm, I probably shouldn't be spending money on new clothes anyway – sale or not.'

'Do you think she's okay?' Audrey asked.

'Harrie?'

'Of course Harrie.'

'She seems fine to me. Why do you ask?'

'She seems a little strange, don't you think? I mean, that outburst the other night – I've never seen her so upset.'

'She just doesn't want you to go, that's all.'

Audrey sighed. 'I think there's more to it than that.'

Lisa pulled out a tiny pink-and-white striped blouse and put it back when Audrey shook her head.

'I've not noticed anything different about her. But she's lost weight, that's for sure. Lucky sod.'

'Yes,' Audrey said. 'She's not eating much either.'

'She ate a pretty big slice of cake last night.'

Audrey smiled at memory. 'We all did, but she's not eating much else. She loads her plate up, but she just tends to pick. Haven't you noticed?'

'No, not really.' Lisa ran her hands down the front of a fuchsia top.

'Too low-cut,' Audrey pronounced.

'For you maybe.'

'And for you too.'

'Spoilsport!'

'Come on,' Audrey said. 'I saw a cute little cafe down the street and I'm dying for a cup of tea.'

They left the boutique, blinking in the bright light of the seafront.

'I hope she's okay,' Audrey said.

'She said it was just a headache.'

'No, I mean in general.'

'Why wouldn't she be?'

'I don't know. I can't quite put my finger on it, but – well – this whole thing seems odd to me. Hiring the priory and summoning us here. Don't you think it's odd?'

'I hadn't really thought about it.'

'Hadn't you?'

'Nope! It's probably just a middle-age crisis or something. She's worked hard for so many years and, after her divorce and everything, I just think she wanted to splash out a bit and treat her friends.'

'Yes, you're probably right.'

'You worry too much,' Lisa told her.

'I know.'

'You're good at it, mind.'

'Thanks!' Audrey said with sarcasm.

'You're welcome.' Lisa linked her arm through her friend's and they headed into the cafe.

If Harrie was one for biting her nails, they would have been down to the quick by now. She knew it was unfair of her not to have told her friends that her daughter, Honor, was coming to stay, but she'd worried that, if she had, Audrey would then want to invite Jack and Lisa would insist on a guest as well, and Harrie had wanted the holiday to be just the three friends. And Honor. It might have been a selfish decision, but she hoped they wouldn't mind. She couldn't bear to be away from her daughter for so long – not when every single moment was precious – and she'd given her friends more than two weeks of her exclusive company. Actually, since Audrey had announced that she would be leaving for a few days, Harrie was feeling less guilty about having Honor to stay. The plan had been that Honor would join them at about the midway point but, after last night, Harrie had texted her daughter and she had rung right back and Harrie hadn't been able to hide the tears.

'I miss you so much!' she'd cried down the phone, wishing her daughter was with her right there so she could hug her close.

'I'm coming tomorrow,' Honor had insisted.

Harrie had protested for a few useless moments, but the truth was that she needed her daughter. Oh, how she needed her little girl with her.

Honor had graduated from university two years before but, unlike her mother, hadn't wanted to study teacher training. Instead, she'd taken a job at a local stately home, working for a family who were trying to save their home by opening it to the public. Her salary was appalling, but she adored the work and the quirkiness of the family and the splendour of the Georgian manor. The family had also been so understanding about Harrie's condition, and Honor had never had any trouble taking time off to accompany her mother to hospital appointments or to help her during the rougher days of her treatment. Harrie didn't know what she would have done without her and was grateful beyond words.

She smiled as she thought about some of the fun times they'd shared recently – days when they'd just taken off in Honor's little car, leaving their worries and fears behind for a few hours. Like the day they'd driven down to Lyme Regis. They'd browsed in a second-hand bookshop, bought fossils from another shop, eaten ice cream on the front and then walked out along the Cobb, taking photos and posing at the end of it like the French lieutenant's woman. They'd then climbed down the steps known as the Granny's Teeth in a rather poor imitation of Jane Austen's heroine Louisa Musgrove, who had leapt from the top.

'Less dangerous this way,' Honor had said.

'Exactly. We don't want any unnecessary trips to the hospital, do we?' Harrie had meant it as a light-hearted comment, but she'd seen the cloud pass over her daughter's face and had known that it had ruined a perfectly lovely day. Cancer had a way of doing that, didn't it?

But now she had to focus on the present. Audrey and Lisa had gone shopping the morning Honor was due to arrive. Harrie had made her excuses, saying that she'd join them next time. There'd been some words of protest and Harrie had been forced to feign a headache. Honestly, this lying business was becoming too much of a habit, she thought guiltily.

Now, she buzzed around the priory, needlessly tidying things up as she waited for her daughter's arrival. Mrs Ryder, who'd turned up at the crack of dawn it seemed, was keeping her eye on Harrie.

'Something's going on here,' she said as Harrie entered the kitchen.

'Yes, Mrs Ryder. My daughter's coming.'

'A little bit of notice would have been welcome. I don't know if I've got enough food in now.'

'There's plenty,' Harrie assured her, 'and we can always go out to eat.'

Mrs Ryder shook her head as she filled the dishwasher. 'I don't like disorganisation.'

'I'm sorry. I didn't know myself until last night.'

'Hmmm, well, that's just bad planning.'

Harrie smiled to herself. There was no arguing with Mrs Ryder sometimes. She always had to have the last word. Anyway, it was worth putting up with her wrath to have her beloved daughter there.

'When's she arriving then?' Mrs Ryder asked.

'Well, she left pretty early so any time soon,' Harrie said, looking out of the kitchen window once again as if Honor might be walking up the garden path at that very moment. 'Actually, I'll go and check.'

Opening the front door, Harrie made her way into the garden, partly to escape Mrs Ryder and partly in the hope that her daughter really was there already. She walked down the pathway lined with lavender and humming with bees, reaching the great wooden door set in the high stone wall, opening it and looking out into the track.

'Honor!' Harrie cried, spotting the small blue car parked parallel to an ancient wall. Honor didn't appear to have heard and Harrie watched for a moment as her daughter sat very still in the car. Was she on the phone? Or was she just psyching herself up for her visit? Harrie couldn't help wondering.

At last, her daughter seemed to rouse herself and opened the car door, spotting her mother standing there.

'Mum!'

'Darling!'

Honor, who was twenty-three, looked just like her mother. She was tall and slim-built with straight fair hair and honey-brown eyes. Her skin was pale like her mother's too. She was wearing a simple summer dress and a pair of trainers and she looked absolutely scrumptious to Harrie.

'I've missed you so much, darling!' Harrie told her, kissing her cheeks with a resounding smack.

'Oh, Mum!' Honor cried, but she was laughing. 'How are you? I mean, how are you really?'

'I'm good. Really good.'

'Yeah? No pain?'

'No pain.'

'But you're still taking—'

'I'm taking as much as I need to.'

'I don't like the sound of that,' Honor said, sounding so much more like a parent than a daughter. 'It's a good thing I've arrived.'

'Honestly, Honor – there's nothing to worry about. I feel absolutely fine. Positively radiant, in fact. I get a little tired occasionally, but that's probably all this fresh air.'

'Well, you do look good, I have to admit.'

'It's all this living outdoors. I can't wait to share it all with you. The gardens are so beautiful and we've got our very own orchard and swimming pool. Wait till you see it! Let me help you with your things.'

'Absolutely not!' Honor said. 'Besides, I've only got one little suitcase.' She returned to the car and opened the boot, reaching inside for her modest luggage.

'Is that all?' Harrie asked.

'It's only light summer clothing,' Honor told her. 'I managed to squash it all in.'

'We could always go shopping.'

'We really don't need to, Mum.'

'But I want to treat you!'

'I don't want you tiring yourself out going round shopping centres. I have everything I need.'

'You won't tire me out. I'm not an invalid yet, you know.'

'I know.'

'And no woman ever has enough clothes,' Harrie told her.

'I do.'

Harrie shook her head. 'You are a *very* unusual young lady.'

They walked through the gate and Harrie closed it behind them, turning to watch her daughter's expression as she saw the priory for the first time.

'Wow! This is completely outrageous, Mum!' She gave a laugh.

'I know!'

'When you showed me the photos, it looked amazing enough, but it's something else in the flesh.'

'Nothing really prepares you for it, does it?' Harrie said. 'It's been my home for two weeks now and yet it still gives me chills when I look at it. I sometimes sneak outside first thing in the morning or last thing at night and just look at the shadows and the silhouettes, and breathe in all its beauty.'

'It's like something out of a fairy tale. I thought you were mad to book it, I have to say.'

'I knew you thought that,' Harrie said. 'Why didn't you say something?'

Honor shrugged. 'I figured you knew what you were doing.'

Harrie smiled. 'Haven't I always?'

Honor gave a sideways glance. 'Erm, not always!'

Harrie gasped. 'I need evidence before you accuse me of such a thing!'

'Well, what about that time you booked us on a boating holiday on the Broads and we crashed into that bridge?'

'Ah, yes! I don't think I'm a natural when it comes to boats.'

'And when you booked that cottage on the Welsh coast and we ended up in the wrong village twenty miles away.'

'That wasn't my fault,' Harrie said. 'That was the unreliable satnav.'

Honor laughed and they entered the cool of the kitchen, where Mrs Ryder was wiping down the table.

'Honor, this is Mrs Ryder,' Harrie said. 'She's taking care of us whilst we're here. Mrs Ryder – this is my daughter, Honor.'

'Pleased to meet you, I'm sure,' Mrs Ryder said.

'And you,' Honor said.

'I haven't had time to prepare a room for you. Your mother sprang your arrival on me just ten minutes ago.'

'It's okay, Mrs Ryder. The twin room's already made up,' Harrie said.

'Could've freshened the bedding.'

'It's fine,' Harrie assured her.

Mrs Ryder mumbled something as she turned away, grabbing a tea towel, and Harrie placed her hand on Honor's shoulder and steered her out of the room and up the spiral staircase to the first floor.

'She's a bit scary, Mum,' Honor said once they were out of earshot.

'Oh, she's a sweetheart really. You okay with that suitcase?'

'I'm fine. I'm glad I packed light, though. I didn't know I'd have to negotiate spiral staircases.'

'Not much further,' Harrie told her as they walked out onto the landing. 'I'm afraid you don't get your pick of the rooms, but it's a very pretty twin that I think you'll be comfortable in.'

Harrie turned left and opened the door.

'It's gorgeous, Mum!' Honor put her suitcase down and did what every single person did when they entered a room in the priory: she walked to the window to look outside.

'Isn't it lovely? Our very own orchard for the summer.'

'It's beautiful,' Honor agreed.

'There's a footpath that runs right through it and out into the lane. I like to walk there early in the mornings when it's still misty. There's a blackbird that sings in one of the ancient apple trees there.' She pointed.

'Are you having trouble sleeping?' Honor asked her.

'A little.'

'You should tell your doctor, Mum.'

'I don't want to waste my time sleeping, darling!'

'But it's important. You need to rest, Mum.'

'I need to *live*!'

The two women starred at each other and Harrie flinched when she saw the tears in her daughter's eyes.

'Hey!' she said. 'What's the matter?' Harrie crossed the space between them and folded her arms around her slender shoulders. She felt Honor's arms tighten around her waist.

'You've lost more weight,' Honor told her.

'Not much,' she said, doing her best to be brave when, in fact, her daughter's tears tore the very heart out of her.

Honor sniffed. 'Don't lose any more.'

'Hey, I'm eating like a pig!'

'Why don't I believe you?'

'There's cake in the kitchen.'

'Really?' Honor leaned back and mopped her eyes with a tissue from her pocket.

'I was thinking of making a treacle tart too. You used to love those, remember?'

'With lots of yellow custard?' Honor asked.

'With whatever you want!'

'You'll have some too?'

'Try and stop me!'

Honor laughed and Harrie smiled before turning to open the bedroom window.

'You've not told them, have you?' Honor suddenly said.

'Pardon?'

'You've not told Lisa or Audrey.'

'What makes you say that?'

'Because you look too relaxed. I don't think you'd be so relaxed if you'd told them.' She came forward and looked directly into her mother's face. 'Have you?'

'No,' Harrie admitted. 'The time's not been right. These first two weeks have flown by and I wanted to enjoy them. I wanted them to be a cancer-free zone.'

Honor nodded in understanding.

'I will tell them, but in my own time.'

'How do you think they'll react?'

Harrie puffed out a breath. 'God knows! They might run a mile.'

'They won't!'

Harrie smiled. 'No, they wouldn't do that.'

'Unlike Linda then,' Honor said.

'Ah, Linda!' Harrie nodded. 'It's funny, isn't it? The people you think you can trust with your problems often turn out to be the ones who simply can't cope.'

Harrie thought of the colleague she'd worked with for so long and how she had simply vanished from her life the moment Harrie had told her of her condition. Harrie had tried to reach out to her, but her calls had gone unanswered and she'd been forced to walk away from that particular friendship even though it had cut her to the core. She'd experienced it since then in others too. It was sad to acknowledge the fact that some people simply didn't want sickness in their lives. They didn't know how to cope with it. They didn't know what to say and they certainly didn't know what to do with a friend who was ill, and that was fine. Well, it wasn't. If Harrie was being perfectly honest, it was downright weird. It angered her immensely. After all, she was the one with the battle on her hands. Why should her friends feel threatened and afraid? But there was nothing she could do about it. Slowly, she had learned to accept that being ill was an isolating experience and that not everybody would be there for you.

'Well, you can do without people like Linda in your life,' Honor told her.

Harrie nodded. 'I have you and my two best friends. What more could I ask for?'

Honor smiled. 'There's something else I need to get from the car. Stay here. I won't be a moment.'

Harrie watched as her daughter left the room. It felt so good to have her there. Harrie had missed her so much over the last two weeks, but hadn't said anything to Audrey and Lisa for fear of giving herself away.

As she thought of the fun that lay ahead of them that summer, her gaze fell to her daughter's suitcase. Perhaps she could help her unpack.

She unzipped her suitcase and opened it, smiling at the pastel-coloured fabrics which her daughter favoured, her hand reaching out to touch the delicate material of a sundress she hadn't seen before. It was very pretty and Harrie found herself searching for the label but, instead of finding a label, her hand uncovered a book.

Cancer. What To Do When It Strikes Your Family.

Harrie cursed, her hand starting to shake slightly. She'd slowly come to accept the cancer on her own behalf, but she still railed against it for the effect on those around her. Why should they have to suffer along with her? Why should *their* lives be torn apart just because the disease had destroyed hers? She still had nightmares about Honor's reaction to her news and would often wake up in a cold sweat, the image of her daughter's distraught face hovering before her. It truly was the most brutal part of this journey, she thought, holding the book in both hands and wanting to hurl it across the room. Of course, she didn't do that and, as she heard footsteps along the corridor, Harrie covered up the book with the dress and zipped the suitcase shut, moving quickly away to stand by the window and look outside once more as her daughter entered the room.

'Here it is,' Honor said and, once she was sure she had her emotions under control, Harrie turned around, frowning when she saw Honor with a large carrier bag.

'What have you got in there?'

'Come and see.'

Honor sat down on the single bed and fished inside the bag, bringing out three large photo albums.

'Oh my goodness! What on earth did you bring all these for?' Harrie asked with a laugh.

'Because I wanted to look at them with you.'

'I haven't looked at these for years.'

'Exactly!' Honor said.

'Did you go round to my house to get these?'

'Of course I did.'

Harrie smiled. 'You always did like looking at all the old photographs, didn't you?'

'You mean like your wedding photos?'

Harrie nodded.

'I couldn't find those,' Honor said. 'You haven't thrown them away, have you?' A little crease formed in between Honor's brows.

'No, of course not,' Harrie said. 'I've just put them somewhere where I don't have to see them every day.'

Honor seemed to visibly relax at hearing this. 'Good,' she said, and then she opened the first of the photo albums.

'Oh, look at you!' Harrie said, sighing with pleasure as she gazed at the photo of her baby girl at three weeks old, wearing the sweetest little bonnet trimmed with lace.

'I look like Little Bo Peep!'

'You look like an angel!'

'You always made me look like a doll.'

'I didn't! You managed that look all by yourself!'

Honor shook her head, but Harrie could see that she was smiling.

'Isn't this my first school photo?' Honor asked.

'Yes! Remember you cut your own fringe? I'd bought you a little pair of scissors because you really loved to cut coloured paper into shapes. I never imagined you'd use them on yourself!'

'So that's why my hair is such a mess!'

'Preserved forever by the school photographer,' Harrie said with a laugh. 'And, if I remember rightly, you also gave one of your dolls a nice haircut too.'

'I did not!' Honor protested.

'You don't remember what you did to Ruby?'

Honor frowned. 'Erm, something's coming back to me.'

'Which is more than can be said for her hair!'

They both laughed and turned the pages of the album.

'I love the feel and weight of a real photograph album, don't you?' Honor said.

'Everything's digital now,' Harrie said. 'You have to make a real effort to print photographs out and have them framed or put into albums.'

'But it's worth doing.'

'Absolutely.'

'We'll have to take plenty of photos here, won't we?'

'Yes,' Harrie said, feeling the subtext of the conversation, as she so often did these days.

'Make sure we get some of us together,' Honor said. 'It always seems to be either you or me in the pictures because one of us is taking the photo.'

'We can get Audrey and Lisa to take some, okay? As many as you want.'

'I want to fill a whole photo album.'

'That's a good idea.'

'So that we'll never forget this summer.' Honor's voice was little above a whisper now, and Harrie could see the tears glistening in her eyes, making them so very bright.

'We're going to have a wonderful time, darling. No time for tears, remember?'

'I know.'

But, as she put an arm around Honor's shoulder and squeezed her tight, she knew that she could do absolutely nothing to stop either her daughter's tears or her own that were now threatening to fall.

Chapter 9

It might not have been a very successful shopping trip as far as Lisa was concerned, but it had been a lot of fun. Lisa liked Audrey when she loosened up a bit. You just had to get her away from her laptop and spreadsheets for long enough and the funny, sunny Audrey would emerge. Lisa was certainly going to miss her when she left.

The car bounced down the track that led to the priory, turning the final corner.

'Whose car is that?' Lisa asked.

'Another gardener's?' Audrey suggested, parking neatly beside the mystery car. The two of them got out and Lisa looked into the driver's window.

'I don't think this is the car of a gardener,' she said.

'Why not?'

'Because there's a bottle of pink nail varnish on the passenger seat.'

'Why can't a gardener wear nail varnish?'

'Just doesn't seem practical,' Lisa pronounced.

'Well, who can it be then?'

'There's one way to find out.'

The two of them went through the wooden gate and walked along the path towards the front door of the priory, entering the kitchen a moment later.

'I guess we can't ask Mrs Ryder,' Lisa said, acknowledging the fact that the housekeeper had left for the day. 'Harrie?' she called up the stairs. 'We're back!'

'Lisa? Audrey?' Harrie's voice came from upstairs.

'We're in the kitchen!'

Harrie appeared a moment later, a big grin on her face. 'I've got a surprise for you,' she announced.

'Whose is that car out there?' Audrey asked.

'That's part of the surprise.' Harrie turned around just as Honor entered the room.

Lisa gasped. 'Honor!'

'Hi, Lisa! Hi, Audrey!'

Lisa raced across the room to embrace Honor. 'What a surprise!'

'It's so lovely to see you,' Audrey said. 'You look so well, Honor.'

'Thanks.'

'How's work going?' Audrey asked.

'Very well.'

'Oh, Aud! You always zone in on work,' Lisa chastised. 'She doesn't want to talk about work!'

'I really don't mind,' Honor insisted. 'I love my job.'

'But I don't want to hear about work,' Lisa said. 'I want to hear about your love life!'

'Lisa!' Harrie cried.

'What? Come on! We all want to know about that, don't we?'

Honor laughed. 'There's really not that much to tell. I go to work, I come home.'

'Oh, nonsense!' Lisa said. 'You're a beautiful young woman. There must be someone out there who's caught your eye by now?'

Suddenly, everybody's eyes were on Honor, who was beginning to look decidedly uneasy.

'You don't need to answer that, darling,' Harrie said, touching her daughter lightly on the shoulder.

'It's okay, Mum. Actually, there is somebody.'

'Really?' Lisa said excitedly.

Harrie did a double-take. 'Is there?'

Honor smiled. 'Kind of.'

'*Do* tell!' Lisa said.

'When did you meet him?' Harrie felt just a little hurt that she hadn't been told this news until now.

'It was only recently.'

'What's his name?'

'Benny.'

Audrey turned to put the kettle on and got four mugs out of the cupboard.

'Tea?' Lisa said. 'Don't you think this calls for wine?'

Harrie smiled and nodded.

'We could take it outside,' Audrey suggested as she went to the fridge for a bottle of white.

'Lovely idea.' Harrie was still reeling from the fact that her little girl was seeing somebody. Somebody she might go on to have a relationship with. Someone who might give her Harrie's grandchildren. She swallowed hard. She was getting carried away and yet she couldn't help it. That was the way her mind was working these days – taking flights of fancy into a future where she wouldn't exist.

Shaking these thoughts off, she followed the others into the garden, each carrying a glass of wine. They sat on the two benches in the herb garden: Harrie and Honor on one and Lisa and Audrey on the other.

'Right, back to Benny,' Lisa prompted.

'Well, I met him at work,' Honor began. 'He's the same age as me and he's really nice.'

'Got a photo?' Lisa continued.

'Lisa!' Audrey cried.

'Oh, come on! You want to see him too, don't you?'

Honor surprised them all by getting her phone out of her pocket. A moment later, she showed it to her mother and then turned it around so that Lisa and Audrey could all see the screen, and there he was. Benny.

'Honor!' Lisa cried. 'He's gorgeous!'

'Let me see again,' Harrie said, and her daughter turned the phone around. 'I'd love to meet him, darling.'

Honor turned to her. 'You will.'

'Soon.'

'Yes.'

'Bring him here!' Lisa suddenly said.

'Oh, no.' Honor shook her head and switched her phone off quickly.

'Why not? We'd all love to say hello.'

'It's too soon,' Honor insisted.

Lisa sighed. 'Well, if you're still together at Christmas, maybe we can all have a get-together. What do you think?'

Honor glanced at Harrie. Lisa couldn't quite read the look that passed between them, but she couldn't help feeling like an outsider.

'You're already doing something then?' she asked.

Harrie nodded.

'Don't worry,' Lisa said. 'Another time.'

The four women sipped their wine, taking in the glory of the afternoon garden. Somewhere in the tower, a pigeon was cooing and a pair of swifts flew overhead, filling the sky with their happy shrieks.

'Benny and Honor,' Lisa said after a moment. 'Honor and Benny. I think it's got a nice ring to it.'

Harrie almost spluttered on her wine. 'Don't marry her off yet!' She turned to her daughter. 'You're not, are you? Thinking of getting married, I mean?'

'No, of course not! But . . .'

'What?' all three of them said once.

'We are thinking of going travelling.'

'Really? When?' Harrie asked.

'I don't know. Not for a while.' Honor reached across the bench and took her mother's hand in hers. 'Benny suggested next summer, but I'm not sure yet. What do you think?'

Lisa watched the pair of them carefully. Despite her maturity, Honor looked entirely unsure of herself at that moment.

'What do I think?' Harrie repeated. 'I think it's a *wonderful* idea!'

'You do?'

'I really do! You should definitely go. It'll do you the world of good.'

'I think it sounds like a terrific idea,' Audrey chimed in.

'And you never took that gap year, did you?' Harrie said. 'You were always so busy.'

'I didn't mind,' Honor said.

'Oh, look! Harrie's getting all emotional!' Lisa clasped her hands to her heart dramatically as she spotted the tears in her friend's eyes. 'Your little girl is growing up.'

'I know!' Harrie said.

'Mum! I *am* grown up!' Honor protested.

'I know you are.' Harrie touched her cheek and smiled through her tears.

The four women sat in companionable silence for a little while longer and then Harrie got up and walked back inside with Honor. Lisa stretched her legs out in front of her and gazed up into the sky.

'You okay?' Audrey asked.

Lisa nodded. 'I don't want to seem mean,' she began, 'and I really am pleased to see her, but I kind of wish that Honor hadn't shown up like this.'

'Really?'

'Does that sound selfish of me?'

'It does a little,' Audrey admitted.

'It's always – well – it's always just the three of us, isn't it? The whole point of this time is that we get away from family and home and just be

123

us again! You, me and Harrie. It isn't fair that she thinks she can break that rule. If she does it one year, we'll all be doing it and this thing we've got – this special thing – will be broken.'

'Harrie obviously wants her here,' Audrey said. 'She's paying a lot of money after all. I think she has the right to invite who she wants.'

'But she should've told us, don't you think? It's only right when we're staying here. The whole dynamic's going to change now, especially with you leaving.'

Audrey shrugged. 'Well, just think of Honor as taking my place for a while.'

'But she's Harrie's daughter. It won't be the same. I'll feel like the odd one out.'

'We've always got on with Honor, though.'

'Yes, I know.'

'And you seemed pretty happy to grill her on her love life.'

'I adore her,' Lisa confessed, 'and it's really great to catch up with her, but I can't help feeling we've lost a little bit of Harrie now.'

They sat a moment, contemplating it all.

'I wish you weren't going,' Lisa said at last.

'Now, don't start all that up again. Just roll out your yoga mat, light a few of those incense sticks you like so much and take a few deep breaths.'

Lisa nudged her in the ribs.

'You'll be fine and I'll be back in no time.'

'Promise?'

'I promise.'

Audrey said her goodbyes as quickly as possible later that evening. Harrie made a token effort to keep her from leaving, but she didn't seem quite as distressed by her going now that her daughter was there.

Now, sitting in the car for the one-hundred-and-fifty-mile journey back to the London suburbs, she couldn't help feeling a tiny bit guilty for her prompt departure, but it simply couldn't be helped. She needed to go back. It had been unrealistic of her to think that she could go a whole six weeks without working. She'd done her very best to kick back and relax, to switch off from the hectic life she led, but it had been impossible. She found ways each and every day to sneak in just a little bit of work. She'd been careful about it, making phone calls from her en suite where she couldn't be overheard by Harrie or Lisa, and catching up with emails late at night, switching her laptop on once her friends were safely tucked up in bed. It had taken its toll on her, though, and she'd found it difficult to sleep after looking at her laptop screen for half the night. She'd found herself nodding off in the garden, hiding behind her sunglasses and pretending to be doing nothing more innocent than sunbathing.

It had been a very unsatisfactory way of trying to keep on top of things and it was always going to be only a matter of time before she left to check up on things properly.

The last streaks of light were fading from the sky as Audrey arrived home, pulling into the suburban street lined with 1930s terraced houses as far as the eye could see. How strange it was to be back in the crowded street after the graceful space of the priory. Everything felt so crowded and claustrophobic, and she remembered the conversation she and Mike had had just before she'd left for Somerset. He'd been trying to persuade her to move out of London for some time, but she'd never really listened to him. He had a mad dream about living in a small village surrounded by fields and trees and, for the first time, she could understand the appeal.

There was no point thinking about that now, however. Finding a parking space ten houses down from her home, Audrey got out of the car, grabbing her things from the boot and walking the short distance to number forty-seven. Quietly, she took the key out of her handbag and let herself in. The lights were on and she could hear the faint noise of the TV coming from the living room.

'Mike?' she called, dropping her luggage.

'Audrey?' He appeared in the hallway a moment later. 'Aud! What are you doing back?'

'Aren't you pleased to see me?'

'Well, of course I am!' he said, wrapping her up in a big hug and kissing her. 'It's just so unexpected. You should have called me!'

'You would have tried to talk me out of coming back, wouldn't you?'

He grinned at her. 'Probably.'

'Which is why I didn't call you.'

'I bet Harrie wasn't pleased.' The two of them walked into the living room and Mike turned the television off.

'Harrie's okay. Honor's there with them now. It was Lisa who got all uppity.'

'But you're going back?'

'Of course. As soon as I get a chance to check in with everyone.'

'I had a feeling this would happen. You're such a control freak.'

'Yes, but you still love me.'

He hugged her again. 'We are managing, you know.'

Audrey nodded. She didn't say anything because she didn't want to undermine her husband, who was helping out at the school part-time, but she needed to be there at the helm of her business. She trusted him, of course, but using anybody else, even one's own husband, wasn't the same as doing a job yourself, was it?

She checked her watch. 'Actually, I was thinking of driving into the office tonight.'

Mike ran a hand through his hair. 'You're kidding!'

'No.'

'You've just driven across the country. I've not seen you for over two weeks. It's after nine at night and you're going into work?'

'There are just some things I want to check on.'

'Which can wait until morning.'

'I won't be long, I promise.'

'Aud, you always say that and you're always wrong. Now, take your shoes off. Have you had anything to eat? Can I make you an omelette or something?'

Her stomach gave a rebellious rumble at the mention of food.

'Just as I thought,' Mike said. 'You're not going anywhere. Now, sit yourself down and I'll get things moving in the kitchen.'

Audrey sighed. There was no point in fighting. She was pretty tired too, she had to admit.

'All right,' she said, 'but I'm getting up extra early tomorrow morning.'

Lisa said she was going upstairs for a long bath with a good book. It was kind of her, Harrie thought, to give her and Honor some private time together and Harrie was making the most of it. Despite the heat of the day, the evening had cooled and Harrie had insisted on making hot chocolate for the two of them and they were now snuggled up on one of the big squashy sofas together.

'This is some place, Mum,' Honor said, looking up to the high ceiling above them with its elaborate plasterwork.

'Not too shabby, is it?'

'I've stayed in worse,' Honor said, and they both laughed. 'It's a shame Audrey left,' Honor added. 'I hope it wasn't because of me.'

'No, darling. She'd been planning on leaving from the start,' Harrie said with a sigh. 'The traitor.'

Honor smiled at that.

'She's a workaholic, that one,' Harrie went on. 'I wish she hadn't gone. Out of all of us, I think she needs this holiday the most.'

Honor shook her head. 'Not the most, Mum,' she said, and Harrie gave a gentle, knowing smile.

'We all need this holiday,' Harrie said. 'That's the truth.'

'Perhaps we can find a way to stay here forever?'

Harrie stroked her daughter's hair, the silky strands so cool and comforting in her fingers.

'It would be nice, wouldn't it?' she said. 'But, we'd probably get bored after a while.'

'No, we wouldn't,' Honor said earnestly.

Harrie took a sip of her hot chocolate, luxuriating in its creamy texture as she gazed around the room, taking in the beautiful curtains and comfy soft furnishings, the chunky, centuries-old furniture and the portraits of long-forgotten people hanging in gilded frames.

'No,' she said at last. 'We wouldn't, would we?'

Chapter 10

It was only eight in the morning and Audrey was already on the verge of a nervous breakdown. Everything was a mess. If she'd had any idea, she would have come home a lot sooner. Or perhaps she would never have left in the first place. That was the truth, wasn't it? She'd been reluctant to leave her work even for her two best friends in the world.

Mike had done his best to hold the fort, but he had a job of his own to juggle too, so she couldn't really expect him to take care of every little problem.

The main concern was staffing. They were two teachers down and the classes were in disarray, and, on top of that, there were unpaid bills and the landlord was threatening to throw them all out. What a homecoming, Audrey thought, trying to prioritise the long list of things she needed to do that day to prevent her world from imploding.

She lost track of the time as she busied herself around the office, only half aware that the noise of the traffic was building up outside as the commuter rush began. She was so totally consumed in her work.

It was as she was staring at her computer screen that she became aware of her vision beginning to blur. That was strange, she thought, because she was wearing her glasses. She blinked and a sudden light-headedness assailed her and her heart started to beat faster. She felt incredibly hot, and her breathing was coming thick and fast, as if she couldn't quite get enough air into her lungs. She began to feel afraid and wondered if she should call out for somebody, but that was silly, wasn't it? She was just sitting down at a desk. She wasn't exerting herself. It wasn't a particularly hot day and she had the window in the office open.

She tried to calm herself down with some deep breaths, thinking of what Lisa might advise.

In through the nose. Out through the mouth. Big, deep, settling breaths.

It wasn't working. Her heart was still racing madly.

And then everything went black.

When Audrey's eyes opened, everything seemed white. From black to white. And then she saw Mike standing beside her bed. Only it wasn't *her* bed.

'Where am I? What happened?' The clichéd questions left her mouth before she had time to check them.

Mike expelled a loud sigh. 'You're awake. Thank goodness!' He leaned forward and kissed her cheek. 'How are you feeling?'

'I'm not sure. What's going on?'

'Aud, you passed out. One of the students found you on the floor in the office at the school. God only knows how long you'd been like that. It's lucky someone found you in time and called for an ambulance.'

Audrey shook her head. She had no recollection of hitting the floor or a student finding her or the ambulance. What had happened to her? For a moment, she couldn't help wondering who it was who had found her and if they'd tried to administer mouth-to-mouth. Surreptitiously, she wiped her hand across her lips.

'You've been overdoing things, Aud. Everybody told you.' Mike gently squeezed her hands in his as he perched on the edge of the bed.

'But I was only in the office for – what? An hour?'

'Doesn't matter. You've been stressed for months, haven't you?'

'No!'

Mike shook his head. 'You're heading for a heart attack.'

'Nonsense.'

'That's what the doctor said.'

'But I didn't have one.'

'But you *nearly* did and you might if you don't slow down.'

'That's rubbish.' Audrey was getting annoyed now. All this fuss over a little fainting spell.

'I'll go and get the doctor for you if you like and then he can tell you.'

'No!' she said in a panicked voice. 'Don't leave me.'

'I won't leave you.'

Audrey took a deep breath and then wished she hadn't. She hated the smell of hospitals. She looked around, wondering if there was a clock and if she could get out of there and back to the school before classes finished for the day. There were a couple of teachers she wanted to see.

'Don't even think about it,' Mike said.

'What?' she said innocently.

'I can see you working out how soon you can get back to the school.'

'I wasn't!'

'Love, I *know* you! I know what you're thinking.'

Audrey considered this. If she was going to make it back to work, she was going to have to slip past her husband.

'Shouldn't you be at work?' she asked.

'Nice try,' he said, shaking his head. 'I'm not going anywhere. Not for a good long time.'

She sighed. 'But there's nothing wrong with me. It was just a little episode,' she insisted. 'I probably just need a few early nights and a glass of wine more often.'

'Don't joke about this,' Mike said. 'You need a hell of a lot more than that.'

'What do you mean?'

'I mean, you need to seriously slow down, Audrey. I've been telling you for weeks now. Months. I've been worried about you. I know this new school is important to you, but I wouldn't be doing my job if I didn't tell you that *you* are important to *me*. And your health and well-being are certainly more important than some school.'

'But it isn't just any old school,' she told him. 'It's *my* school.'

'I know it is,' Mike said, 'but I don't want it . . .' He paused.

'What?' she asked, seeing the anxiety in his face and feeling a slight tremor in the hands that held hers.

'I don't want it being the death of you.'

Audrey almost gasped at the severity of his words. 'Don't be silly!'

'I'm not being silly.' He looked at her and she recognised that look. It was the one reserved for when he was being earnest. Her darling Mike. He let her get away with so much. She steamrollered her way over him sometimes to get her own way, she knew that, but she also knew when not to push her luck with him and now was one of those times.

'I know it's hard,' he began, 'but I need you to listen to me. You've got to stop working.'

'What do you mean, *stop*?'

'I've spoken to the doctor and he says you need complete rest.'

Audrey shook her head.

'Slowing down just isn't going to be enough,' Mike went on. 'You've got to have a real break.'

Words of protest tumbled around Audrey's mind in a chaos of confusion. 'But I'll die if I don't work.'

Mike shook his head. 'No, you won't, but there's a jolly good chance that you might if you don't stop working.'

'No, no,' she said. 'I'm . . . I'm in my forties – that's the prime time for a woman, isn't it? I'm still young. Ish. And I feel great. Honestly, I really do.'

'Can I just point out to you that you're in a hospital bed?' Mike said gently.

'Yes, but it's not serious!'

'You could have had a heart attack.'

'But I didn't.'

'You're heading that way. Your blood pressure's off the scale, your sleep is shot to pieces and you're not eating properly.'

Audrey's mouth gaped open at that.

'Don't deny it. You've been eating on the run since you started that school. I haven't seen you sit down to a proper meal for ages.'

'I was eating proper meals at the priory. Ask Harrie and Lisa.'

Mike lowered his head as if in despair. 'You need to listen to me, Aud, please. This is serious. You've been so focused on your new business that you've simply forgotten to take care of yourself. It's easily done. The doctor says you're not the first and you won't be the last person to put work before everything else, but I can't let you do that anymore. You're killing yourself.' He gently picked her hands up again and stroked them in the comforting way that he knew she liked.

'This is what we're going to do,' he told her. 'You're going to stay here for as long as you need to and then you're coming home with me, where you're going to do precisely nothing.'

Audrey looked up at him and, for the first time in a long time, she found that she was crying.

'Hey, hey!' he whispered, snuggling up next to her on the bed. 'It's okay. Everything's going to be okay. I'm going to take the very best care of you, all right?'

She nodded through her tears. She felt ridiculous for crying, but she felt so very vulnerable, lying helpless in the hospital bed, unable to remember exactly how she got there. She'd always been so in control of her life, feeling that she had boundless energy and that she was capable of anything, and it came as a shock to her to realise that she did, indeed, have limitations. Her will was strong, but she now knew that it couldn't completely override the needs of her body, and that she had to start paying it more attention before it was too late.

Lisa was missing Audrey more than she could have guessed. They might have had their differences, but Lisa wished with all her heart that her friend was still there. Of course, it was lovely to see Harrie so happy with her daughter, and she was being very sweet in trying to include Lisa in their conversations, but she still couldn't help feeling like a spare part. It was only the second day of Audrey's absence, but Harrie and Honor still hadn't caught up, it seemed. Right now, Lisa was half listening to their conversation about somebody in their home town called Lionel who was going out with a woman called Jacqueline. The story didn't seem very funny to Lisa, but Harrie and Honor couldn't stop laughing. Was there anything worse, Lisa thought, than being unable to take part in an apparently hilarious conversation?

And then there'd been the times when she'd come into room to find them engaged in some deeply serious conversation in low voices. They'd look up, seemingly startled by her presence, as if anxious that she might have overheard them. But then Harrie would plaster a huge smile across her face and encourage Lisa to join them. Lisa didn't take well to being the odd one out. It wasn't what she wanted from her summer holiday.

She was just about to give them some privacy and leave the room when Harrie's mobile rang.

'What?' she said a moment later. 'No! How is she?'

Lisa frowned at the serious expression on Harrie's face.

'Okay,' Harrie went on. 'Keep us updated, won't you? And send her our love.' She hung up.

'What is it?' Lisa asked.

'That was Mike.'

'Is everything all right?'

'Not exactly. Audrey was rushed to hospital.'

'What?'

'She collapsed at work.'

'Oh, my god!'

'She's at home now and Mike's taken some time off work to look after her. But she needs complete rest.'

'She should come back here,' Lisa declared and, for once, she wasn't just thinking about herself. 'This is the best place for her, isn't it? I mean, it's so peaceful and quiet.'

'I think Mike wants to keep an eye on her,' Harrie said. 'You saw how she'd practically set up an office in her bedroom here when she'd promised him she wouldn't be working at all.'

Lisa nodded. That was true enough. 'Should we go and see her?'

'I'm not sure Mike would want that.'

'Well, he can't keep her all to himself. We're her best friends and, if she's not well, she needs us there with her.'

Honor glanced at her mother and Harrie cleared her throat. 'I think Mike probably knows best.'

Lisa swallowed hard, feeling that Harrie wasn't telling her everything. She hated that feeling of being locked out and she definitely felt it with Harrie and Honor right now.

'I'll be out in the garden if you need me,' Lisa told them, leaving the kitchen quickly.

It felt good to be outside. It was warm, but there were just enough wispy white clouds around to ensure that the sun's rays were more gentle than they had been recently. Lisa had already been out in the garden that morning, performing her sun salutation and having a quiet meditation amongst the herbs. As ever, yoga was her escape, her salvation, and she returned to the mat, which she had left out on the lawn.

Sitting herself down, she crossed her legs and placed her hands on her knees, her thumb and forefinger touching lightly as she practised her breathing, the gentle cycles calming her mind and body.

After a few moments of this, she started her physical practice and how good it felt! She was happy Lisa once again, the disappointments of the world forgotten as she bent and stretched and breathed.

'What's that?' a male voice suddenly asked from somewhere behind her. It was Alfie. She could see him from between her legs. Typical that he should approach her when her bottom was saluting the sky.

'It's downward dog,' she stated, pushing herself into an upright and slightly less revealing stance.

'Nice,' he said. 'I mean – it looks like a nice stretch.'

'It is,' she told him, thinking how easy it would be to flirt with him, but refusing to do so.

He nodded and then rolled his shoulders.

'You feeling tight?' she asked him.

'Pretty much.'

She walked behind him and reached up to feel his neck and shoulders.

'God, you really are,' she said. 'Come on – get on the mat.'

Like before, Alfie removed his boots and socks before stepping onto Lisa's mat. Lisa stood in front of him, her feet embracing the coolness of the grass. She then took him through a series of simple stretches, adjusting his movements slightly so that he got the best results. He was tall and strongly built, just as a rugby player should be, but it was obvious that the sport had done his body no favours at all and that he was now paying the price for his passion.

'Better?' she asked him when they came to the end of their practice.

He rolled his shoulders again and stretched his neck.

'Feels pretty good to me, thanks.'

'We could do a short breathing exercise to calm down if you like, but I expect you'll want to be getting back to your gardening.'

'I'd love to.'

'You would?'

'Got plenty of time for the garden with these long days.'

'Okay,' Lisa said, her eyes meeting his brilliant blue ones.

She showed him how to sit and watched as he winced, encouraging him to kneel instead. They then closed their eyes and she led him through a series of breathing techniques. It felt strange to be in such close proximity with a stranger while she was going through what she felt was an intimate routine. But it was a good sort of strange because she knew that she was sharing something really special with somebody who would truly benefit from it.

'And wriggle your toes and fingers and slowly blink your eyes open,' she said at last.

Alfie took a long deep breath and sighed it out.

'Good?'

He nodded, a satisfied smile on his face. 'I'm going to have to take this up.'

'You do mean yoga, don't you? And not taking up the fact that an old woman is distracting you from your duties as gardener.'

He frowned. 'You're not an old woman.'

Lisa got up from the grass and Alfie stood up from her mat.

'I'm forty-six,' she told him, not quite sure why she felt the need to.

'I'm twenty-four.' He shrugged. 'Have you been to the Golden Swan in the village?' he asked as he bent to put his socks and boots on.

'No. Not yet.'

'It's a nice pub. Good pints.'

'I don't drink pints. Not since my student days anyway.'

Alfie nodded. 'Would you like to come out for a drink with me?'

Lisa hesitated, but then she thought of her holiday companions. There was Audrey, who was now with Mike, and Harrie, who now had Honor. She was just Lisa. On her own.

'Yes,' she said, surprising herself with her alacrity.

Alfie grinned. 'Great! I can pick you up at eight tonight—'

'It's okay. I'll meet you there.'

'Oh, I see.'

'What?'

'You don't want your pals here at the priory seeing me picking you up.'

'That's not it at all!' Lisa protested. 'I just like being independent.'

'Oh, right. So, if you decide you don't like my company, you can leave immediately.'

She gave a tiny smile. 'Something like that.'

'Fair enough,' he said. 'But you're going to like it.'

'What?'

'My company.'

'You're very sure of yourself.'

He flashed her a smile. 'I'll see you there.'

Harrie was worried about Lisa. She was worried about Audrey too, but at least she could be sure that Mike was taking good care of her. But she hadn't seen Lisa for a good few hours now and she'd searched the garden for her too. She'd found her yoga mat rolled up in the herb garden, but there'd been no sign of her. Where could she have gone?

Harrie went back into the priory to make a start on dinner and, ten minutes later, Lisa waltzed in.

'Hey! I was getting worried about you!'

Lisa looked surprised. 'Really? I didn't think you'd notice if I was here or not.'

Harrie sighed. 'Oh, Lisa – of course I'd notice.' She addressed her friend with great caution, knowing she could be a drama queen when feeling hurt.

Lisa slunk around the kitchen for a moment and Harrie instinctively knew that she was fishing for an apology and, because she was in a giving vein, she gave her one.

'I'm really sorry if you're feeling left out, Lisa.'

'I'm not feeling left out.'

'No?'

Lisa pouted. 'Well, maybe I am.'

'I should have told you and Audrey about Honor coming,' Harrie admitted. 'I'm sorry I didn't. But I didn't think it would upset things between us. I thought it would be a case of the more the merrier.'

Lisa glanced down, picking at her nails, and Harrie quickly wondered what she could do to make up for her obvious gaffe.

'Is there anything special you'd like for dinner tonight? I'm cooking.'

Lisa shook her head. 'Actually, I'm going out.'

'Really?'

'Yes.'

'Are you going to tell me where?'

'Just to the local pub.'

'On your own?'

'I'm going on my own, yes, but I'll be meeting somebody there.'

'Oh!' Harrie couldn't help but sound surprised. 'Would you care to elucidate?'

'No, not really,' Lisa said, quickly crossing the room and making her way up the spiral stairs.

It was then that Honor entered from the living room.

'What's going on?' she asked.

Harrie placed her hands on her hips. 'You know, I'm not really sure.'

Entering the pub at exactly eight o'clock, Lisa spotted Alfie leaning up against the bar, his broad back towards her as he laughed at something a man standing next to him had said. He was wearing a pale-blue shirt and smart, clean jeans. She took a deep breath, suddenly wondering if she'd made the right decision in coming tonight but, as Alfie turned around and spotted her, she realised it was too late to change her mind.

'Lisa!' he called, beckoning her over. 'What can I get you to drink?'

'Oh, erm – a glass of white wine,' she said, defaulting to her old standby. Heaven only knew that she needed something to still her nerves.

A couple of minutes later and they were both seated at a table next to a window at the back of the pub which overlooked a pleasant garden.

Lisa looked across the small table at Alfie and wondered what on earth she was doing there.

'You look . . .' He paused.

'I look what?' Her right hand flew to her face in fear that she was having a hot flush. 'Red? I look red?'

He smiled. 'No! I was going to say that you look pretty, but I wasn't sure if that would offend you.'

'Why would you think that would offend me?'

He shrugged. 'I don't know. It's hard to know what to say to a woman these days.'

'You can still tell a woman she looks pretty,' Lisa told him.

'Yeah?'

'Yes.'

There was a pause.

'Well, go on then.'

'What?' he asked.

'Tell me I look pretty!'

He laughed. 'You look pretty.'

Lisa beamed and they both relaxed a little.

'So, what made you become a gardener?' she asked him, thinking it best to turn the attention away from herself.

'I'm not.'

'Oh,' she said. 'Well, you seem to be doing a pretty good impression of a gardener.'

'I'm just filling in,' he said. 'It's a summer job.'

'I see,' she said, taking a sip of her wine. 'So, what are your plans after the summer?'

He shifted his feet under the table. 'Going to join my dad at his company.'

Lisa watched the expression on his face change. 'You – er – don't seem too happy about that.'

'Yeah, well, it is what it is.'

'Can I ask what his company is?'

Alfie shrugged. 'Office supplies. Equipment, stationery, that sort of thing.'

'Quite different from gardening then.'

'You could say that.'

'You like gardening, don't you?'

'It's okay, yeah.' His smile had returned now. 'I've been trying a few things out, you know? I did a bit of travelling after university, did odd jobs here and there – some bar work – that kind of thing. I suppose I've been delaying the inevitable.'

'You mean, working for your dad?'

'I'm his only child. I'd be letting him down if I didn't work for him there. I've been putting it off for as long as possible and he's been good to let me try a few other things out, but it's always been with the understanding that I'd work for him one day.' He took a sip of his drink.

'But you can't do a job that you're not going to be happy in,' Lisa pointed out to him. 'That's your father's dream, not yours.'

'Yeah, but he'd be devastated if I didn't take the job.'

Lisa sighed. 'Well, if you don't mind me saying, I think it's a bit mean of him to push you like this. I mean, can't he find some other young man who has more of an affinity with stationery?'

Alfie chuckled. 'Maybe I could develop a fondness for envelopes.'

Lisa couldn't help but smile. 'You're joking about this now, but just you wait a few years. You'll be sitting at some desk in a stuffy office, watching the hands of the clock crawl around, your skin grey from a lack of sunshine and wondering what on earth you've done with your life.'

'So what do you suggest? I can't hurt the old man's feelings.'

'Are you sure about that? Are you sure you want to hand your life over like this? I don't want to incite rebellion, but this is something I feel really strongly about. You've got to go after your dreams, Alfie.'

'Like you did with acting?'

'Exactly!'

They were quiet for a moment.

'Alfie, if you could do anything, what would it be?'

'Why is this so important to you?' He looked genuinely puzzled.

'Because you only get one life and you have to make it count. You don't realise that when you're young but, the older you get, you know that you have to grab hold of every opportunity.' She took a sip of her wine. 'I want to tell you something. Something I don't usually talk about.'

'Okay.'

She swallowed hard. 'My mother died when she was thirty-nine. I was at university when it happened. She'd been ill for a while. Cancer.'

'I'm sorry.'

Lisa paused, her fingers tight around the stem of her glass as she recalled the darkest period of her life. She still felt the loss of her mother so keenly, even though it had happened nearly thirty years ago, and she found Mother's Day impossible to get through unless she kept her distance from social media and all the photographs of people celebrating the day with their beloved mothers. Did they know how lucky they were, she thought, to still have their mothers to show their love to?

Looking at Alfie now, she continued, 'My mother confided in me just before the end. She said that, although she'd led a happy life, she'd never felt completely fulfilled. She'd always wanted to sing' – Lisa smiled at the memory – 'but circumstances and her own lack of courage seemed to get in the way. But she'd held that dream in her heart her whole life, always hoping that fate would step in and present her with some miraculous opportunity. Only it didn't, or at least that was what she'd thought. It wasn't until right at the end of her life that she

142

could look back and see that there had been plenty of opportunities, only she hadn't recognised them. Maybe she'd been too afraid or too busy, maybe she'd made excuse after excuse, but they'd been there and she'd overlooked them. Who knows what she could have done if she'd only set her mind to it?'

Alfie reached across the table and took Lisa's hand in his and she instantly felt tears rising at the sweetness of his gesture.

'But what if you don't have a dream?' he asked her.

She frowned. 'You've *got* to have a dream! You can't just drift through your life with no direction.' She blinked her tears away and took a deep breath. 'Right!' she said, getting into teacher mode. 'We're going to discover *your* dream.'

'What?' He sounded incredulous.

'We're not leaving this pub until you've told me what makes you happy.'

He laughed and shook his head. 'Being here with you makes me happy.'

'Well, that's very nice, but you can't make a living from that.'

He puffed out a sigh, obviously sensing that she was being serious now.

'Okay,' he said, looking thoughtful. 'What makes me happy?'

'That's right. It can be anything. Just think.'

'Rugby used to make me happy until the injury. I like gardening, but I can't really see myself doing that. I'd never remember all those Latin names for a start.'

Lisa nodded. 'Good, you're thinking.'

He gave her a funny look.

'Sorry, that's me being a teacher.'

'It's okay,' he said. 'I like it.'

She smiled, relieved that he hadn't found her patronising.

'I did once work for a family friend who runs an outdoor-activity centre for kids. That was fun,' he revealed.

'Yeah?'

He nodded. 'I liked the kids. Some of them were from the city and had never seen the countryside before. It was great taking them into the woods camping. They learned how to pitch a tent and make a fire and how to cook. We did orienteering too.'

'So what happened?'

'I gave it up.'

'Why?'

He shrugged.

'Oh, Alfie!'

'I've never really stuck at anything for long because I've known I was going to be working for my dad one day.'

'Well, at least we've found something you're passionate about,' Lisa said.

He held her gaze for a moment.

'There are other things I'm passionate about,' he said.

Lisa almost spluttered on her wine as he winked at her.

'I think *one* passion an evening is enough to be getting on with,' she told him with authority, the teacher in her rising once again, firmly quashing the woman.

Chapter 11

At first, it was a novelty to have a long lie-in and be brought breakfast in bed by a husband who hadn't had to run out of the door at first light. But, after twenty-four hours of being housebound, Audrey was ready to scream. Mike had taken some time off from work and was proving worse than any gaoler, sitting in a chair opposite her, pretending to read the newspaper when he was only really there to make sure that she didn't sneak onto her laptop as soon as his back was turned.

It just seemed crazy to her to sit around doing nothing. Surely sending a couple of emails or making a few phone calls couldn't do any harm. She truly believed that she was getting more stressed by wasting time than by filling it, but Mike was having none of that. He meant her to have total rest and so her home became the sofa with a pile of magazines and books beside her and an endless stream of cups of tea which he provided.

It was on the third day when she dared to broach the subject.

'You know what?' she said, trying to sound as casual as possible. 'I think I might be better back at the priory.'

Mike's startled face appeared around the side of his newspaper. 'What?'

'I've been thinking about it and I really believe it would do me the world of good to spend time in the garden there. We don't have much of a garden here, do we? And the neighbours' kids are always so noisy at this time of year. I really think I could benefit from the grounds at the priory and even get some swimming in. The doctor said swimming was good for me, didn't he?'

Mike nodded, but he was looking guarded.

'And being with my friends. That could only help, couldn't it? And you must be bored sitting here with me all day. It can't be much fun.'

'I'm not bored,' Mike assured her.

'No?'

'I could sit here for the rest of my life and be quite happy.'

Audrey was aghast at this. 'If you really mean that, I'll have a heart attack right here and now and end it all!'

'Don't say that!'

'I mean it, Mike. I don't how much longer I can sit like this.'

Mike ran a hand across his jaw and then nodded. 'I know, Aud.' He stood up.

'Where are you going?'

'I'm going to ring Harrie.'

'But I can do that.'

'Let me handle this,' Mike said.

'I *can* make a phone call, you know. I'm not a complete invalid.'

But Mike had left the room and Audrey could do nothing but wait and send a telepathic message to Harrie, begging her friend to encourage her return.

It didn't take long before Mike was back.

'I've spoken to Harrie and she's keen to have you back and assures me that she'll keep an eye on you.'

'Of course she will. You won't need to worry.'

'I haven't said you can go yet.'

'Oh, Mike!' Audrey stood up and gave him a hug. 'I'll be absolutely fine. I'll be better than fine there. You know I will. And you could come and settle me in and make sure I'm okay.'

Mike was still looking uncertain about the whole thing. 'Now, I don't want you getting any ideas about working there. If I do let you go, it's for total rest, okay?'

'Okay.'

'You won't be taking the laptop.'

Audrey gasped at that.

'No laptop, Audrey, I mean it.'

'But you'll let me go if I don't take the laptop?'

'And if you report in to me each day.'

She grinned. 'You make it sound like I'm on parole!'

'You are, and Harrie's on my side, you know. She's going to ring me the minute she thinks you're not relaxing.'

'You mean if I dare to get up and fetch myself a drink?'

'Exactly!'

'Can we go today? I mean, right now? I'd better go and pack!'

'*I'll* pack,' Mike said. 'I don't want you sneaking any gadgets into your luggage.'

'As if I would!'

'You most certainly would. As soon as my back was turned, you'd be filling your suitcase with paperwork.'

Audrey rolled her eyes at him, secretly loving that he cared so much.

Harrie had been sitting by the swimming pool when Mike had rung. She'd been watching her daughter swimming laps, her body sending perfect ripples into the turquoise water of the pool.

When Honor got out, Harrie handed her a towel.

'Mike just rang. Audrey's coming back.'

'Really? Is she okay?'

'Mike made me promise to keep a careful watch on her. I think he's still really worried.'

'I bet he is.'

'She's always had a habit of overdoing things and working until she's physically broken,' Harrie told Honor. 'Even at teacher-training college, she took on the running of so many after-school activities that she had no time left to recuperate from the day's teaching and was left writing up the next day's lesson plans in the early hours. She really ran herself down. Lisa and I both warned her at the time, but you know what Audrey's like when she takes on a new project – it's always head first at a hundred miles an hour, and I don't think she's slowed down over the years!'

Honor dried her long hair and rubbed her limbs before applying some lotion and settling back on the sun lounger next to her mum.

'What is it?' Honor asked a moment later. 'Are you worried about Audrey too?'

'No. Well, a little maybe. But it's made me think.'

'What about?'

Harrie pursed her lips and wondered how she was going to say this. 'I've come to a decision.'

Honor's eyebrows rose a fraction. 'Now, you're worrying me.'

Harrie took a deep breath. 'I've decided not to tell them. I can't. Not now.'

'What do you mean?' Honor sat upright, swinging her legs over the side of the sun lounger and facing her mother.

'I mean, it wouldn't be right. Not with Audrey feeling the way she does. She needs to recuperate. I've made a promise to Mike that I'll look after her.'

'But what about *you*, Mum? Isn't this what the holiday is all about? It's *your* time, not Audrey's. She's a bit stressed, that's all. That's *nothing* compared to what you've been through.'

'Stress can be as much of a killer as cancer.'

'That's rubbish!'

'No, it's not!'

'But I don't think she's in imminent danger, do you?'

'Please keep your voice down.'

They exchanged a heated look.

'My mind's made up, Honor. I'm not going to tell them.'

Honor stood up, looking furious. 'Well, yours might be, but I could still tell them.'

'Honor! You're not to tell them anything, do you hear me?' Harrie cried.

Her daughter looked full of thunderous thoughts at that moment and Harrie wasn't totally sure what she was going to do or say.

'Darling—'

'It's not fair, Mum! This is *your* time. God only knows you've got little enough of it and you told me that you needed to tell them.'

'I know I did, love, but things have changed now.'

Harrie stood up and reached out to hold her daughter's hand, encouraging her to sit down again.

'But you've been through so much and I just think it's unfair that they weren't there for you,' Honor said.

'But they would have been, you know that.'

Honor's lower lip was trembling and Harrie knew that she was on the verge of tears.

'I still don't understand why you never told them.'

Harrie sighed. 'I guess I saw it as a way of protecting them. They didn't need to be a part of all that ugliness and, believe me, if I could have got away without telling you, I would have done. I saw what it all did to you.'

Honor shook her head. 'I was fine.'

'Don't get upset, darling!'

'I'm not upset! I'm mad. I'm *really* mad that you're here thinking about them and offering to take care of Audrey when she wasn't there for you!'

Harrie sat next to her daughter on the sun lounger. She was crying now and Harrie brushed away the tears with her fingers, feeling tears of her own threatening to spill.

'This is the hardest thing I've ever done and I need you on my side, not fighting against me.'

'Oh, Mum!' Honor threw her arms around her and, suddenly, they were both crying. 'I'm not fighting against you. I'm fighting *for* you!'

For a few moments, the two of them allowed the tears to fall. It was a pattern that kept repeating itself; they'd found that they could only go for so long putting on a brave face to the world and to each other and, every so often, they would just break down, acknowledging the true darkness of the thing that lay between them.

'Listen, Honor,' Harrie said, leaning back and drying her eyes, hoping that Lisa wouldn't make an appearance. 'I can't change the decision I made in the past. I chose not to tell them and I stand by that decision because I think it was the right thing to do – the *kindest* thing.'

'But you should tell them now,' Honor said.

Harrie gazed out across the blue water of the swimming pool. 'I can't.'

'Mum!'

'Honor, listen to me.' She held her daughter's hands in hers. They were cool from her dip in the pool and Harrie held them oh-so-tightly. 'You have to trust me, okay? I've got to do what's right or at least what feels right to me. You do understand that, don't you?'

'No!'

'Yes, you do,' Harrie said. 'I know you do.'

Honor shook her head. 'Maybe I do, but I'm not going to pretend that I like it.'

Harrie leaned forward and kissed her cheek. 'Just trust me, okay?'

It was mid-afternoon when Harrie realised that it had been a while since she'd seen Samson. She'd been so wrapped up in her daughter's arrival and then recovering from their emotional outburst that she'd forgotten her old friend.

Old friend. She smiled at that. She barely knew the man and yet there was something about him that made her feel as if she did, and she had to admit that she missed her strange one-sided conversations with him. With that in mind, and with Honor keeping Lisa company in the garden, Harrie made two cups of tea and walked through the cloisters to where Samson was working in the tower.

'Hello there! I have some tea for you,' she called up the scaffolding before actually locating him. 'Samson? You up there?'

The raucous call from a jackdaw in the tower greeted her, but there didn't seem to be any sign of Samson.

She rounded the corner to the grandest part of the priory and there he was, gazing up at the ceiling.

He shook his head slowly. 'Frustrating,' he said without looking at her.

'What is?'

'All the repairs this place needs.'

Harrie didn't know much about architecture, but she could appreciate the beauty of the ancient building from its stone tracery to its fan-vaulted ceiling. The creamy gold of the stone was so lovely but there were so many places where the plasterwork had crumbled to reveal the bare brick behind it and, as beautiful as this hapless disarray was, it must have pained somebody like Samson to see it.

'Is there anything you can do?' she asked him.

'I've just got my little corner to do, but there's easily half a decade's work here.'

'Really? As much as that?'

She handed him the mug and he took a long slow sip, nodding at her in appreciation.

'Do you walk around old buildings assessing the work that needs doing?'

'Pretty much, and this is a gem.'

'Maybe the trust that owns this place will get around to these other repairs one day soon. They've done a pretty good job with the rest of it.'

'I was telling my granddad I was working here and he said he could remember it when it was almost completely a ruin. He said that he and his friends would cycle down the lane and throw stones at the broken windows.'

'That's terrible!'

'It's what little boys do.'

'But surely you didn't do anything like that. Not with your sensibilities!'

'I threw my share of stones. Not here, though.' He took another sip of his tea. 'Anyway, I'm making up for any damage I might have done now.'

He gazed up again at the tracery windows high up in the tower. The lower, larger windows had glass in them, but the ones higher up didn't, which was how the jackdaws and pigeons got in.

'I wish I could get up there and sort it out. It could look so beautiful.'

Harrie craned her neck back, trying to see the place as Samson might. 'But it is still beautiful, isn't it?'

'Oh, sure, but it's like . . .' He paused as if searching for the right words. 'It's like leaving a priceless painting out in the rain. It seems unthinkable to me that it should be left in such a state.'

'All the same, it's survived all these centuries and will live long after we've gone,' Harrie said, swallowing hard.

'I know, but it still needs attention.'

'I once read something that said there was no such thing as restoration. Isn't that depressing?'

Samson frowned. 'What do you mean?'

'Well, I think it meant that any repair work isn't the same – it's not original.'

'Of course it isn't.'

'It's a new artist or craftsman's work.'

Samson's eyes had darkened. 'Are you saying restoration is worthless?'

'No!' Harrie cried. 'I'm only saying what I read.'

'But you believe what you read?'

'Not at all. I'm all for saving these places and works of art. I think you're doing a really important job.'

'If these places weren't restored, they'd crumble and disappear.'

'I know.'

He nodded and handed his mug back to her. 'Thanks.'

'You're not cross with me, are you?'

'No.'

'Are you sure? You wouldn't be the first person I've upset today. My daughter's in the most terrible mood with me.' She thought, again, of Honor's tear-streaked face and closed her eyes for a moment. When she opened them, Samson was heading back towards the scaffolding and Harrie knew that her little slot of time with him was fast coming to an end.

'I told her I was going to do something and now I've gone back on my word, but I swear it isn't my fault.' She cursed under her breath. 'I don't know what's the right thing to do anymore.'

Samson paused as he reached the ladder and Harrie could have sworn he was going to say something, but he didn't.

'Why is life so complicated?' she went on. 'And why do you say so little?'

He looked taken aback at this. 'I don't need to say a lot. You do all the talking.'

Harrie's mouth dropped open at his cheek. 'Well, I'll stop and give you a chance then.'

He cleared his throat and Harrie waited.

'I guess it's why I like stone,' he said after a moment.

Harrie frowned. 'What?'

'It's uncomplicated. You know where you are with a block of stone. People – they confuse me.'

'So you're not married then?'

He shook his head.

'You don't want children?'

'Who says I haven't got children?'

'Oh, you have?'

His lips twitched in amusement. 'Nope.'

Harrie grinned. 'Well, I get about as much out of you as I would a block of stone.'

Samson smiled at that and that made Harrie smile too. She'd finally reached his sense of humour.

'Why are you here all summer?' he suddenly asked.

Harrie was surprised by his question. 'Why not?'

'Well, it's unusual, isn't it? I mean, people normally only book these places for a week or two.'

'Yes, but I'm not most people,' she said.

There was a pause.

'Now who's proving hard to talk to?' Samson said.

Harrie laughed. 'I'll leave you to it,' she said and watched as he slowly climbed the ladder, up to his safe, solid world.

It was late afternoon when Mike's car pulled up in the driveway. Harrie, Lisa and Honor were all sitting in deckchairs in the south garden and heard the car at the same time, leaping to their feet in an instant.

'Audrey! We were so worried about you!' Harrie cried, running towards her friend and flinging her arms around her as soon as she appeared. 'It's so good to have you back.'

'It's good to be back. I really missed this place!'

'Oh, charming!' Lisa said. 'She missed the priory but not us!'

'You know what I mean,' Audrey said, coming forward and hugging her friend.

'I want to hear you say it,' Lisa insisted.

Audrey gave her a funny look. 'Oh, all right then – I missed you guys! There, will that satisfy you!'

'Welcome back, Audrey!' Honor chimed as she received her hug. 'How are you feeling?'

'A lot better, thank you.'

'Don't let her fool you,' Mike said, coming forward with Audrey's luggage. 'She still needs plenty of rest.'

'How are you, Mike?' Harrie asked. The two embraced.

'Good. You look well, Harrie.'

'Thank you.'

'And Lisa – it's been a while, hasn't it?'

'Too long, gorgeous man!' Lisa said, giving him a resounding kiss on the cheek.

He laughed. 'Hello, Honor.'

The five of them walked into the priory together.

'Audrey's been driving me nuts!' Mike confessed. 'Who would have thought that doing nothing could be so hard?'

'I did!' Audrey said. 'Doing nothing absolutely terrifies me.'

Mike glared at her.

'But I'm learning to adapt,' she quickly added.

'Let's get the kettle on,' Harrie suggested.

'Kettle?' Lisa cried. 'Shouldn't we be opening some wine? You are allowed a little tipple, aren't you?'

Audrey looked to Mike and he pursed his lips.

'I'm not sure that's a good idea,' he said. 'Not just yet.'

'But surely wine helps you to relax?' Lisa said.

'A cup of tea,' he said. 'For now.'

Audrey sighed, but nodded.

'Now, let's get you unpacked,' he said. 'Which way is it?'

'Up the spiral stairs,' Audrey said. 'Come on. I can't wait to show you around. I'm still in the same room, aren't I, Harrie?'

'Of course.'

'Just making sure Lisa didn't pinch it whilst I was gone.'

'I did no such thing!' Lisa protested. 'Although I might have had the odd shower in your en suite.'

'This place is amazing,' Mike said as he followed her up the spiral staircase.

'You see why I wanted to come back?'

'It's certainly beautiful.'

They reached the landing and Audrey crossed towards her bedroom and smiled as Mike whistled.

'You've got your own fireplace!' he cried. 'And look at that window.'

'I wish you'd stay the night,' she said to him.

He put his hands on her shoulders. 'I wish I could too, but I should get back. But, first, I'm going to get you all sorted here.'

She watched as he walked across the room and unzipped her suitcase.

'Mike, I can do that, really.'

'It's okay.' He took out her clothes and laid them on the bed before opening the wardrobe door and hanging up her dresses. There would be no arguing with him. Even though he had the long drive home, he insisted on her not lifting a finger.

Finally, he crossed the room and wrapped his arms around her.

'Promise you'll call if you're worried about anything. Any time – night or day.'

'I promise.'

'And remember—'

'No working! I got it!'

'I have all my spies in place,' he told her. 'The first sign of you sending an email or ringing the school and I'll be back here in a heartbeat.'

They returned to the kitchen, where Harrie had tea and biscuits ready on a tray to take into the garden. Mike immediately cut in, taking the tray from Harrie, and they all enjoyed their treat as the sun slowly slipped behind the great tower of the priory.

'Well, I'd really better be off,' Mike said, getting up at last.

'You sure we can't tempt you to stay, Mike?' Harrie asked.

He looked up at the building behind him and shook his head ruefully. 'Afraid I'm needed in London. Maybe another time, eh? Be sure and book it again.'

Harrie smiled at him and nodded. 'I'll try and do that.'

Audrey watched the exchange and couldn't help noticing Honor glaring at her mother in an odd manner but, before she could question it, Mike was on the move and everyone was saying goodbye.

She walked with him to his car and they embraced.

'Love you, Aud.'

'Love you, Mikey.'

They kissed.

'Call me once you're home.'

He nodded. 'And you call me every day and any time you need me, okay?'

'I promise.'

She watched as he left and then turned and walked back through the garden to her friends.

'Thank goodness for that!' she said. 'Right, who's got a laptop I can borrow? I need to get some work done.'

Harrie held her hands up. 'No way, Audrey! I'm under strict instructions not to let you work.'

Audrey laughed. 'I was joking!'

Harrie examined her closely. 'I can never quite tell with you.'

Audrey felt restless that first night back at the priory. Mike had rung as soon as he'd arrived home to make sure that she was comfortable and feeling well. It had taken about twenty minutes of constant reassurance before he was happy enough to hang up.

Switching on her bedside lamp, Audrey got out of bed. The night was warm and she tiptoed across the floorboards to open the casement window, praying for some cool air to find her as she sat on the large window seat. She felt like a romantic heroine from a Tennyson poem and smiled at the notion. It was a long time since she'd felt romantic. That was something which had definitely been missing from her life of late and she knew that the fault lay with her because she'd been so horribly busy.

All those little romantic things she and Mike used to do together, like taking a walk at dusk along the river or making time to visit a favourite restaurant, had fallen by the wayside when she'd started her school. Just before she'd left for the holiday at the priory, she'd arrived home after nine one night, several hours after the school had closed, to find Mike brooding on the sofa. When she asked him what was wrong, he'd motioned to the kitchen and Audrey had then remembered. It was their wedding anniversary and she'd forgotten. Mike hadn't forgotten, though. There'd been an uneaten meal in the oven and a bunch of red roses in the sink.

She still felt awful about that and she'd offered to take Mike out the following night, but he'd declined and, in all honesty, she'd been glad because she had so much to do at work.

When had that happened, she wondered? When had she started to choose work over her husband? It wasn't that there was anything wrong with her marriage. They were still very much a loving couple. But it might not always be that way, she warned herself. Not if she continued to put her work first and Mike a very poor second. Maybe her episode, her health scare or whatever it was, was a wake-up call. It wasn't too late to change things, was it? Mike was still very much there for her, but how long would he put up with things? He'd already told her that things had to dramatically change. He hadn't really gone into any detail about that when she'd questioned him and she had to admit that it worried her. Her work was so much a part of her that she sincerely doubted there'd be very much left of her if it was taken away.

Hopping down from the windowsill, she pulled on a cardigan and slipped her feet into the comfortable slippers Mike had bought her after she'd come out of hospital. He'd bought her a lot of things: a stack of magazines, a box of her favourite chocolates, a huge bunch of flowers, the silver earrings she had admired in the local jeweller's as well as the velvety soft slippers. Oh, yes, Mike was still there for her. It was *she* who had moved away.

Quietly, opening her bedroom door, she tiptoed across the landing, stopping when she heard a strange noise. It took her a moment to work out what it was. Crying. She cocked her head to one side. It was coming from Honor's twin bedroom. Moving closer to the door, Audrey hovered, her hand in the air ready to knock, but something stopped her. She didn't feel it was her place to intrude.

It was probably boy trouble. Maybe Honor and Benny had been fighting, Audrey told herself, continuing to the kitchen. There she poured herself a glass of water and returned to her room, picking up one of the hardbacks which Mike had packed for her. She smiled. It was one of the books he'd bought her last Christmas. Or was it the Christmas before? She couldn't remember. But, one thing was for sure, she hadn't had time to read it. She had time now, though, she thought, as she climbed into bed.

Audrey wasn't the only one who was having trouble sleeping. Lisa had opened her window before getting into bed and, although there was a light breeze now, it was still unbearably hot.

She got out of bed and threw on a light kaftan, padding across the floor in bare feet. The floorboards felt wonderfully cool, as did the stone steps of the spiral staircase as she made her way downstairs. What to do in a priory in the middle of the night, she wondered? A priory with no TV. There were books, plenty of books, that was for sure, but she really didn't feel like reading. Actually, she was feeling a little bit peckish, she realised, moving towards the fridge. Opening it, and bathing herself in the delicious coolness for a moment, she stared at the contents. There was nothing but salad, smoothies and fruit juices in there.

'Thanks, Harrie,' Lisa groaned, closing the door.

It was then that she remembered something: the birthday cake. Now, where was it hiding? It certainly hadn't been in the fridge. Hadn't Harrie put it in one of the cupboards?

Lisa started opening a few and soon found the box the cake had come in. With careful hands, she lifted it and took it to the table, opening it up a moment later. And there it was: a single slice of cake. It was a pretty generous slice, it had to be said. You could probably get two decent slices from it, but you'd have to look for a knife and that wouldn't be as simple as plonking it on a plate and eating it. But, could she, in all consciousness, eat that last slice of cake?

She looked around as if somebody might be watching her from the dark corners of the large kitchen. Maybe this was some sort of test, she thought, but how very tempting it was and she couldn't actually remember eating any more of the cake since that first night so surely everybody else had had seconds and even thirds. Anyway, it was probably going a bit stale by now, she told herself, giving it an experimental poke with a finger. She'd be doing everybody a favour by eating that last slice. It would probably prevent it from being ravaged by mice or from causing an outbreak of mould in the priory. Nobody would want that, would they?

Sitting down at the table, Lisa pulled the opened box closer to her and picked up the slice, nibbling the triangular corner. Nothing had ever felt as decadent as eating that big slice of birthday cake in the middle of the night. The light sponge, the sweet jam and the smooth icing tasted so good that she refused to feel guilty about it. Harrie and Audrey would have done exactly the same thing, she reasoned.

Still, she couldn't help thinking that some long-departed monk was frowning down on her, shaking his head at her having given in to temptation. But it was too late for guilt now. The damage was done and, within a few minutes, there wasn't even a single crumb left; she'd made sure of that.

Getting up, she carefully folded the now empty box and put it into the bin and brushed down the table. All evidence of her greed must be removed. With any luck, nobody would remember that there'd been a slice left at all.

Chapter 12

Harrie was the first one up the morning after Audrey came back. It was a beautiful day and there was a freshness to the air which allowed a delightfully cool breeze to find its way into the priory through the windows that had been left open during the night. She liked these quiet moments and having the gentle old building to herself for a while. She walked around it now, barefoot, wincing slightly at the ancient coldness of the stone floors, but revelling in it too. She'd learned that feelings – even if they were unpleasant or even painful – meant that she was alive and that was always good. And so she strode across the floors, a big smile on her face as she admired the quirks of the property, peeping into alcoves, trailing her fingers across the crumbling brickwork, staring up into chimneys and listening to the squeaks of her favourite doors.

After an hour or so of this happy pastime, Harrie made it into the kitchen, where she was surprised to see Mrs Ryder.

'You're very early,' Harrie observed.

Mrs Ryder nodded. 'Got a dentist appointment later so thought I'd get my hours in here first,' she explained. 'Can I make you some breakfast? I've done a top-up shop and have plenty of eggs and bacon and—'

'Did Lisa give you another list?'

Mrs Ryder pursed her mouth and Harrie grinned.

'She seems to have a heartier appetite than you.'

'There's nothing wrong with my appetite,' Harrie protested, even though she knew it was a lie. It hadn't been the same for months now. For a while, everything she'd eaten had tasted of salt. It had been weird and unsettling and had put her off eating altogether and she'd lost so much weight and hated the way she could feel her ribs through her clothes. Since the whole salt disaster, her appetite had definitely shrunk, although she was careful to get plenty of good natural nutrients into her system. And the occasional piece of cake. Harrie smiled. She wasn't sure what had suddenly made her think of the birthday cake, but now she couldn't shake it from her mind and went to the cupboard where she'd placed it, opening the door and then frowning.

'Mrs Ryder, have you seen the birthday cake?'

'You're eating cake for breakfast?'

'No. I mean, I was just looking for it. It was in this cupboard with my blender, but now it's gone.'

'I've not touched it.'

Harrie searched a few of the other cupboards and then opened the fridge, but there was no sign of the cake. Then her eye caught the bin and she went over to open it. Sure enough, there was the neatly folded box inside.

'Looks like somebody's enjoyed the last slice.'

'Were they not meant to?' Mrs Ryder asked.

'Oh, it's okay,' Harrie said. 'I'm just wondering who it was and when it happened.' She laughed. 'It's fine.'

'I'll make you a cup of tea,' Mrs Ryder said.

'I'll get a juice.'

'One of them sickly-coloured things you've got in the fridge?'

'There's nothing sickly about them,' Harrie told her. 'They're packed full of goodness.'

'They look like liquid grass to me.' She pulled a face to show her disgust. 'No wonder your complexion looks green all the time.'

'What?' Harrie felt stunned by this observation.

Before she knew what was happening, Mrs Ryder had crossed the room and had caught Harrie's face in her chubby hands. Harrie gasped and went rigid, her eyes wide in alarm at this unprovoked move.

'You're not well, are you?' Mrs Ryder said, standing back now and letting her hands drop.

Harrie turned away from her inquisitor and opened the fridge for the express purpose of hiding her face inside it.

'My sister – she – well, she was ill,' Mrs Ryder continued.

Harrie grabbed one of her juices. One of her green juices. She knew she'd have to come out of the fridge at some point, but she was kind of hoping for an intervention before she did. Maybe Lisa would come bounding into the kitchen or maybe the tower would crash down. That would be a good distraction.

'I'm right, aren't I?' Mrs Ryder's voice sounded as if it was just the other side of the fridge door. Harrie took a deep breath and closed it. She wasn't sure what she was going to say, but there was something in Mrs Ryder's face that made her feel as if nothing but the truth would do.

'How did you know?' Harrie found herself saying, realising that her hands were trembling.

'You have that same other-worldly look about you that my sister had.'

Harrie's mouth had gone quite dry now.

'Your friends don't know, do they?'

She took a few big gulps of her juice before answering. 'Audrey suspects something.'

'The serious friend?'

'Yes.'

'But you haven't told them?'

'No.'

Mrs Ryder looked concerned by this. 'But you are going to, aren't you?'

'I was, but I'm not so sure now. Audrey's been sick, you see.'

'Not as sick as you by the looks of things.'

'That's what my daughter keeps saying,' Harrie admitted.

'Cancer?' Mrs Ryder whispered.

Harrie paused before answering. Oh, how she hated that word – that soul-crushing, mind-paralysing word. 'Yes,' she said, her voice little more than a peep.

'I thought so.'

'Is it *really* so obvious?'

'There are a few signs if you know what you're looking for.'

'And your sister?'

'She passed,' Mrs Ryder said matter-of-factly.

'I'm so sorry.'

A moment of stillness and wordlessness passed between the two women. It was a strange feeling because Harrie didn't feel any sort of closeness to Mrs Ryder, but this confession – this sharing of intimate pain – now connected them. Harrie had found that her journey with cancer had linked her to so many people in this way – people she probably would never have spoken to. She remembered that strange waiting-room camaraderie and the little looks that passed between people that said, I'm here too, I understand. Something similar was happening with Mrs Ryder now.

'But you're okay now?' Mrs Ryder asked, her voice catching slightly.

'No.' The blunt word seemed to pop out of Harrie and she swore she could see tears rising in Mrs Ryder's eyes.

'You must tell them,' Mrs Ryder said gently.

Harrie shook her head. 'I can't. I thought I could, but not now.'

'You might regret that.'

'I won't get much time to regret anything,' Harrie said grimly.

'But your friends would want to know, wouldn't they?'

Harrie drank some more of her juice.

'Let me feed you up a bit,' Mrs Ryder said, pulling a face at Harrie's green glass.

'Really, my appetite isn't good.'

'But you haven't given me a chance,' Mrs Ryder told her, her hands on her hips now. 'I bet I could tempt you with something. I make a pretty good cottage pie.'

Harrie couldn't help smiling. 'You know I'm a vegan!'

'Why deprive yourself? Especially now.' Mrs Ryder paused. 'I mean . . .'

'I know what you mean.'

'Well, you should be enjoying yourself.'

'But I am.'

'What – with them awful juices?'

'They're not awful! You should try one.' Harrie returned to the fridge and opened the door, pulling out one of the juices.

Mrs Ryder flinched and shook her head. 'No, no, no! I'm not pouring that horrible green thing into me. I'll tell you what. I'm going to leave you one of my meat pies with the golden crusts.' She raised a plump finger in the air as Harrie was about to protest. 'You can eat it or not, but I'm making it all the same. Your friends can enjoy it even if you don't.'

Harrie gave in with a sigh. 'Fine. Make it and leave it if it makes you happy.'

Mrs Ryder looked pleased at this and it was then that Audrey and Lisa came into the kitchen.

'Good morning!' Lisa chimed. 'What are you two chattering about?'

'Nothing!' Harrie said, exchanging a little glance with Mrs Ryder, who quickly turned her back on her and busied herself at the kitchen sink. 'I was just trying to persuade Mrs Ryder to enjoy a green juice with me.'

'Ewwww! What did she do to deserve that fate?' Lisa asked. 'It's like something you'd find in a student fridge at uni.'

'Like that gone-off milk, remember?' Audrey said, screwing up her nose.

'Don't remind me,' Lisa said. 'I poured it into my coffee and it came out in huge blobs.'

'Why didn't you sniff it first?' Audrey asked.

'I was half asleep. I thought it would be fine.'

'Remember we used to have to write our name on things in the fridge?' Harrie said. 'You used to write with a big red angry pen, Lisa.'

'And even that didn't stop people from stealing,' Lisa said, 'but fear not – we will not be stealing your green juice!'

Harrie smiled. 'Isn't Honor up yet?'

'I haven't seen her,' Lisa said.

'Did you sleep well, Aud? Wasn't it hot?'

'I had to get up for a cold water.'

Harrie nodded, wondering if it was Audrey who had eaten the last slice of cake. Well, if she had, she couldn't begrudge her for it after what she'd been through.

'I'm going into town this morning. Can I pick up anything for you?' Harrie asked. 'Oh, there you are, darling.'

Honor entered the kitchen, her eyes looking red and sore.

'Are you okay, sweetie?' Lisa asked.

'I'm fine,' Honor said, but she didn't look fine to Harrie, who approached her now and gently stroked her hair.

'Did you not sleep?'

'I slept fine.'

Harrie examined her daughter's face and could see the pain clearly etched there.

'I fancy French toast,' Audrey announced. 'Anybody else?'

Honor moved towards the cupboard and reached in for a box of cereal.

'I was just saying that I've decided to go into town,' Harrie said again. 'Does anybody need anything?'

'Oh!' Lisa immediately cried. 'Can you get me some coffee? You know the sort I like?' Lisa went to one of the cupboards and pulled out her almost empty jar of coffee to show Harrie.

Harrie nodded. 'Got it. Anything else?'

Both Lisa and Audrey began to list some things and Harrie grabbed a notebook and pen from out of her handbag.

'I'm running out of toothpaste,' Audrey said.

'And I'd love some more of that coleslaw from that deli if you're passing,' Lisa said.

'Oh, if you're going past that little bookshop, could you pop in and see if they've got the new Susan Hill? But only if you're going past.'

'Hang on a minute. Let me get this all down.'

'Perhaps we should get some more wine in too?' Lisa suggested.

'Never a bad idea,' Audrey said.

'Hey!' Honor suddenly cried.

'What is it?' Harrie asked, looking up. 'Did you want something too?'

'If I *did*, I'd get it myself. I wouldn't bother you, Mum, and neither should you two. She's not here to be at your beck and call.'

'Honor – I offered to go. I don't mind.'

'But you shouldn't be waiting on everyone like this.'

Audrey was looking pointedly at Harrie now. 'Why shouldn't she, Honor?'

Harrie glared at her daughter. 'I really don't mind.'

'Well, *I'm* minding for you,' Honor said.

Everybody was staring at them now and Harrie felt horribly uneasy, as if she was under a microscope. It was Mrs Ryder who came to the rescue.

'I'll help,' she said. 'I'm going into town too and can help your mum.'

'I don't need any help. It's only a bit of shopping. Why is everyone making such a fuss?'

Her question hung in the air for a moment.

'Right, let me get my handbag,' Mrs Ryder said. 'I'm all done here anyway.'

Quickly, before anybody could say anything else, Harrie left with Mrs Ryder.

Audrey had been watching Honor for a while as she swam angry lengths in the pool. She'd never seen anyone swim with such fury before. It was as if she was fighting the water with each and every stroke. Lisa, who was sitting with a pair of earphones on, didn't seem to notice or wasn't saying anything if she did.

It was almost three hours since Harrie had left to go shopping and Audrey was still perplexed about Honor's earlier outburst. She'd tried to question her about it, but Honor had disappeared into her room with her breakfast as soon as her mother had left and then she'd walked straight between Audrey and Lisa settled by the pool and jumped head-long into the water. She'd been swimming now for a good ten minutes. She was going to have to stop sooner or later and then Audrey would try to talk to her again.

Something was definitely going on, Audrey knew that. Perhaps Honor resented her mother's two best friends being there. Perhaps she wanted her mother to herself. But Honor wasn't really that kind of person. She didn't have a selfish bone in her body and it wasn't like her to be possessive.

Audrey watched as she continued to slice through the water. Lisa was still locked away in her world of music, her head nodding to her latest favourite band. Unless she was chanting to something yogic. No, Audrey thought, the beat was too fast.

She returned to watching Honor. She must be getting out of the pool soon. Audrey was beginning to get annoyed, which probably wouldn't do her blood pressure any good. She took a moment, taking in some slow deep breaths and breathing them back out again.

It was then that Honor emerged from the pool, her long limbs dripping in the sunshine. Audrey suddenly felt nervous about confronting the young woman even though she'd known her all her life. But there was something different about her now. All the joy seemed to have been sucked out of her and Audrey had to find out what was going on.

'Honor?'

Honor had grabbed the towel she'd brought out with her and was roughly drying her hair.

'What?'

'I'd like to talk to you.'

'What about?'

'About your mother.'

'Why?'

'Because I think there's something going on here.'

Honor continued to dry her hair, seemingly taking an unnatural amount of time over it.

'Honor – will you please look at me?' Audrey was almost shouting now.

'What?' Honor yelled back. This caught Lisa's attention and she took her headphones off.

'What's going on?' she asked.

'That's what I'm trying to find out.'

'Nothing's going on!' Honor cried.

'Yes, well, that's where I think you're not telling the truth,' Audrey said. 'For one thing, you're behaving like a teenager. I've never seen you like this before even when you *were* a teenager.'

'Is everything okay?' Lisa asked.

Honor flashed her a wild look. She looked both vulnerably young and horribly aged.

'What is it?' Audrey asked. 'Has something happened between you and your mum that you're not telling us about?'

Honor stared at her for a moment. She looked as if she was on the precipice of confession. Indeed, her lips parted as if she was about to speak, but then she swallowed and looked away.

'You'll have to ask Mum what's wrong. It's about time she told you.'

Audrey was just about to question her about this when she heard the cheerful voice of Harrie ringing out across the garden. She turned to look and there was her friend, her shopping bags in her hands.

'Hey!' Harrie called as she approached. 'I managed to get everything. Well, apart from your coleslaw, Lisa. They'd run out. But I got you a little pot of olives instead. I hope that's all right. They looked so gorgeous.' Harrie stopped talking and looked at everyone, a frown etching her face. 'What's the matter?'

'That's what we're trying to find out,' Audrey said.

'What do you mean?'

Audrey was getting frustrated now. 'I want to know what's going on, Harrie.'

'I don't understand.'

Audrey was looking closely at Harrie, and she saw the exact moment that her expression changed from bemusement to fear.

'Honor?' Harrie said. 'What have you told them?'

'Nothing! I've told them nothing.'

'Honor said that *you* should tell us something,' Audrey said. 'What did she mean, Harrie? What's going on?'

Lisa was sitting up. 'You guys are worrying me.'

Harrie dropped her shopping bags and perched on the edge of one of the sun loungers, her eyes large in her pale face.

'Harrie?' Audrey pressed again.

Harrie sighed. 'There's something I've been meaning to tell you.'

Chapter 13

It wasn't quite the scenario Harrie had painted in her mind when she'd thought about this moment. She'd imagined it taking place at night for some reason, all cosy in the living room of the priory, the curtains drawn, with everybody feeling mellow after a few glasses of wine. Instead, they were all sitting outside in the glaring sunshine. There was no way to hide out here, she thought. She felt as if the sun was a gigantic spotlight pointing directly at her. She was alone in this and she had to do it because she was causing everyone so much distress by not telling them. She could see that now. Honor was angry and Audrey was suspicious and Lisa was looking as if she might possibly faint. It was time.

'Harrie? Whatever it is, I think we need to know,' Audrey said gently.

Harrie nodded. 'I know you do.'

Wrapping her towel around her body, Honor took a seat next to her mother and held her hand.

'It's the right thing to do,' Honor said encouragingly.

'Yes.'

Harrie looked at the anxious faces of Audrey and Lisa, knowing that this was their last few moments of being blissfully unaware of what was happening. She'd hoped to keep this from them for as long as possible. Indeed, she'd changed her mind about telling them at all.

'Harrie?' Lisa prompted, and Harrie took a deep breath.

'You're right,' she began. 'I wanted us to spend this summer together because there was something I was going to tell you. But then – well – you've been through so much, Aud, and I didn't want to add to that burden so I changed my mind.'

Harrie closed her eyes, wishing she could slowly disappear and re-emerge somewhere far from this place. This wasn't how it was meant to happen. She didn't feel ready. But, if she was perfectly honest with herself, when would she be ready? When would be the right time? There was no right time for something like this, was there?

She opened her eyes and looked at the beautiful faces of her friends again. They had no idea what was coming, did they? She held the power right now in this moment. But, the time had come. It was why she'd gathered them here, after all.

'I'm not well.'

The words sounded so strange to her still. As long as she didn't say them aloud, she could almost believe it wasn't true.

The silence that greeted her was almost overpowering.

'Say something,' Harrie whispered. 'Please!'

'What exactly do you mean by "not well"?' Audrey asked, leaning forward slightly and shielding her eyes from the sun.

Harrie saw the fear in her friend's face and, as much as she hated to go on, she knew she was committed now.

'Cancer.'

'What?' Lisa cried.

'Breast cancer,' Harrie went on, feeling Honor gently squeezing her hand. 'I had a double mastectomy, chemo, radiotherapy . . .'

'So the scar I noticed earlier was to do with that?'

Harrie nodded. 'The mastectomy was four years ago now.'

'Why didn't you say something before?' Audrey asked.

Harrie sighed. 'I couldn't.'

'Why not? Aren't we your friends? I don't understand how you kept this from us for so long. To go through all that . . .'

Harrie could see the tears sparkling in her friend's eyes.

'I wanted to spare you. I thought – I *knew* I could cope.'

'But nobody should have to just *cope*,' Audrey pointed out.

'I had Honor,' Harrie said. 'She's been such a star. I couldn't have done it all without her.'

'You could have, Mum. You're stronger than you think.'

Harrie turned to look at her daughter and they shared a sad smile.

'So that's it, then? You've had all the treatment and you're okay?' Audrey asked. It was the question Harrie had been dreading and which she'd known would come.

'I'm afraid not. I went into remission and had three cancer-free years, didn't I?' She turned to Honor, who nodded, her eyes shiny with tears. 'We did all sorts of fun things, didn't we? And I'm so glad we did. But, just before Christmas, I had a scan and they found another tumour.'

'Oh, Harrie!' Audrey cried. Suddenly she was on her knees in front of her, her arms wrapped around her in a tight embrace. Harrie wasn't sure what she'd been expecting, but it wasn't this. Audrey was normally so reserved. It was Lisa who was the demonstrative one, but their roles seemed to have been switched with Harrie's revelation, and Lisa sat stone-still on her sun lounger.

'Mum?' Honor said. 'I'm going to take the shopping in, okay?'

It was sweet of Honor to give her some time with her friends, Harrie thought. She could be so wonderfully mature like that sometimes.

'You should've told us!' Audrey said again, once Honor had left them. 'I can't believe we didn't know what you were going through.' She cursed. 'We've been terrible friends!'

'No, you haven't!'

'We shouldn't have lost touch like we did.'

'But we didn't. We've been busy, that's all. We've all been leading our own lives.'

'That's no excuse! We should have been there for you, Harrie.' Audrey loosened her embrace and sat back. 'Are you having treatment for this tumour?'

Harrie shook her head. 'The cancer's spread now. It's too late for treatment to be successful even if I wanted to go through it, which I don't.'

'Really?' Audrey's voice was incredulous.

'I've decided to go for quality of life over quantity this time,' Harrie told her.

'But surely there's a chance it would work? Shouldn't you at least give it a try?'

Harrie shook her head. 'The chemo made me feel so ill before and I didn't want to go through that again.'

'But what have they said? What *exactly* did they say?' Audrey persisted.

Harrie knew what she was asking. 'You mean how long do I have?'

She saw Audrey swallow hard.

'My oncologist didn't want to give me a timeframe. Everyone's different, you see. It's impossible to know really, but I did press for an estimate and he was a bit vague. He told me that I'd be able to enjoy the summer, but that it was unlikely that I'd see Christmas.'

Audrey's mouth fell open, but no words came out.

'It's fine,' Harrie said. 'I'd kind of been expecting it.'

'Fine?' Audrey's voice was a squeak. 'How can you say that? It's not *fine*!'

'But I feel good. I really do,' Harrie assured her. 'I just get a bit tired, that's all. But I've got my medication and . . .' Her voice petered out as she saw the pain in Audrey's face. She turned to Lisa. She still hadn't said anything.

'Lisa?'

Lisa stared at Harrie for what seemed an inordinate amount of time and then she got up.

'Where are you going?' Audrey asked, grabbing her by the hand as she passed.

'I'm going for a swim.' She shook her hand free of Audrey's and Harrie watched as Lisa walked to the edge of the pool and jumped in.

Audrey got up as if to stop her. '*Lisa!*'

'Leave her,' Harrie said. 'She just needs time. I've kind of sprung this on you.'

'I'm going after her,' Audrey said.

'You're going to jump in the pool?' Harrie asked with a laugh. 'Just leave her, Aud. She'll process it in her own way.'

Audrey turned to her, her eyes like large wounds in her face. 'How can you be so calm about all of this?'

Harrie took a moment before answering. 'Because I've had time to think about it. I mean, *really* think about it.'

Audrey took a seat beside her. 'Please tell me that your sense of humour has taken a real dive over the years and that this is some kind of horrible joke.'

Harrie shook her head. 'It isn't a joke. I wish it was.'

'Harrie!'

Harrie took her friend's hands in hers. 'It's okay,' she assured her.

'How can it be okay? You're dying!'

'We're all dying.'

'Yes, but not before Christmas!'

'Maybe not,' Harrie said. 'You know, I once looked up the number of deaths from cancer each year in the UK. It's over one hundred thousand. Isn't that astounding? So I won't be the only one and there'll be a mighty fine welcoming party for me wherever I'm heading. And, believe it or not, there's actually a strange kind of comfort in knowing when your time's coming.'

For a few awful moments, Audrey could do nothing but cry and Harrie let her, stroking her dark hair and telling her that it was all right. This was exactly what she'd done her best to postpone for so many years.

When she'd first been diagnosed, she hadn't wanted her friends to know the fear she'd felt, and then her natural optimism had kicked in and she'd sincerely hoped that they'd never need to know because she would be all right, and indeed she had been for a while.

Audrey gave a gargantuan sniff. 'So that scar I saw? That was just the beginning for you, wasn't it?'

Harrie nodded. 'I'm sorry I lied to you. I hated myself for doing that.'

'I can see why you did.'

'You can?'

Audrey nodded. 'I might have done the same.' She gave her a strange little laugh. 'I probably wouldn't, though. I'm too much of a coward.'

'You'd be amazed at how brave you can be when you need to be.'

'Oh, god, Harrie! I can't bear it. The thought of you—'

'Don't say it!'

'You're too young. It's not fair!'

'There are plenty younger than me that have been taken.'

'Yes, but they're not my best friend!' Audrey stated. 'Oh, my god! Honor! How is she coping?'

'She's been pretty amazing actually,' Harrie said. 'We've had our moments, of course, but she's really been there for me.'

'That's why she was so angry at us before – when we were barking orders at you for shopping.'

'You weren't barking!'

'She was so defensive of you.'

'I know. I've had to rein her in a bit.'

Audrey's eyes were filling with tears again. 'Harrie!'

Harrie opened her arms and hugged her friend as she sobbed. 'I'm so sorry. I really didn't want to do this to you. You're meant to be relaxing. Mike would kill me!'

Audrey leaned back and dried her eyes on the light sleeves of her blouse. '*You're* worrying about *me*?'

'Of course I am! I'm pretty much done with worrying about myself.'

'Really?' Audrey's face creased into disbelief.

'Well, I've come to . . .' Her voice petered out again. 'I've come to an understanding about it. It's exhausting being worried all the time when there's nothing that can be done.'

Audrey looked truly amazed by this statement. 'You're incredible, Harrie. If I was you, I'd be going out of my mind.'

'Oh, I've done that a few times already.'

Audrey gave a rueful smile. 'Are you sure they haven't made a mistake? I mean, is there somebody else you can see? Some specialist in America or Europe or somewhere?'

'Or someone who sits cross-legged on a mat in India?' Harrie suggested.

'Yes!' Audrey cried. '*Anything!* I'll pay for the flight. I'll come with you.'

Harrie shook her head. 'I've spent hour upon hour on the Internet. I've researched everything you can think of and then a bit more.'

'But you're still eating all that health food. Do you think that might cure it?'

Harrie shook her head. 'Nothing's going to cure it.'

'So why put yourself through the horror of kale?'

Harrie had to laugh at that. 'Believe it or not, I've rather developed a taste for greens and it feels good to eat them. It's a strange way to look at it, but having cancer has made me the healthiest I've ever been! It's made me want to fight for my body in ways I've never done before. They say that you take your health for granted and that's really true. I know just how badly I was abusing my body before I got ill. I was running on empty. I just assumed it would do exactly what I needed it to do without putting any real goodness into it.' Harrie shook her head. 'When I think of all the junk food I used to eat!'

Audrey nodded. 'I think I might be guilty of that too.'

Harrie took hold of her friend's hands again. 'But it's not too late for you, is it?'

'You mean I should eat kale?'

'Why not?' Harrie laughed. 'Although I ate bloody heaps of the stuff and the cancer still came back.'

Audrey winced and Harrie leaned towards her. 'Just promise me you'll take good care of yourself.'

Audrey nodded and her eyes were shiny with tears once again. 'I will.'

'Because I'll come back and haunt you if you don't.'

'I believe you.'

'You'll be sitting on the sofa about to swig your third can of cola of the day when I'll drop a fat apple into your lap!'

Audrey laughed, her tears spilling down her cheeks. 'You do that! But, in the meantime, I'm going to look after you.'

Harrie shook her head. 'Absolutely not. I can take care of myself.'

'Well, at least let me make you a cup of tea?'

Harrie smiled. 'You go ahead and have one. I'm going to sit here a while and see if I can talk to Lisa.'

Audrey got up and walked to the edge of the pool. 'She's got to surface at some point.'

'And I'll be right here when she does.'

Audrey bent down close to the water.

'What are you doing?' Harrie asked.

'I'm going to get her for you.' Audrey was on her knees now.

'You'll get wet!'

But Audrey wasn't deterred. 'LISA!' she cried as their friend approached the shallow end. 'Get *out* of the water!'

'She won't hear you,' Harrie said.

'She can hear me just fine. She's only pretending she can't.' Audrey took a deep breath and tried again. '*LISA!*' She dipped her right hand into the pool and banged on the side, sending angry little waves up her arm.

'Leave it, Aud. Please.'

Audrey turned around and stood back up. 'She's being ridiculous.'

'She's just handling it differently. You know what happened to her mother and how awful that was for her.'

'Yes, I do, but this isn't about her – it's about *you*.' Audrey moved forward and gave Harrie another big hug. 'You are *so* kind. I don't know how you can be so patient with her.'

'Not patient,' Harrie said. 'I understand her a little, that's all. You know, if I could have got away without telling you both, I would have done, but Honor kind of forced my hand, didn't she? I really wanted to spare you both. I've been dreading – absolutely dreading – telling Lisa. Remember all those sleepless nights she had when she'd just cry and cry? And we couldn't do anything to help except hold her?'

'I remember.'

'So I think we should try and understand how she might respond to all this now.'

Audrey sighed. 'You're amazing, Harrie.'

'I thought you were going to make some tea.'

Audrey looked at her quizzically. 'You're not going to use this cancer to boss us all around, are you?'

'There have got to be *some* benefits!'

Harrie watched as Audrey walked back to the priory and then she turned towards the pool. Lisa was still swimming mad lengths, her arms slicing through the water. She'd always been a natural swimmer – graceful and fast, she made it look effortless. Harrie, on the other hand, moved through the water with all the grace of a truck. It wasn't her natural element and, although she liked to swim, she knew her limitations.

Harrie stood and walked to the water's edge, wondering how long it would be before Lisa stopped swimming and started talking to her. She could only imagine what was going through her mind. Once again, she hated the cancer for what it was doing not only to her but to those around her. What was it somebody at the hospital had once said to her? 'Cancer – the gift that keeps on taking.' If Harrie could have kept her condition to herself she would have willingly, but that hadn't been possible with all the hospital appointments. She had needed to turn to her daughter and now she felt she needed her friends too.

'Lisa?' she called as she reached the shallow end. 'You can't ignore me forever.'

Lisa placed her hands on the edge of the pool and hauled herself out, grabbing her towel a moment later and drying herself quickly.

'Lisa?' Harrie persisted. 'Did you hear what I said?'

Still, Lisa didn't look at her.

'I need to know—'

'I heard you!' Lisa cried, and the two women stared at each other for a long moment.

'Okay,' Harrie said. 'I just wanted to make sure . . .'

But Lisa didn't seem to be listening now. Instead, she leaned down to pick up her belongings and, without saying another word or looking at Harrie again, headed towards the priory.

Chapter 14

Audrey cried for most of the night and her ribs felt sore by morning. She'd never felt so wretched in her life. Nothing could have prepared her for Harrie's news. It just seemed so unfair. Harrie was too young and too nice to be taken. What kind of a crazy world took somebody like Harrie? If Audrey had believed in God, she would have been furious with him.

When she had left Harrie by the pool to try and talk to Lisa, she found Honor in the kitchen putting her mother's shopping away. Honor had turned around to reveal a red and tear-streaked face and Audrey had run to her.

'Honor!' she'd cried. 'How have you coped?' she'd asked as her own tears began to fall again.

'I haven't. Not really.'

'But you *have*! Your mum's so proud of you, you know that? But I wish you'd reached out to us.'

'I wanted to, but Mum wouldn't let me.'

'I know. I know.' She'd stroked Honor's hair. 'I blame myself now. We should have made more of an effort to keep in touch. If we had, we'd have known something was going on.'

'She wouldn't have let you know. She'd have made some excuse not to see you.'

'Really?'

Honor had nodded.

'You might be right,' Audrey had said at last. 'She didn't even want to tell us now, did she?'

'I think I kind of forced her hand.'

'I'm glad you did,' Audrey had said.

They'd spent a further ten minutes crying and embracing. Audrey had been so desperate to comfort Honor, but had also needed comforting herself.

Now, lying in bed with the morning light spilling onto the dark floorboards, she felt that she had to talk to somebody about it and she knew who that person should be.

Finding her phone and switching it on, she rang Mike. It was early and he would still be at home. Sure enough, a moment later, he answered the phone.

'Audrey! Why didn't you ring me last night? I was worried sick! I told you that you were to keep in touch.'

'Mike – listen! I couldn't call you.'

'Why? What's happened? Are you okay?'

'Yes, yes! I'm fine.'

'Then what is it?'

She felt the tears rising once again and a large lump formed in her throat. 'It's Harrie,' she managed. 'She's dying, Mike!'

'What?'

'She told us yesterday. She's been hiding it from us for years! I can't believe it. Why wasn't I there for her? I'm such a bad friend!'

'Aud, love! Slow down. You're not making any sense.'

Audrey took a deep restorative breath, trying to corral her thoughts, and then she told Mike what had happened the day before. When she'd finished, he swore and she could hear that his voice was thick with emotion.

'I can't believe it. I don't want to, Mike.'

'Come home.'

'What?'

'You should come home.'

'I can't do that! I can't leave Harrie – not after what she's just told me. Why would I do that?'

'Because I'm worried about you. It's too stressful.'

'But you don't understand – this is her last summer.'

'I understand perfectly. It was nearly your last summer too, remember?'

'That's rubbish.'

'Have you forgotten you ended up in hospital?'

'No, of course not. But I feel fine and I'm staying here to be with Harrie.'

Mike swore again.

'Don't fight me on this, Mike, because you won't win. I've got to be here for her, especially with the way Lisa's behaving.'

She heard him sigh and imagined that he was pacing up and down the front room, raking a hand through his hair.

'We're losing her, Mike. I have to be here with her. It's what she wants. It what *I* want.' Saying the words made her feel suddenly very calm. She knew that, whatever Mike said, she would be spending the rest of the summer with her dear friend.

'All right,' Mike said at last. 'If you're sure it's what you want and that you're okay.'

'Of course I'm sure.'

'Because I can be there—'

'I know – you can be here in the blink of an eye and whisk me away.'

'I'm just worried about you,' Mike said. 'I was worried enough before this bombshell.'

'She needs me,' Audrey said. 'She needs her friends around her and the peace of this place. I can see why she booked it now. She planned this. You know, she was going to tell us and then changed her mind when she found out about my episode? That's the kind of a friend she is – putting others before herself even when she's dying.' The words caught in Audrey's throat and she had to will herself not to burst into tears again. 'It's not going to be easy, but I'm going to do my very best to be what she needs. You understand that, don't you?'

They talked for a little while longer and then Mike hung up. Audrey sat perfectly still for a while, the air seeming to hum with her emotions, but she really did feel strangely calm now and that's what had struck Audrey most about Harrie – she too had been so incredibly calm. She'd told them that she was dying as if she might have been telling them that she'd just had a nose job. It was no big deal. But maybe she'd already cried herself out. Maybe she was being calm for her friends' sake. And that's when something struck Audrey. *She* had to be calm and strong for Harrie now. There would be time enough for tears later. This holiday, this special holiday which Harrie had arranged for them, had to be happy. Harrie wouldn't want to see her and Lisa crumbling around her.

With that in mind, Audrey left her room and walked across the landing towards Lisa's, knocking lightly on the door. There was no response and so she turned the handle and pushed it open.

'Lisa? Are you awake?' She tiptoed across the room towards the bed. Lisa's back was to her and she didn't seem to respond when Audrey touched her shoulder, which told her that Lisa was either a very heavy sleeper or was just as awake as she was. Audrey suspected the latter.

'I've been thinking about Harrie.' She sighed. 'How can I think of *anything* else now? We need to be really strong for her. I know this is going to be difficult and there are going to be tears. I don't think I've cried as much in years, but she doesn't want to see our miserable faces, I'm sure of that. She doesn't want to watch us having a meltdown, okay? She hired this place to be happy, to have fun with us. One last time. One last summer.' Audrey felt a lump in her throat. 'And we've *got* to make that happen. It's going to be hard and I know what you went through with your mum, Lisa, but we've got to push aside our own needs now and be there for her.'

She paused. 'Lisa? I wish you'd talk to me, goddamn it! I don't want to be alone in this. I need you.' Audrey reached out again and squeezed her friend's shoulder. 'Are you even *listening* to me?'

Lisa didn't respond and, feeling angry, disappointed and horribly isolated, Audrey left the room.

'What are we going to do about Lisa?' Audrey asked the next day. It was late afternoon and Lisa had done her best to avoid them both, breakfasting early and spending her time in the secluded corners of the garden.

'I don't think there's anything we can do,' Harrie said matter-of-factly.

'Are you going to try and talk to her again?'

'I don't know. She didn't respond well yesterday. I think she's shut herself down and I'm not sure I'll be able to get through to her no matter what I say.'

'But this is ridiculous! She's behaving like a child.'

'Don't be cross with her.'

'How can I not be cross? She shouldn't be treating you like this, Harrie. It's unacceptable.'

'It's fine. It's just her way of coping with all this.'

'Well, it's not good enough.'

It was later that evening when Lisa came downstairs. Harrie, Honor and Audrey were at the trestle table, having just polished off the very fine meal Mrs Ryder had left for them. Audrey, who was facing the door, spotted her first.

'Hi!' she cried. 'Come and join us.'

Lisa paused for a moment but, instead of joining them, she walked to the fridge, took out a bottle of wine and then headed back up the stairs.

'Lisa!' Audrey called after her, rising from her seat. 'Hey! I'm talking to you!'

'Leave her,' Harrie said, reaching a hand out to try and settle Audrey.

'Are you crazy? She's going to drink herself into a stupor.'

'She's a grown woman, Aud,' Harrie said.

Audrey shook her head, her face reddening with anger.

'I'm going to talk to her, Mum,' said Honor. 'This has gone on long enough.'

'No. Just leave her for now,' Harrie told her. 'I'll try her again later.'

It was almost ten o'clock when Harrie tried the door to Lisa's bedroom and found it unlocked. She hesitated for a moment, almost too nervous to venture inside.

'Lisa?' Harrie whispered, peering around the door.

Lisa was lying on her bed, her face buried in her pillow.

'I don't want to talk to you,' she said, her voice muffled.

'I wish you would.' Harrie walked inside and moved towards the bed, noting the empty bottles around the room. 'We've been worried about you. Have you eaten anything today?'

Lisa didn't respond.

'You must be starving,' Harrie continued, 'and it's stifling in here.' She went to open one of the windows and was greeted by a blessedly cool breeze. 'There, that's better.' She looked around the room again, trying to gauge exactly what Lisa had been up to. She couldn't see any evidence of food other than an empty packet of chocolate digestives. The bedding was a messy tangle and, when she peered into the en suite, she saw that all the towels were on the floor.

'Oh, Lisa!'

Suddenly, her friend sat up on the bed, her eyes bright with tears in her swollen face.

'I don't want to lose you!' she cried.

'But you haven't!' Harrie said. 'I'm right here. *Right now!*' She sat down on the bed and, as she'd done with Audrey, just let her friend cry for a while. 'It's okay.'

'It's not fair!' Lisa said, sniffing loudly. 'Why did this have to happen to you?'

'I don't know,' Harrie said honestly. 'I wish it hadn't, if only so I wouldn't have to hurt you all like this.'

Lisa inched back a little, turning her bright, teary eyes to Harrie. 'You always think of others, Harrie!'

'But I know what you've been through already.'

Lisa closed her eyes for a moment and nodded. 'It took me right back there – that moment when you so casually said you had cancer out in the blazing sunshine.'

'I thought that's what had happened.'

'I couldn't face it.'

'It's okay.'

'I'm sorry!' Lisa said at last. 'I didn't know what to do.'

'It's all right.'

'No, it's not! I've wasted all this time when I could've been with you. You needed me and I turned away from you.'

Harrie hugged her close. 'You needed to process it, that's all. I understand and I know what you went through with your mum. It's okay.'

'I still remember when Mum sat me down to tell me her diagnosis. It was so horrible. It was such a shock. We'd just been eating chocolate ice cream.'

Harrie blinked. She'd never heard this story before. 'You had?'

Lisa nodded. 'I've never been able to eat it since.'

Harrie wasn't quite sure why. Maybe it was the way Lisa had said the line – like she was an actress in a cute romantic comedy – but a tiny smile tickled the corner of Harrie's mouth and she couldn't stop it from spreading.

'What?'

'Sorry!'

Lisa sniffed again and wiped her eyes. 'It's not funny.'

'I know it isn't. It's just the way you said it.'

The tickly smile seemed contagious and Lisa's lips twitched with it now. 'Stop making me laugh.'

'I'm not!'

Lisa took a tissue out of a box by the side of her bed and pushed her hair away from her face. 'Do I look a mess?'

Harrie smiled. The old Lisa was resurfacing. 'I've seen you looking better.'

A smile spread across her friend's face.

'Listen!' Lisa said. 'I've been thinking. I've not been comatose the whole time I've been in here.' She paused and Harrie couldn't help wondering what she was going to say next. 'I can help you.'

'What do you mean?'

'I mean, I can help you beat this thing.'

Harrie shook her head. 'No, Lisa.'

'Yes – yes, I can!'

'I've tried everything, believe me.'

'But *I* haven't tried!' Lisa cried.

'Lisa, aligning my chakras and teaching me how to breathe through one nostril isn't going to save me.'

'Don't say that!'

'This thing's got me good and proper.'

'I won't believe that.' Her tears rose again. 'We've got to fight it!'

Harrie took hold of Lisa's hands and squeezed them, speaking slowly to her. 'Listen, I know this is going to sound slightly crazy, but I'm at peace with this now. I've done all the fighting I'm going to do.'

'How can you be so calm about all this?' Lisa cried.

'Because I've been through all the other emotions,' Harrie explained. 'Believe me, I've sunk to the very bottom with this but, somehow, I've bobbed back up – maybe not to the top – but I'm in a good place now.'

'Really?'

'Yes! Truly.'

Lisa shook her head. 'But there must be something . . .'

'I would have found it. Trust me on this.'

'But we could try—'

Harrie squeezed her hands again. 'Please, just be with me now. That's all I want.'

They embraced again and Lisa wiped her face with the back of her hand and sniffed.

'Are you okay?' Lisa asked at last. 'I mean, I know you're not, but – oh, god! I'm not saying this very well.'

'I'm okay,' Harrie told her. 'Sometimes, my mind can't help but dwell on all the things I'm doing for the last time – like seeing my last cherry tree in bloom or birthdays and anniversaries, but there are compensations too, believe it or not.'

'Like what?'

'Like never having to go to the dentist again.'

Lisa laughed and Harrie was pleased to see her friend smiling again.

'And really, it's a blessing in so many ways,' Harrie went on.

'How do you mean?'

'I mean I can plan things – make sure everything's in order for Honor and the rest of my family. It's the poor sods who die on the spot of a heart attack or who get run over by a bus that I feel sorry for.'

Lisa looked aghast for a moment, but Harrie gave an encouraging smile and, luckily, Lisa mirrored it back to her.

Honor was delighted to see Lisa up and about and there was a tearful reunion in the kitchen where Lisa apologised to both her and Audrey. But Audrey was still angry with Lisa.

'You shouldn't have locked yourself away like that,' Audrey told her. 'Not when Harrie needed you.'

'I've said I'm sorry,' Lisa said.

'I hope you've told Harrie how sorry you are.'

'Of course I have!'

'She needed you, Lisa, and you shut her out.'

Lisa looked at Audrey, her eyes bright with tears. 'I'm here for her now and, unlike you, she's accepted my apology.'

Mrs Ryder was also not in the mood for forgiving, it seemed.

'Had a little party, did you?' she asked later that day, eyeing up the bottles which had been rounded up from Lisa's bedroom.

'Not exactly,' Harrie said.

'Oh, I see. You told them, didn't you?' Mrs Ryder said.

'I did.'

Mrs Ryder nodded. 'Good girl.'

Harrie found it strange to be called a girl when she was, in fact, a forty-six-year-old woman, but she rather liked it.

'Let me help you with the bottles.'

'There's no need,' Mrs Ryder said. 'I've only to take them to the recycling.'

'But I can help carry them.'

'Suit yourself.'

Harrie and Mrs Ryder took their share of the bottles and left the priory, walking down the drive to where the bins were stored.

'So, what did they say when you told them?' Mrs Ryder asked.

'Audrey cried a lot and Lisa went into meltdown. She shut herself in a room and, well, drank.'

'All this was *one* person?'

'I'm afraid so. You see, her mother died of cancer and I don't think she's ever really got over the loss.'

They'd reached the bins now and carefully placed all of Lisa's empties into it.

'You can see why I've delayed telling them now,' Harrie continued.

'You did the right thing,' Mrs Ryder assured her.

'Yeah?'

'They needed to know and I think you probably needed to get it off your chest.'

Harrie gave a little grin. 'Don't talk to me about getting things off my chest. I've had my fill of that already.'

Mrs Ryder looked quite shocked by Harrie's black humour and had to have a smile nudged out of her.

'They say laughter is the best medicine,' Harrie added, 'but I don't think it's going to cure what I've got.'

Chapter 15

A couple of quiet days went by at the priory. More tears were shed and Harrie received more hugs in those forty-eight hours than she had ever before in the rest of her life. She felt so humble and grateful for her dear friends and for the daughter who was being so strong for her.

Things were still a little tense between Audrey and Lisa, Harrie couldn't help noticing, but she was confident that they'd be back to normal in time. She had been taken aback by Audrey's anger at Lisa. She'd never seen her friend so riled before and, while it was wonderful to be the recipient of Audrey's protectiveness, she couldn't help feeling sorry for Lisa being on the receiving end of so many warning looks.

Another thing she was truly grateful for was the fact that her friends weren't overly mothering her. She would have hated it had they started treating her as an invalid, fussing over her and not letting her get on with things as normal. Okay, they'd insisted on making her endless cups of tea, but they also gave her the space she needed.

And that reminded her. She owed somebody a phone call. Just the night before, she'd received a text from Dr Russell asking her to get in touch. Harrie knew that her call was overdue, but she'd been putting it off – not wanting to break the holiday mood by talking about her health.

Making her way to her room, she closed the door and rang the number. She was put straight through to Dr Russell and immediately felt at ease when she heard her warm voice greeting her.

'Harriet – how are you?'

'I'm good.'

'Yes?'

'Yes!' Harrie replied. 'Truly. I was going to message you so you wouldn't worry. I'm feeling really great. Maybe I'm getting a bit more tired than usual, but then I'm walking more and I'm even swimming every day too.'

'That's fantastic.'

'It is,' Harrie said, and then paused. 'Is that . . . *normal*? I mean, feeling as well as I do at the moment?'

'Like I told you, everybody's different. If you feel well, then *that's* normal. Don't let what you have stop you from doing what you want to do – not if you have plenty of energy.'

'But I sometimes feel like a fraud telling people I've got terminal cancer and then jumping into a swimming pool.'

'I'm sure people don't want to see you sitting around doing nothing with a blanket on your knees.'

Harrie laughed. 'No, I'm not quite ready for that.'

There was a pause and Harrie couldn't help wondering how far along the horizon that awful fate was, just waiting for her. She shivered. Well, it wasn't here today, that was for sure.

They talked for a few minutes about Harrie's medication – the pills she was currently taking and what was available to her when she needed it.

'You can ring me any time,' Dr Russell said. 'Just let me know what your needs are. And Harriet?'

'Yes?'

'Enjoy your summer.'

The two women said their goodbyes.

Harrie sat for a moment on the edge of the bed. The room was warm and sunny and she looked out into the tops of the trees beyond. Talking to Dr Russell always left her feeling anxious. She felt like she was being pulled into a world where she still didn't belong; a world she didn't want to be a part of.

She glanced towards the bottles of pills she'd brought with her on holiday. She'd noticed that Dr Russell had told her what would be available when she needed them. *When*, not *if*. Like she was hurtling head-on into a future she couldn't stop.

Harrie took a deep breath and repeated the little mantra that only just managed to control her emotions when she felt so vulnerable and when she couldn't help dwelling on the dark future that lay ahead. She knew she'd have to face it, but not today.

But not today. But not today.

It was late one evening as the sun was setting over the garden. The women had been sitting by the pool, having enjoyed a cold buffet left by Mrs Ryder.

'I have a plan,' Lisa declared, swatting a moth away from her face in disgust and standing up. 'Go and get changed into something loose-fitting and keep out of the chapel.'

'What are you up to?' Audrey asked.

'You'll see soon enough.'

Fifteen minutes later and Lisa met them in the kitchen, leading the way through the cloister to the chapel.

'We'll have to ignore the scaffolding, I'm afraid,' Lisa told them as she opened the great wooden door into the oldest part of the priory.

Harrie, Honor and Audrey gave a collective gasp.

'Lisa!' Honor cried. 'It's beautiful.'

Harrie looked around in wonder. There were candles everywhere: on the bare stone windowsill, on saucers along the floor and on a little table which Lisa had set up with a jar of fresh flowers from the garden, a little collection of gemstones, some meditation beads, a copy of a book called *The History of Now* and a rather spooky statue of the god Ganesh.

'Nothing should have quite as many limbs as that,' Audrey whispered to Harrie, who let out a giggle. 'Personally, I've never trusted anything with a trunk.'

'Are those arms or legs?' Honor asked. 'I've never really known.'

'I think they're all trunks,' Harrie said.

'Come and sit down,' Lisa interrupted. 'We need to make a start.'

It was then that Harrie noticed the yoga mats set out. There was Lisa's pink one, a green one and two blue ones.

'Where did you get all these mats from?' she asked.

'I usually carry these two around with me,' she said, pointing to the pink and the green, 'but I bought the others online and got next-day delivery after' – she paused – 'after we had our chat.'

Harrie smiled. 'It's a lovely thought.'

'I think it's important to take time out – for everyone – not just Harrie,' Lisa blurted. 'We all need to de-stress, and decompress.'

'I definitely need to decompress after that second helping of chocolate cheesecake,' Honor said.

Harrie and Audrey laughed, but Lisa was in teacher mode by this stage and Harrie could see that she was only just managing to resist clapping her hands for attention.

'Let's sit,' she said, lowering herself beautifully onto her pink yoga mat. 'Find a comfortable position that you can maintain for a few minutes whilst we relax.'

It had been a long time since Harrie had sat on a yoga mat and she took a few moments to find a position that suited her. She definitely couldn't curl her legs inward as Lisa and Honor had done, so she chose a kneeling position which Audrey had adopted too. How stiff she felt.

Stiff and awkward. Even with all the walking she did, she couldn't help feeling that she was still in pretty bad shape even if it wasn't for the cancer. Was that inevitable with the onset of middle age, she wondered? Lisa certainly seemed to be very flexible, but that took work and dedication and, although Harrie admired it and hankered after a portion of it, she really didn't want it enough to put the hours in. Not when she didn't know exactly how many hours she had left. Since her last diagnosis, she'd had to learn how to prioritise things, but there was a wonderful calmness that came from yoga, she knew that, and it would be most welcome in her life now. Perhaps it was something she could ease into over the rest of the summer. After all, that was part of the reason she'd booked the priory – to find ways to relax and simply be.

'Take a deep breath in and sigh it out through the mouth,' Lisa said.

Harrie did as she was told, inhaling the centuries-old atmosphere of the chapel, and wondering if Samson was aware of that glorious smell while he worked. How could he not be? He seemed to her to be very sensitive to his environment, in tune with the stone and his tools.

'Focus only on your breath,' Lisa told them. 'In and out – two more times and then let your breath settle into a natural pattern.'

Harrie did her best to focus on the movements of her body as she breathed. She wondered if Samson had ever done yoga. She couldn't quite imagine it, but the thought amused her. The image of his great bulk sitting cross-legged on a mat made her smile.

'If your mind strays away from your breath, which is only natural, bring it back,' Lisa said, interrupting Harrie's thoughts. 'Acknowledge the thoughts you are having and then let them drift away and come back to your breathing.'

Goodbye, Samson, Harrie said to herself. It was funny that she had been thinking about him but, then again, she was sitting in his workplace. She thought of the chapel as being very much his space. She hadn't seen him since she'd first imparted the news about her cancer to Audrey and Lisa and now she found herself wondering if she should tell him. Did he count as a friend? Would he want to know? Would he feel uncomfortable if she told him something so personal? He might think her strange to be revealing something like that. It might make him uncomfortable, and yet she couldn't help feeling that there was more to him being there than mere coincidence.

'Slowly blink your eyes open and, when you're ready, come onto all fours,' Lisa said. Harrie looked across the space of the cold stone floor between them. Lisa was backlit by candles and her wavy chestnut hair looked so pretty – like a Botticelli angel's.

Your mind's drifting again, Harrie told herself, taking another deep breath to try and regain control. She really was terrible at this yoga business.

Lisa then took them through a series of stretches, all the time reminding them to link everything to their breath, and Harrie lost herself completely in the movements, her arms reaching up towards the fan-vaulted ceiling, her eyes adjusting to the candlelight as the evening darkened beyond the windows and her breath finding a purpose that linked the mind and the body in perfect harmony.

Harrie felt amazingly focused. Since her last diagnosis, she had been looking for ways of escape. Although she had calmly accepted what was happening to her, she still found that she sometimes needed to leave her own mind behind and sink into the world of a beautiful novel or a moving film. She was finding that the yoga practice was having the same effect – that she was able to forget about herself for a while and focus entirely on just being.

But then the practice ended and Lisa encouraged them to lie back on their mats. As soon as Harrie stopped moving, she found that her mind was crowded with thoughts once more.

'Let's return our focus to our breathing again, letting go of our physical practice tonight. Think about how your body is feeling. Perhaps you feel lighter, looser, warmer.'

Harrie was only half listening to Lisa's voice because she had caught sight of something high up on the wall near Samson's scaffolding. She hadn't spotted it before but maybe it was only visible to those on the scaffolding or flat on one's back. She squinted up at it now, but it was hard to see in the semi-darkness. However, she was pretty sure it was some kind of face. A gargoyle, perhaps, although it looked more beautiful than a gargoyle.

'In and out.' Lisa's voice suddenly cut into Harrie's thoughts. She'd drifted again and, like before, her thoughts had turned to Samson, wondering if he was restoring this particular feature, and then she remembered that he had said something about an angel. Was this the angel? She would have to ask him. She was quite determined to make it up the scaffolding and see exactly what he was up to.

'Let your breath come easily. It shouldn't be laboured or forced, but natural. The rhythm of life.'

Focus, Harrie, she told herself, and she managed to for about twenty seconds, but that's when she lost it. She just couldn't help it. Her nose was making a funny sort of whistle and it set her off giggling, which, in turn, set Honor off. They were meant to be lying down with their eyes closed, but they kept peeping at each other and that made things even worse, especially when Audrey's eyes opened too and she joined in with the laughter.

It was unstoppable, infectious laughter and there was nothing that Lisa could do to control it.

'Hey!' she cried. 'What's going on?'

'I'm sorry!' Harrie said, happy tears streaming down her face. 'It's my nose! It's whistling and I can't stop it!'

That set Honor and Audrey off even more.

'Oh, you lot are impossible!' Lisa said, getting up from her mat. 'We're meant to be relaxing.'

'No, no! Don't give up on us!' Harrie said, wiping the tears from her face.

'We're meant to finish in a calm, serene state, not rolling around the floor laughing like hyenas!'

That set everybody off even more and the ancient walls of the chapel seemed to reverberate with the laughter. There was a sound of fluttering wings from high above from some disgruntled roosting pigeons. It was time to go.

'I'm so sorry, Lisa,' Harrie said, moving forward to hug her friend.

'It was a brilliant session,' Audrey said as she stood up.

'Yeah?' Lisa said.

'You're a really good teacher.'

Lisa looked genuinely surprised. 'Thanks!'

'You know what?' Audrey said. 'I really fancy a glass of wine after that.'

Harrie looked at Lisa, wondering if it was a good idea to open a bottle of wine after her recent binge.

'Anyone else?'

'Love one,' Honor said. 'I feel wonderfully mellow and a glass of wine would be perfect.'

Honor helped Lisa to blow out all the candles and then the four of them went into the kitchen, where Audrey opened the fridge.

'You can thank me for having the foresight to chill a few bottles later,' she said.

'Are you allowed to drink?' Harrie asked her.

'Do you mean has Mike told me not to?' Audrey asked. 'He advised against it, which is really silly because wine relaxes you, doesn't it? Isn't that exactly what I need at the moment? What we all need?'

Harrie looked across at Lisa, who was picking at her nails. 'I'll just have one glass,' she said.

With their wine glasses filled, they walked through to the living room and Honor switched on a couple of the great fat lamps. The sound of an owl hooting came from the garden as Harrie drew the curtains against the inky night.

'So, you really enjoyed the yoga?' Lisa asked.

They all spoke over one another, eager to show her that they had.

'Perhaps that young gardener can join us next time,' Audrey teased.

Lisa instantly blushed.

'He's having special private tuition,' Harrie said.

'Not special,' Lisa was quick to point out. 'I'm just helping him out.'

'That's nice,' Honor said.

'Yes, it is.'

Lisa nodded. 'Yoga can help everybody. It really can.'

'Well, it's got rid of some of the cricks in my neck,' Audrey admitted. 'Or maybe that's the wine beginning to work.'

They talked some more, their conversations rambling from subject to subject as more wine was poured and enjoyed. Finally, Audrey yawned and got up from her place on the sofa.

'I am completely done in,' Audrey said.

'Me too,' Honor agreed, and the two of them said their goodnights and left the room.

It was only then that Harrie realised she was alone. At some point, Lisa had got up to go to the kitchen. She was meant to be bringing nibbles back but, so far, they weren't forthcoming.

Putting her wine glass down, Harrie went in search of her friend, finding her with her head in the fridge.

'There you are! Where did you get to?' she asked.

Lisa visibly jumped and span around and Harrie could tell immediately from the pink of her cheeks that it hadn't been nibbles Lisa was after from the kitchen.

'Have you been drinking again, Lisa?'

'Just a *little* bit!'

'Oh, no!'

'Oh, *yes!*'

'I thought you were hunting for peanuts or something.'

'Listen – come here,' Lisa said, hiccupping dramatically.

'How much have you had?'

'I – erm – I'm not sure. Not enough probably.' She swayed a bit and put an arm around Harrie's shoulder. 'I've got a brilliant idea. It's *so* good, you're not going to believe it.'

'Really?'

'Yes, really.'

'And are you going to tell me this idea?'

Lisa frowned. 'What idea?'

'The idea you just said you'd had.'

'Oh, the *idea*! Yes, yes!'

'Well?'

'I'm going to shout at it.'

'What?'

'*It* – the cancer. I'm going to *shout* at it!'

Harrie laughed. 'What are you talking about?'

'I'm pretty bossy, you know. Pupils tell me I'm scary when I want to be. So I'm going to shout at this cancer. Scare it away,' she said, jabbing a finger into Harrie's shoulder. 'Sorry.'

'It's all right.'

There was a pause and Harrie was quite convinced Lisa was about to swoon onto the kitchen floor, but she seemed to right herself.

'Come on!'

'Where are we going?' Harrie asked.

'To the chapel to shout.'

'The chapel's too echoey. We'll wake the whole of Somerset if you start shouting in there.'

'Where shall we go then?'

'I don't think we should go anywhere other than up to bed. I really think you need to lie down.'

'Nonsense! We're going to shout at this thing, okay?'

Harrie took a deep breath. There was no arguing with Lisa when she was like this. 'Okay,' she said, thinking it best to get it over and done with.

'Let's go outside, come on!'

Harrie couldn't help smiling at her friend's determination as they headed out into the darkness. The lights from the priory lit their way as they crossed the garden and then an obliging moon allowed them to make a silvery progress into the orchard.

'How about here?' Lisa asked.

'Aren't we still too close? I don't want to wake Audrey or Honor up.'

'It'll be fine. They'll be sound asleep by now after all that wine.'

'And so should you be,' Harrie said.

'I'm not ready for bed. I've got work to do,' Lisa declared.

'Well, hurry and get on with it. I'm getting cold.'

Lisa stretched her arms towards Harrie, resting her hands heavily on her shoulders as if to steady herself.

'Are you ready?' she asked.

'I'm bracing myself,' Harrie said, trying not to laugh.

Lisa took a deep breath, still holding onto Harrie's shoulders.

There then followed a torrent of abuse the like of which Harrie had never heard before. She wasn't aware Lisa knew half of those words, but perhaps her experience of teaching in inner-city Leeds had taught her a few of them.

When she finally stopped, the night air seemed to vibrate with the echo of her words.

Lisa stepped back a little. 'Do you think it's done anything?'

'Well, I think I might have lost part of my hearing.' Harrie laughed and then Lisa laughed too. 'Lisa – your language!'

'What about it?'

'I've never heard you swear like that before.'

'When needs must.'

Harrie linked her arm around Lisa and the two of them walked slowly through the orchard, back towards the garden. The light from the moon had silvered the gnarled trunks of the apple trees and their shadows made the most enchanting of patterns on the grass, like bewitched lacework.

As they walked on, Harrie felt Lisa swaying again.

'I think you should probably have something to eat. Do we have some biscuits or cake or something?'

Suddenly, tears were pouring down Lisa's face. 'I ate your last piece of cake!'

'What?'

'Your birthday cake! I pigged the last slice in the middle of the night!'

'Hey, it's okay!'

'No, it's not! Oh, god! I'm such a bad friend!'

'You're not a bad friend. You're an extremely good one,' Harrie told her.

'I just took it! But I'll buy you another one. A whole cake. A *massive* cake! None of us will go near it. It'll just be for you!'

Harrie laughed. 'You don't need to buy me a cake.'

'I'm so sorry! I'm so sorry!'

'It's okay. Now, let's get back indoors. There are moths about.'

'What?' Lisa started swatting the air with her hands. 'Get me inside!'

They rushed across the lawn, stumbling in the half-light towards the great front door, which Harrie was relieved to close behind them. Lisa looked exhausted and Harrie pushed the tendrils of hair away. They'd been sticking to her friend's cheeks, wet with tears.

'Let's get you to bed, shall we?'

Lisa nodded and stumbled as she made her way towards the spiral staircase. Harrie placed a hand in the small of Lisa's back as she swayed on reaching the landing.

Once in Lisa's bedroom, she pulled down the duvet and plumped the pillow and Lisa got in without protesting, snuggling down under the bedclothes.

'I haven't done my bedtime meditation,' she said, suddenly sitting bolt upright.

'I think you'll be okay without it tonight.'

'Will you stay with me until I fall asleep?'

'Of course I will.'

'You're my best friend, Harrie. You've always been my best friend.'

Harrie leaned forward and kissed Lisa's warm forehead, and then sat with her until she was quietly snoring before tiptoeing out of the room. She wondered how much of the night Lisa would remember in the morning. Probably not a lot, but Harrie would certainly never forget it.

Chapter 16

Audrey met Lisa out on the landing the next morning. She'd already had her breakfast, taken a walk and read two chapters of her Susan Hill novel. Lisa, it seemed, wasn't having such a productive morning.

'God, you look dreadful!' Audrey told her.

'Gee, thanks!'

'I'm guessing you stayed up and had more wine?'

'Very likely.'

'You don't remember?'

'I have a vague recollection of shouting at Harrie.'

'What?' Audrey was appalled. 'Why?'

'I think I was trying to scare the cancer away.'

Audrey stared at her friend. 'Seriously?'

'I thought it was the right thing to do at the time.'

'You thought shouting at Harrie was a good idea?'

'Not Harrie – the *cancer*.'

'You've got to stop drinking, Lisa,' Audrey said, the warning tone back in her voice. 'It's not good for you and it's certainly not good for Harrie.'

Lisa nodded and then clutched her head as if regretting the movement. 'I don't feel so good.'

'You should go back to bed.'

'I think I feel worse lying down.'

'Hey, I saw your young gardener friend. He was asking how you were. I think he's waiting for his yoga lesson.'

'Oh, no!' Lisa groaned. 'I completely forgot about that!' Her hands flew up to her hair. 'Can I use your shower? Please!'

'Go on – it's all yours.'

'Thanks!'

Audrey watched as Lisa returned to her room and came out a second later with a towel and some bottles.

'Tell him I won't be long,' Lisa said.

'Lisa?'

'Yes?'

'Are you okay now? I mean, about Harrie?'

Lisa's eyes widened and Audrey could see them sparkling with tears. 'I'm never going to be okay with this.'

Audrey nodded. 'I know. Me neither. But we've got to do our best to be strong for her this summer.'

'I know,' Lisa said in a very small voice. 'But I just can't think about anything else except the cancer now. It's just sitting there between us and I can't even look at her sometimes, let alone speak without fearing I'm going to break down any minute.'

'That's probably why she didn't want to tell us – because it changes everything, doesn't it? I've been thinking about this and I truly believe that she doesn't want to see our miserable faces. She was trying to save us from the pain of telling us for as long as possible, wasn't she?'

'I don't know how she did that,' Lisa said. 'I would've rung you both at the first sign of trouble.'

'Me too,' Audrey said, 'but this is our Harrie. She's always been the strong one, but she needs us now and we've got to be there for her, okay?'

Lisa nodded. 'I know.'

'No more wine, Lisa, I mean it. And no more shutting yourself away. I know this is hard. It's probably one of the hardest things we'll ever have to get through, but we've got to make this the most wonderful summer ever. If you keep away from the wine and I keep away from laptops and spreadsheets, I think we can really be there for Harrie when she needs us most, just as she's always been there for us in the past.'

Lisa closed the space between them and hugged her. Audrey got a faceful of Lisa's bath towel, but she didn't care. All the anger she'd felt about Lisa's response to Harrie's cancer ebbed away from her in that moment and compassion flooded her heart.

'I'm going to be there for her,' Lisa told her. 'I promise. And for Honor and for you.'

Audrey did her best to blink her tears away. 'I know you will.'

Harrie was sitting in the garden with one of her green smoothies. Honor was having a swim, Audrey was reading in a deck chair in the shade and Lisa had finally surfaced and was doing something yogic with the gardener. Audrey kept peering over her sunglasses at her and, because Harrie was wearing sunglasses herself, she probably didn't think she'd noticed, but she had. It was sweet that her friend was concerned about her, but she couldn't help feeling awkward at being stared at like that – as if she might die on the spot at any moment.

When she'd first announced her diagnosis to her friends and colleagues at home, there'd been a strange sort of stampede. Suddenly, everyone had wanted a piece of her. It was part of the reason she was hiding away at the priory. As soon as she'd told people she was ill, they'd flocked to her, which was nice, of course, but they hadn't wanted to spend quality time with her when she was fit and well so it seemed odd that they wanted to see her now. Was that how lottery winners felt, she wondered? A little bit of money suddenly turned you into a human magnet. The same thing seemed to happen with a death sentence. You suddenly became everybody's favourite person.

Harrie was not the sort of person to want a fuss. She'd never felt comfortable being the centre of attention. Her own wedding had been a massive embarrassment to her, with cameras poking in her face and relatives everywhere. The only time she felt at ease being looked at was in the classroom and that was because she became somebody else then. Teaching was a kind of performance. But being so closely monitored by people because she was sick was nothing short of unnerving.

She tried to ignore Audrey, hoping her friend would go back to her book and let her get on with her aimless daydreaming. More and more, she found she just wanted a place to sit and dream, to watch the clouds chasing themselves across the sky, to listen to the wren, the robin, the blackbird, and the cawing of the jackdaws, the cooing of the pigeons. She wanted to watch the wind playing in the trees. Simple, everyday things that she might once have missed because there was never enough time to just be still and observe them. It astonished her how much pleasure you could get from such things. Why didn't more people know about it? Why was everyone always rushing? Harrie smiled to herself; her illness was turning her into a philosopher, although she wasn't enjoying how tired she was feeling lately.

She closed her eyes against the sun and against Audrey, revelling in the warmth and the soothing call of a nearby dove from its home at the top of the tower. It was then that she remembered the face in the chapel.

'You okay, Mum?' Honor asked from the pool as Harrie got up from her chair.

'I'm fine.'

'Where are you going?' Audrey asked.

'Just to see Samson.'

She made her way quickly into the priory, where she had a drink of water in the kitchen before going through the cloister and into the chapel. Her sun-warmed limbs cooled down now that she was inside the ancient building.

As usual, he was hidden from view when she first approached.

'Hello?' she called up. 'Anybody there?'

A sandy head popped over the scaffolding and he nodded an acknowledgement.

'Can I come up?'

Samson didn't answer, but Harrie soon heard the heavy tread of his boots as he descended, coming to earth with a light jump a moment later.

'Is that a no?' she asked him.

'Have you a head for heights?'

'I think so.'

'It's very delicate up there – delicate and dangerous.'

'Okay. I promise not to touch or trip over anything.'

Samson gave her a look as if he didn't know if she was joking or not.

'I'll beg if I have to,' she said. 'Come on! I've been bribing you with tea for weeks now.'

He scratched the back of his neck and looked distinctly ill at ease. 'Follow me,' he said at last, and Harrie only just managed to stop herself from punching the air in glee.

She'd never climbed through scaffolding before and, although she wished she wasn't wearing a sarong, she was glad that she at least was wearing trainers instead of flip-flops. Even though she'd told him she was good with heights, she still did her best not to look down.

'I see what you mean about having a head for heights!' she joked now. Samson turned around and glared at her.

'You're not going to pass out on me, are you?'

'No!' Harrie cried, but she clenched hold of the sides of the ladder all the more as she continued to ascend, her hesitant steps following Samson's sure ones.

'So this is your office,' she said once they'd both made it to the safety of the top.

'I guess it is,' he said.

Harrie looked around, trying to take it all in at once, from the pale golden stone in front of her to the incredible view of the fan-vaulted ceiling. She saw his tools laid out, his denim jacket folded neatly and his lunch box and flask. Everything he needed.

'I just love this stone,' she said, her hand instinctively reaching out to touch it and then pausing just short of contact. 'May I?'

Samson gave a single nod. 'Yellow Triassic limestone,' he said.

'Is it?'

'It's the period before the more famous Jurassic. Over two hundred and fifty million years ago.'

'How amazing.' Harrie looked at the stone with a new appreciation, and then she saw it – the face. It wasn't any ordinary face and it certainly wasn't a gargoyle.

'It's an angel,' she said, her fingers inching to touch it. 'Can I?'

Samson nodded. 'She's survived all that time. I think she can survive a quick poke.'

Harrie laughed. 'I wasn't going to *poke* her!' Her fingers gently caressed the stone, appreciating the lines carved so many centuries ago. 'I saw her from below. Well, I noticed a vague face, but I couldn't make out what it was. But she's lovely! I had no idea you were hiding something so precious up here. You should have told me about her even if you didn't want to show me.'

'I wasn't hiding her from you,' he said, sounding surprised that she should think that.

'I know,' she told him with a smile. 'It's just that you don't think to – well – share things, do you?'

'What do you mean?' he asked, narrowing his bright eyes a little.

'I mean, you're pretty self-contained, aren't you?'

'I don't understand.'

'You do your job. You put your head down. You don't get involved with people, do you?'

'There isn't usually anyone to get involved with.'

Harrie mused on this. 'I suppose not, but I'd like to get involved.' She looked at the angel again and then something occurred to her. 'I mean, to get involved with what you're doing. I didn't mean to get involved with you or anything like . . .' She paused, seeing colour creep into his cheeks. She was embarrassing this poor man.

He cleared his throat. 'I'm glad you're interested.'

'Really?'

He nodded and she thought she saw the tiniest of smiles tickling the corner of his mouth.

'One of the reasons I booked this place was because I'm fascinated by the past. I'm always nosying around old churches. It drives my daughter mad. We can be driving back from somewhere and I'll see an old church and just have to pop inside and see what's there because you never know what you're going to find, do you?'

Samson seemed to be taking all this in. 'You like misericords?' he asked.

'Pardon?'

'Misericords – they're the carvings on the underside of a folding seat. You find them in churches and monastic buildings.'

'*Misericords*,' Harrie repeated slowly. 'What a *gorgeous* word! I've never actually seen one. At least I don't think I have.'

He looked surprised by this admission. 'There are some in St Michael's just down the road from here.'

'Really?'

'I can show you if you like. I think they're some of the best in the country.'

'I'd *love* to see them.' She grinned. 'Is this you proving to me that you *can* get involved with people?'

'I thought you said you didn't want to get involved with me?' His eyes sparkled as he spoke.

'Well, I didn't mean *that* exactly,' she said, struggling to work out what she did actually mean. 'I meant – well – never mind. I'd love to see these misericords.'

'Okay.'

She smiled and he gave a half-smile in return. Or maybe it was a muscle twitching.

'So, when would you like to show me these misericords?'

'After I finish here for the day?' He looked at his watch. 'A couple of hours? Meet me by my van.'

Harrie nodded. 'Right.'

They looked at each other and Harrie wondered if he was going to say anything else. No, of course he wasn't.

'Well, I'd better leave you to it,' she said.

Samson gave her a little nod then turned his back to begin his work again and Harrie couldn't help smiling because she felt she was finally chipping away at the surface of Samson Haverstock.

Lisa took one final breath and slowly opened her eyes. Alfie was sitting in front of her, his eyes still closed, his legs crossed and his palms facing upwards on his knees. She watched him for a moment, the afternoon sun the colour of golden syrup on his face.

'When you're ready, open your eyes,' she said softly.

Alfie did as he was told, his blue eyes focusing on her.

'Wow! I've never felt so calm,' he said.

'Meditation is a powerful thing.'

'I'm not used to looking inside, you know?'

Lisa nodded, remembering the miraculous journey she had taken when she'd first started to meditate.

'It's like floating away,' he added. 'I thought I might actually be floating at one stage and that this yoga mat had turned into a flying carpet.'

Lisa smiled at the notion and, for some reason, she began to cry.

'Hey!' Alfie leaned towards her and wiped the tears from her face with his fingers. 'What's the matter? Is it something I said? Something I did?'

'No!' Lisa shook her head. 'I didn't mean to cry. It's just that sometimes meditation can bring the emotions up to the surface, you know?'

'I'm beginning to.'

She dared to look at him, wiping the tears from her eyes with a tissue from her pocket.

'I'm trying to be happy,' she whispered. 'I'm trying to be brave for her, but I'm not doing a very good job.'

'Who are you trying to be brave for?'

She sniffed. 'Harrie. She's ill. Really ill.' The tears began to rise again.

'Oh, god!'

'And I'm so scared. I don't want to lose her, Alfie!'

'Hey!' he said, moving closer and wrapping his arms around her. Alfie rubbed a hand up and down Lisa's back in a soothing motion.

'You know what she once did for me?' she said. 'We'd gone to London to stay with my uncle. He had this really cool flat with a spare room and we went to see a play in the West End. Well, after the show, I wanted to hang around the stage door to see if we could meet the cast. The guy playing the lead was from a big US TV show I was crazy about at the time. Anyway, it was absolutely freezing and I was shivering so Harrie ran off somewhere and got me a cup of coffee. I still remember how blissful that moment was when I clasped it in my cold hands.'

'And did you get to meet your star?'

'Kind of. There was a pretty big group of us waiting by the time he came out and he signed a few autographs. He was a bit grumpy actually. I went right off him after that, but it was still a buzz to see him. Anyway, that meant we were late and we missed the last bus that would have taken us to my uncle's place and we had to walk. I can't remember how far it was, but it felt like miles in the dark and it was so cold. We held onto each other because the pavements were so slippery. Harrie slipped over once and I did twice. Anyone seeing us must have thought we were drunk.' Lisa giggled at the memory.

'When we finally made it back, my uncle was furious. He'd been waiting up and was about to call the police. He was really scary when he was mad. He wouldn't calm down, but then Harrie put a hand out and touched his shoulder. I remember the look of complete serenity on her face as she apologised to him. She told him that it was *her* fault we were late back. She said *she'd* wanted to wait by the stage door and how I'd kept telling her that we'd be late. Then she went on and on about the star of the show, who she really wasn't that mad about – it had been me persuading her to see him in the play. And what could my uncle do? Harrie knew that he'd lay into me far worse than he would her, and so she made sure that she put herself in the line of fire.'

'Wow!' Alfie said.

'I've never told anyone that before – not even Audrey. But that's the sort of person Harrie is!'

'She sounds like a good friend.'

Lisa's tears really began then and Alfie continued to hold her until she calmed down a little.

'I hate this,' she said. 'I hate feeling so helpless. It was the same when my mum got cancer. I didn't know what to do and Audrey keeps telling me that I've got to be strong for Harrie and that she doesn't want to see my tears. But I'm *not* strong and I don't know if I can cope with this!'

Alfie kissed her forehead. 'You know what?' he said gently. 'You're stronger than you think.'

'I'm not.'

'Yes, you are! Anyone with the capacity to sit so calmly and to help somebody else learn to meditate – I'd say that's a kind of strength. You're succeeding where dozens of others have failed before. I've been crippled with pain for years now, but you've really helped me work through that.'

'I have?'

'You really have.'

'But that doesn't make me strong.'

'It does as far as I'm concerned,' he told her. 'You have a strength of personality. You don't give up. Like waiting outside that theatre in the freezing cold. Even though that star was an idiot, you had the tenacity to wait and find that out for yourself.'

Lisa gave a tiny smile.

'And from what I've seen of Harrie, and from what you've told me about her, she seems like a really nice and decent person.'

'She's the best there is.'

'Then I'm sure she won't want you hiding your feelings from her. Bottling up all these emotions isn't good for you. If I was her, I'd want to know *exactly* how my friends were feeling. I'd want the truth – not some facade.'

'You would?'

'Definitely.'

'But Audrey said—'

'But you're not Audrey. You're Lisa,' he said, as if that needed explaining to her. 'Let Audrey get on with things her way and you do your things your own way.'

Lisa finally nodded and then stood up from the yoga mat. 'You won't tell Audrey about this, though, will you? I mean about me crying? She'll just get annoyed with me all over again.'

'Hey – what happens on the mat stays on the mat!' Alfie told her.

Lisa laughed. 'Why are you so sweet?'

He smiled and gave a shrug. 'You just bring it out in me,' he told her.

Chapter 17

Harrie had changed into a long-sleeved cardigan and a pair of light trousers for her trip to the church with Samson. She was surprisingly nervous, which was ridiculous really because it was just a little trip out together; it wasn't anything to get worked up about and yet she couldn't help it because she really couldn't remember the last time she'd gone out with a man. Not that this was a date or anything. It was nothing more than an outing to see something they both appreciated. After all, nothing could be more innocent than visiting a church, could it? So, there was nothing to get anxious about, she told herself.

He was waiting for her by his van, just closing his doors. The sun was still warm, bathing the priory in a wonderful honey-coloured light, and it seemed a shame to leave the beauty of the garden behind, but Harrie was very much looking forward to her adventure with Samson. Typically, Audrey, Lisa and Honor had been hanging around the kitchen as she'd made her way to the front door.

'I'm just off out,' Harrie had said.

'Want some company?' Audrey had asked.

'Actually, I'm going somewhere with Samson.'

'Oh, really?' Audrey had said with a knowing smile.

'If you must know, he's going to show me some misericords.'

Lisa had frowned. 'Is that a euphemism?'

Harrie had laughed. 'I'll see you later!'

Now, sitting next to Samson in the van, she wondered what her daughter and friends had made of her sudden departure. Well, Lisa had struck up a friendship with the gardener, hadn't she? Why shouldn't she make a friend of her own? She didn't have time to make many new friends, did she?

With that thought in her mind, she turned to look at Samson. Could she really call him a friend? Maybe it was a bit early for that, but she liked the strange, half-silent sort of companionship she had with him and the interests they shared.

They drove away from the priory in silence until he turned onto a road for a mile or so and then took a smaller lane pitted with potholes. It was a sunken lane with high banks either side and grass growing in the middle of it. She wasn't surprised when they saw a horse and rider ahead of them. Luckily, a bridleway opened to the left and the rider turned off, so Samson was able to continue at a pace slightly faster than a rising trot.

He pulled over a moment later by a low wall and Harrie saw the church for the first time. It was a surprisingly large building for the middle of nowhere, but Harrie had learned that villages often moved away from their churches over time. This one was certainly not within easy walking distance of its local community anymore and that was a shame because it was rather lovely with its grey-gold stone and its comically squat tower. It was modest and not as eye-catching as many of the churches Harrie had visited over the years, but she knew that a plain facade might well hide an exciting interior.

They got out of the van and walked through the small churchyard towards the porch and Samson opened the door, stopping to touch the stone arch around it.

'What's that?' Harrie asked, peering closer at the mark on the stone. 'Is it a stonemason's mark?'

'No, it's graffiti.'

Harrie tutted. 'Disgraceful!'

'No, no. It's very old. People used to carve into the stone in places like porches and around pillars. Not much is really known about it, but some marks were believed to ward off evil and others were just records of events or barters between neighbours. Always worth looking out for.'

'I've never noticed them before,' Harrie said, her fingers tracing the circular shape which Samson's fingers had touched just a moment before.

He moved into the church and Harrie followed, closing the heavy door behind her, and they were instantly enveloped in silence and the comforting, slightly musty smell which churches have.

He led the way up the aisle to the choir stalls, passing the medieval font and the fine old pews. Harrie was close behind him, eager to see what he had to show her.

'Well, here they are,' he said, gesturing with a hand.

At first, Harrie couldn't work out why Samson had especially wanted her to see them. He'd talked about carvings, hadn't he? But Harrie couldn't quite see what all the fuss was about. She could see that the seats were lovely, the curving wood gloriously shiny in the sun which entered the church through one of the plain glass windows, but she wouldn't have called them extraordinary.

He seemed to sense her disappointment and gestured for her to come closer. He then lifted one of the dark oak seats and there it was – hiding underneath a little ledge was a magnificent carving. Harrie gasped. She'd never seen anything like it. It was a bird sitting on a nest full of young.

'A pelican,' Samson explained.

'Yes! Feeding her babies,' Harrie said. 'It's charming.'

'She's actually feeding them with her own blood.'

'What?'

'It's a popular religious image called *a pelican in her piety* depicting the mother wounding her chest to feed her offspring.'

Harrie looked again. 'I think I've gone off it now. Are there any more?'

'Why not find out?'

Harrie smiled and moved forward, her hands clenching the seat next to the one Samson had lifted.

'Oh, it's heavy!' The old oak squeaked as she revealed a cross on a shield and two leonine-like heads. 'Fabulous!'

She was excited now, going from seat to seat, lifting each of them up in turn to see what treasures were to be discovered. There were beautiful leaves, strange faces with elongated tongues and odd creatures playing musical instruments.

'What on earth is this one?' Harrie asked, turning her head upside down as if it might help her work it out.

'Ah, yes,' Samson said. 'I looked that one up. It's a wolf carrying a priest. His gown has slipped down around his head, see?'

'How bizarre! I wonder what it means.'

'Probably just a piece of medieval nonsense,' Samson said.

'Oh, I don't know – I'd like to think it means something.'

The seats of the other benches each revealed something quirkily different.

'See how the wood is so much more polished on this one?' Samson nodded to a face which looked like some kind of Green Man.

'It is wonderfully tactile,' she said, reaching out to touch it herself.

'Centuries of fingers have touched it.'

'Yes.' She felt a sudden lump in her throat. It was little things like this that sometimes caught Harrie unawares. There was so much beauty in the world – so many things to see and touch. She couldn't bear that she wouldn't be a part of that anymore. That one day, very soon, all her senses would be shut down and she wouldn't be able to just wander around at leisure, discovering treasures such as misericords.

'They're lovely,' she said, trying to regain her composure. 'Thank you for showing me them.'

'You're welcome.'

'I'll need to revisit all the churches near me now and see if I've missed any.'

'They're rather special, aren't they?'

'How old are they?' Harrie asked.

'Fifteenth century with a few later repairs like some of the hinges and a bit of the wood here and there.'

'And there's nobody here to appreciate them,' Harrie observed. 'There should be queues around the block to see these.'

Samson smiled at that. 'You know, the choir could perch on the upright ledges when they were standing. Apparently, they were designed to crash down heavily and make a horrendous noise if the person perching on them dared to fall asleep.'

'Is that true?' Harrie laughed.

'Who knows?' Samson said with a shrug.

'I'm so glad I've seen them. Thank you.'

'I'm glad you like them,' he said. 'Perhaps I could show you some other churches before you leave Somerset.'

Harrie smiled, thrilled at this new development in their friendship. 'I'd love that.'

They spent a little longer looking around the church, admiring the faded carved figures around the font and commiserating at the loss of the beautiful brass inlay on a tomb.

'These places are so wonderful,' Harrie said. 'I wish they were better protected.'

'So many are locking their doors now.'

'Yes, I've often had to ring for a key to be let in to some of the more rural ones.' She fished in her handbag for her purse and found a few coins to pop into the collection box fixed into the wall by the door. 'Thank you for bringing me here.'

They left the church and returned to the van. The air was fresher now and there was a strange quality to the light. The summer day had been replaced by something slightly more menacing.

'There's going to be a storm tonight,' Samson announced.

'Really?'

'Wind's picked up.'

Harrie looked at a row of wind-tossed trees on the other side of the road. The sky in the direction of the priory was noticeably darker.

'Make sure you've got some candles lit. The priory's susceptible to power cuts.'

'Thanks for the warning,' Harrie said as they headed back down the bumpy country lane.

On arriving at the priory, Samson pulled up and switched off the engine. The sweet song of a robin filled the van and, for a moment, neither of them spoke. Harrie weighed the silence. She'd known so many silences like that in recent months when she'd been in the company of friends and had deliberated whether to tell them or not.

'Samson,' she said at last, feeling that the moment was right, 'there's something I think you should know.'

He didn't say anything and, for a brief moment, Harrie wondered if she should continue because she knew that, once her secret was out, she couldn't take it back. But she felt like she wasn't being honest with him and, for some reason she couldn't explain, she really wanted to be honest with this man.

'I have cancer.'

The words hung heavily between them and he didn't speak at first but simply stared at her.

'Do you want to talk about it?' he asked.

'No, not really.' She laughed at her own bluntness. 'I want to talk about misericords and limestone and angels.'

His face looked solemn and she instantly regretted telling him.

'Just forget it,' she said.

'Forget that you just told me you had cancer? How am I supposed to do that?'

'I don't know – just pretend that this conversation is a figment of your imagination.'

'Harrie – I can't do that.'

She gasped. It was the first time she'd heard him say her name.

'I shouldn't have said anything. I don't know why I did.'

'Do you need me to do anything?'

'No,' she said quickly. 'I don't need anything from you. I don't want anything from you. I just . . .' She paused. 'I just wanted to be honest.'

'I don't know what to say.'

'You don't need to say anything.' Harrie sighed. Why had she told him? Honestly, she did nothing but make this man feel uncomfortable. 'It's just been hanging between us. I've felt awkward not telling you the truth, I suppose. And I thought it might explain some of the slightly odd behaviour around here lately. You know – women bursting into tears and the like.'

'Okay.' He nodded.

The silence had returned.

'I'm sorry,' Harrie said, 'I feel like I've spoilt our day now.'

Samson frowned. 'It's nice that you want to be honest with me.'

'Yeah?'

He nodded. 'I appreciate that.'

Harrie twisted her fingers in her lap, knowing that she hadn't told him everything. 'There's more.' She took a deep breath. 'It's terminal. This time. It's happened before and I made a good recovery, but this time . . .'

He reached across the car and picked up her hand in his and it took all Harrie's strength not to break down in front of him. Instead, they sat in silence for a little while longer, her hand warm and cosy in his as the first drops of rain pattered onto the windscreen.

Samson was right about the storm. The first roll of thunder came a little after nine o'clock and, by half past, the lights were out.

'Oh, great!' Audrey said, quickly switching on her phone's flashlight so she could see what she was doing. 'I was hoping to finish this novel tonight.'

'Well, you still could,' Harrie said. 'You could read by candlelight.'

'That might have sounded romantic twenty years ago, but I'm not sure my eyes would cope with it now.'

'We should get Lisa's candles from the chapel,' Honor said.

'Good idea.' Audrey got up from the sofa.

'Are you kidding?' Lisa cried. 'I'm not going there in the dark.'

'I'll go,' Harrie said. 'It'll be an adventure.'

'I'll go with you, Mum.' Honor retrieved her phone from her pocket and turned the light on.

'Me too.' Audrey held up her phone, which was giving off just enough light to see by. 'I'm armed and unafraid.'

'You can't all leave me in here in the dark!' Lisa said.

'Come with us, then, silly,' Honor said.

'But I really don't want to go in there at night.'

'Afraid of ghosts?' Audrey asked.

'No – bats and moths.'

'Better stay here then,' Harrie said. 'You can have my phone. We won't be long.'

'Wait until I've switched it on!' Lisa cried in panic.

They waited.

'Okay?' Harrie asked once she saw Lisa's face by the cold light from the phone.

'I suppose,' Lisa said sulkily. 'Hurry back!'

Harrie, Audrey and Honor left the cosy cocoon of the living room and made their way towards the chapel. It was slow progress because they were ever mindful of the numerous little steps around the priory, but they finally made it to the great wooden door. Honor opened it and the large, cool space greeted them, swallowing up the light from their phones.

'I think I've changed my mind,' Audrey said.

'Oh, silly!' Harrie said, playfully slapping her. 'Get in there.'

They crossed the space to where their yoga session with Lisa had taken place and started gathering up the candles, placing them in the basket Harrie had collected on their way through the kitchen.

'What was that?' Audrey asked a moment later.

'Probably a bat,' Harrie said.

'I thought you were making it up about bats in here,' Audrey said.

'Well, it was either that or a very large moth.'

'Good job Lisa stayed where she was,' Honor said.

'Let's get out of here,' Harrie said, and they walked cautiously out of the chapel.

Lisa was mightily relieved to see them and the four of them got to work lighting the candles and placing them around the kitchen and living room.

'How long do you think the power will be out for?' Honor asked.

'I don't mind now that we've got light,' Lisa said.

'Candles and cocoa – that's a pretty good combo,' Audrey said. 'Let me go and get us some.'

Soon, the four women were curled up on the two great sofas, mugs of cocoa warming their hands. There was something deeply comforting about candlelight, Harrie thought. Perhaps it was that ancient connection to one's ancestors who only ever knew candlelight. Whatever it was, she was grateful to the storm for giving her this golden moment with her daughter and friends.

'I had a power cut in my flat last month,' Lisa suddenly announced. 'Just long enough to defrost my freezer and cause chaos, but not long enough to stop the band in the flat above from plugging in their instruments and keeping me awake half the night.'

'Poor Lisa – you really should think about moving,' Harrie told her.

'Oh, I think about it all the time. Thinking is free after all.'

'Remember that power cut at uni?' Audrey said with a giggle. 'You were seeing that guy from the maths department. What was his name?'

'Anton,' Lisa said, and groaned at the memory. 'He was explaining algebra or something equally dull and I thought he might stop once the lights went out, but on he went, writing out this boring equation by torchlight. Honestly, I began to doubt my abilities as a young woman that night.'

'English and maths should never mingle,' Harrie said.

'*Mum!*'

'Unless it is to make a perfect daughter,' Harrie quickly added.

'It seems like such a long time ago, doesn't it?' Audrey said.

'University?' Lisa said. 'Yes, thank goodness. I wouldn't want to go back to it all.'

'Really? Why not?' Harrie asked.

'I just remember being so full of insecurity back then.'

'And you aren't now?' Audrey said with a cheeky grin.

'Well, I am,' Lisa agreed, 'but it's a different kind of insecurity and it's one that comes with a pay packet at least.'

'Would you want to go back, Harrie?' Audrey asked.

'No, I wouldn't,' she said honestly.

'Really?'

'I've never wanted to go back. Even now – you know – with what lies ahead.'

Everybody was silent for a moment as if absorbing this information.

'And I don't mean to get maudlin or anything,' Harrie continued. 'I've just never seen the point in going back. I mean, if you could. It's the same with regrets. I think it's sad that people have them because everything we experience, everything we feel, makes us who we are and that's a truly unique person. I wouldn't want to be any different than I am. Sure, I could probably use little bit more money and might have enjoyed a bit more time off work, but I really don't think I can complain.' She smiled, but she saw that both Audrey and Lisa were staring at her with tears in their eyes. 'Don't you dare cry!' she warned them. 'I wasn't turning this into a discussion about me.'

Lisa sniffed loudly and grabbed a tissue from somewhere up her sleeve.

'You're amazing, Harrie,' Audrey said.

'No, I'm not. I just know how to be grateful. I have cultivated an attitude of gratitude!'

Honor tutted. 'Oh, Mum – that sounds so corny!'

'There's nothing corny about it. Everyone knows that they should count their blessings yet how many people actually do?'

'What do you mean?' Lisa asked.

'I mean, how many people sit down and examine the things they're grateful for?' Harrie asked, and was greeted by silence. 'Okay, we'll do it now. It's really best to write a list, but that's not going to be very practical in a power cut, so we'll just go around the room and see what we're grateful for today, okay?'

'She's slipped into teaching mode,' Honor said.

'I'll start,' Harrie said, laughing at her daughter's summation, but not letting it put her off. 'One of the things I'm grateful for today is seeing misericords for the first time with Samson.' She paused. 'Honor? Come on – you've done this with me before.'

'All right. Let me think.' Honor paused. 'Okay – I'm grateful for swimming in the pool and gazing up into the sky to see a pair of white doves flying overhead. Lisa?'

'What?'

'Your turn.'

'Oh, I'm not ready. I'm still thinking this whole thing through.'

'It doesn't have to be anything earth-shattering like winning the lottery or seeing your favourite movie star in the local post office,' Harrie told her. 'It can be really simple things like making a nice meal for lunch or watching the butterflies in the lavender.'

'Okay, then,' Lisa said. 'I'm grateful for my session of yoga this morning with Alfie.'

'Oh, yes?' Audrey said and, even though the light was soft, Harrie could see she'd raised a suggestive eyebrow.

'We made very good progress,' Lisa added.

Audrey grinned.

'Your turn, Aud,' Harrie said.

Audrey tossed her head back and looked up at the shadowy space above them. 'I'm grateful for being here with you all.'

'Oh, that's a cop-out!' Lisa said. 'We're *all* grateful for that!'

'Can you be more specific?' Harrie asked her, taking a sip of her cocoa.

Audrey pursed her lips. 'I read a very good chapter of my book just before the lights went out.'

Harrie laughed as a flash of lightning lit up the room and thunder rolled across the sky above the priory.

'Blimey, that's close!' Lisa said. 'Are we safe here? I mean with the tower and everything?'

'Well, it's stood for the last few hundred years. I don't think it's going to fall tonight,' Harrie said. 'At least, I hope not. I'll ask for a refund if it does.'

They all laughed, the candlelight soft on their faces.

'I'm grateful for this cocoa,' Lisa said, 'and even more grateful that there's a gas stove so we can heat up some more.'

'Yes, time for a top-up,' Audrey said.

'I'll do the honours.' Honor got up and took everyone's mug.

'Ha ha! Honor is doing the honours!' Lisa laughed.

Honor turned to look at her. 'I am so grateful for your sense of humour!' She shook her head as she left the room.

Harrie got up. 'You know what? I'm suddenly starving. Anyone else?'

A moment later, they were all in the kitchen and Audrey made her way to the fridge, shining a candle inside it.

'What do you fancy, Harrie?' Audrey asked. 'There's only a bit of worn-looking salad.'

'Let me have a look.' Harrie pushed Audrey gently aside. 'What's this pie?'

'Mrs Ryder left it, but it's meat,' Audrey said.

'Give me a slice.' Lisa turned round from the cooker. 'I had a piece before and it was delicious. It'll just as good cold too.'

'Anyone else?' Harrie asked. Audrey and Honor said they'd have some and Harrie placed the pie on the table and got four plates out with forks and a large serving knife.

Once the cocoa was piping hot and had been poured into mugs, the women sat at the table. Harrie served up the pie and nobody seemed to notice at first. Perhaps it was because she was half hidden by the flickering candlelight. Honor was the one to raise the alarm.

'Mum!' she screamed.

Harrie's eyes widened. 'What?'

'What are you doing?'

'I'm having a bit of supper.'

'But that's meat!'

'I know,' Harrie said, taking another forkful. 'Oh, wow! That is *so* good!' She closed her eyes to relish the taste.

'Wait a minute – did you just eat *meat*?' Lisa said from across the table.

'What kind is it?' Harrie asked. 'No – don't tell me. I probably don't want to know.'

'Oh, my god!' Audrey laughed. 'It must be the power cut and the fact that she thinks we can't see her.'

'I'm not hiding anything. I'm simply having some pie.'

'You're not vegan anymore?' Honor asked.

Harrie shrugged. 'I think Mrs Ryder actually made this pie for me. It would be rude not to at least try it.'

Honor was still looking shocked, but Audrey was just laughing. 'Good for you, Harrie!'

'What does it taste like?' Lisa asked.

'Pretty similar to yours, I imagine,' Harrie said.

'I bet it doesn't,' Lisa said. 'How long is it since you've eaten meat?'

Harrie shrugged. 'I think I was about fifteen when I gave it up.'

'And you're eating it from now on?' Lisa pressed.

'Don't get excited,' Harrie warned. 'I'm not about to order a rare steak or anything.'

'I can't believe it, Mum.'

'What's the big surprise? I've tried this vegetarian/vegan thing for years now. I just fancied something different. After all, look where so-called healthy eating got me. And I tell you what – I'm going to buy some cookies tomorrow and more cake too. Maybe even a bag of jelly babies. God, I miss those!'

Everyone was silent for a moment.

'Here, Harrie – have another slice of pie,' Audrey said at last, and they all laughed, breaking the tension.

'And let me buy you the cake at least. I do believe I owe you,' Lisa told her, making Harrie smile.

The rain was getting heavier now, battering against the mullioned windows. Harrie got up from the table and walked across the room to look out into the garden, but nothing much was visible.

'Where are you going?' Audrey asked a moment later as Harrie picked up a candle. Audrey did the same.

'Don't you lot go leaving me again!' Lisa said, grabbing a candle herself and following them both.

'What on earth are you doing, Mum?' Honor asked as Harrie moved to the front door and opened it.

'I want to listen to the rain,' she said.

'You can listen to it with the door closed – it's deafening.'

'Yes, but I can feel its mist here on my skin. It's so refreshing!'

Audrey joined her. 'I've never liked storms,' she said. 'They always make me headachy.'

'I love them,' Harrie told her. 'All that passion and emotion. It's like living in a chapter of *Wuthering Heights*.'

'I think it's beginning to ease off now,' Audrey said.

Harrie turned towards her. 'Listen!'

'To what?'

'That soft patter of the rain on the leaves of that tree.'

Audrey cocked her head to one side, listening intently. 'I've never heard that before. It's lovely. We don't have many trees where we live and, if we did, I never have the time to just stand and listen to them.'

'Let's get closer,' Harrie said, suddenly grabbing Audrey's hand.

'What? Oh, no – Harrie!'

Before she could protest further, Harrie had dragged Audrey outside into the rain.

'Harrie!' Audrey yelled.

'Isn't it wonderful?' Harrie cried. 'So refreshing!' She threw her head back, closing her eyes and feeling the rain on her face. It was lighter now and the thunder had rumbled right across the sky to frighten a different county, leaving behind a gentler heaven.

'What on *earth* are you two doing?' Lisa's voice shrieked from the front door. 'You'll get soaked!'

'Come on out!' Harrie called.

'No way! You're crazy.'

'Come *on!*'

'I'm wearing my favourite blouse!'

Just then, the lights in the priory came back on, flooding the garden. Everybody cheered.

'Come *on*, Lisa!' Honor shouted as she herself ran outside.

'Oh, no! *Please* don't make me do this!' Lisa yelled back before shaking her head and running across the lawn to join them, squealing as she went. 'You lot are crazy!' she said, but she was smiling now.

They all laughed and then did a sort of silly, funny dance and, all the time, the rain kept falling, soaking into their clothes and plastering their hair to their faces.

'I'm calling time!' Lisa said at last.

'Me too,' Honor agreed.

'Oh, don't go!' Harrie said. 'I thought we could walk around the garden.'

Lisa laughed. 'In the dark and rain?'

'There won't be any moths in the rain,' Audrey pointed out.

'Don't be long!' Lisa added, leaving with Honor.

'They're not much fun, are they?' Harrie said.

'You really want to walk in the rain?'

'You know what? I think I just want to sit.'

'In the rain?'

'Sure. Why not? Have you ever just sat in the rain before? Without an umbrella, I mean?'

'No, of course not!'

'Neither have I,' Harrie said. 'Come on.' She took Audrey's hand and they sat on a bench dimly lit from the light now spilling from the priory windows. Audrey let out a laugh. 'See? Isn't it amazing?'

Audrey linked her arm through Harrie's and the two of them sat in happy silence together as the gentle rain fell upon them.

Chapter 18

Audrey thought it was probably best that she didn't tell Mike about spending half the night sitting in the rain because he'd only worry about her. So she kept it as a wonderful secret and talked to him about other things instead.

'Jack sends his love,' Mike told her.

'How is he?' Audrey asked.

'He's got a new girlfriend.'

'Really? Do we know her? What's her name?'

'Erm, Pippa,' Mike said. 'Or Poppy.'

'Oh, Mike! Can't you remember?'

'It's Pippa. I'm pretty sure it's Pippa.'

'Well, find out and let's invite them both over for dinner as soon as I'm back home.'

There was a pause and then Mike said, 'There's something I want to tell you and I don't want you to get angry or worried or upset, okay?'

'What is it?'

She heard Mike take a deep breath and there was another pause before he told her what he'd done.

Harrie was in the kitchen when Audrey came downstairs.

'There you are! Did you sleep okay?'

Audrey nodded.

'I'm so glad we had that storm last night,' Harrie went on. 'I've been worrying about things I won't see again.' She looked out of the window. 'I probably won't ever see snow again.'

'Don't say that,' Audrey said. 'We might get some next month, what with global warming and everything!'

Harrie laughed as she turned from the window and then she frowned. 'Hey – are you okay?'

'Not really.' Audrey walked towards the kettle to put it on. 'I've just spoken to Mike.'

'He's not threatening to take you home again, is he?'

'No,' Audrey said. 'Mind you, there might not be a home for me to go home *to*.'

'What do you mean?'

'Mike's had an estate agent round to value our home. Can you believe it? The minute I'm gone, he pulls a stunt like that. And he expects me to *relax*!'

'Why did he do that?' Harrie asked.

'He wanted to see how much the place is worth and, well, it's worth so much more than we thought. It's in between three different tube stations, you see, and the price is ridiculous even though it's the tiniest two-bedroomed terrace.'

'And he wants to sell it?'

'He wants to move right out of London. He keeps talking about Norfolk.'

'Wow! That's – erm – rural.'

'You're telling me! What the hell would I do in *Norfolk*?'

Audrey grabbed a mug from the cupboard, dumped a teabag into it and then poured the freshly boiled water into it.

'It's where Mike grew up and he's got this crazy idea that we should set up a little bed and breakfast by the coast.'

'And I take it you're not as keen as he is.'

'How did you guess?'

Harrie smiled then gestured to the table and they sat down facing one another.

'Have you thought about it?'

'Yes, and it's not going to happen.'

'Why not?'

Audrey almost spluttered on her tea. 'Why not? You *know* why not! I love London and I've just set up my own school.'

'I know,' Harrie said, 'but don't you think it might be fun to try something different?'

'That's what I'm doing with my school.'

'Yes, but that's been so stressful, hasn't it? I don't think it's making you happy.'

'Has Mike been talking to you again?'

'No, of course not.'

'I wouldn't put it past him to put you on his payroll.'

'Oh, Audrey! I'm just thinking about what might be good for you. I'm sure that's Mike's reasoning too. I don't think he's just plucked this Norfolk idea out of thin air. I think he believes it will do you both some good.'

Audrey sipped her tea. 'If only I hadn't fainted. He's totally taking advantage of that when it was just a silly little thing.'

Harrie glowered at her.

'What?'

'It wasn't a silly little thing. It was a warning.' Harrie reached across the table to hold Audrey's hand. 'And I should know. All my life, I've been in this awful rush to get somewhere, to achieve something, to tick things off a list that other people seemed to have written for me. Now, I don't want to become some kind of preacher – that's the very last thing

I want – but we're alike, Aud. I see so much of me in you and I don't want you to make the same mistakes as I have.'

'You think we should move?'

'I think you should think about it.'

'But my business—'

'It didn't exist before, did it? You were fine without it so surely you don't need it now. Not really. Not in the scheme of things.'

Audrey didn't feel happy or convinced by Harrie's argument.

'I've put everything into that school.'

'I know you have and it's zapped all your energy.'

'I can't just walk away from it and leave London.'

Harrie sighed. 'Well, then think about deputising. If you *must* go on working and building the school, hire some more help. Take the pressure off yourself.'

'But that will cut into the profits.'

'What good are profits if you haven't got the time or good health to enjoy spending them? Think about it, Aud. Would you rather be working yourself into an early grave or taking time to enjoy your life? And, before you say it, I know you enjoy your work. We all do. None of us would have gone into teaching unless we loved it. We do it because we're passionate about it, but this business of yours is eating up all your time. That's what Mike's told me at least. He hardly gets to see you and, whenever he does, he says you're so tired that you hardly speak to him.'

'Mike exaggerates.'

'Mike worries, and not without good cause. You're stressed, Aud. I've never seen you look so exhausted, and stress can be just as deadly as the thing that's eating me up from the inside.'

'Oh, Harrie!'

'No, no! Don't make this about me. We're talking about you now. Maybe Mike's Norfolk idea isn't such a bad one. You'd be working together and that would be fun, wouldn't it?'

'Are you sure about that?'

Harrie laughed at Audrey's scepticism.

'You'd also be working from home so there wouldn't be any travel involved.'

'But a bed and breakfast? Is that really us?'

'You won't know until you try.'

'But we wouldn't be able to get away from our work. It would always be there around us.'

Harrie gave a wry smile. 'Unless you haven't noticed, you already take your work home with you now. You even brought it on holiday with you.'

'But that will all calm down soon. A new business is special – it needs all the man hours you can throw at it.' Audrey finished her tea and looked at Harrie. 'What?'

'I think you should listen to Mike. He might be onto something and I think it would be fun to have a change.'

'You seriously think we should pack up and head to Norfolk?'

Harrie smiled again. 'I think you should at least consider it.'

Harrie knew she'd rattled Audrey by being honest with her, but it sometimes took an honest friend to help you see the opportunities right in front of you that you weren't always able to recognise yourself. The funny thing was, she had felt an immediate sense of excitement as soon as Audrey mentioned the Norfolk idea. She could really see her friend living there, working alongside Mike and strolling on the endless north Norfolk beaches, breathing in all that wonderful salty air. Surely that was preferable to being stressed out in a stuffy office or classroom. Harrie knew that her friend had worked hard to build her school and she sincerely admired her, but her dream seemed to have turned into a nightmare and Mike had obviously had enough of seeing Audrey put herself through it all.

Dear Mike. That was something else Audrey had to consider in all this. Marriage was a partnership and compromise was essential in order to make things work, and Harrie could think of far worse things than moving to the country.

She looked out of the kitchen window, where Audrey was walking in the garden. She'd been out there herself, walking through the rain-soaked grass with bare feet and inhaling the air, which was pure and fresh after the storm. There was nothing quite like it – a summer garden after a downpour. The colours seemed brighter, deeper and the scents seemed stronger, especially so when it might be the last summer to enjoy such things, she thought to herself. No, there was nothing that heightened the senses quite like a death sentence.

She'd go back outside in a little while, she told herself, shaking her dark thoughts out of her head. First, though, she'd go and see Samson. She was eager to talk to him again to make sure that things weren't weird between them after she had told him about her cancer. Cancer had a way of spoiling friendships and of making people wary or scared and she hoped the rotten disease hadn't stolen Samson from her.

'There's only one way to find out,' she told herself.

She made her way to the chapel, ready for her second trip up the scaffolding to see what she now thought of as her angel. Although she didn't relish the idea of climbing that ladder again, she believed she would handle the height issue better this time.

She could hear Samson at work as she entered the chapel.

'Hello!' she called.

She heard the tools stop and his sandy head popped over the scaffolding. 'Hello!' he called back.

'Can I come up?' Harrie asked, moving towards the ladder.

'No!'

Harrie blanched, surprised by his response. 'Oh, okay.'

'I mean – not today.'

'What are you up to?'

'Nothing. It's just – a bit delicate. I'll show you another time.'

'I'll hold you to that.'

'I know you will.' He grinned. She liked his grin. She remembered that, not too long ago, he had only ever scowled at her. 'Did you have a power cut?'

'Yes, we did!'

'I trust you were prepared for it.'

'Well, I didn't really believe you, I'm afraid. I mean about the power going. So we had to come in here in the dark to get our candles. It was very spooky.'

'Why didn't you believe me?'

'I thought you might be exaggerating.'

He shook his head in mock despair. 'You're in the middle of nowhere here. If there's a storm, there'll likely be a power cut.'

'I'll remember that for next time,' she told him. 'You want a cup of tea?'

'Sure.'

Harrie left the chapel, breathing a sigh of relief that things seemed pretty normal between her and Samson.

He came down the ladder for his cup of tea and she sipped her own herbal one.

'How's my angel?' she asked.

'Pardon?' He looked a little taken aback.

'The angel you're working on up there,' Harrie said. 'Did you think I was calling you my *angel*?'

'No!' Samson said.

Harrie laughed. 'I can if you want.'

'I'd rather you didn't.'

His cheeks were burning bright and he cleared his throat. 'Your angel is doing fine. A bit more work to do on the stone around her, but she should be safe for another few hundred years after that.'

'Wow! That's amazing. Do you think you could chisel some of the rotten bits out of me and give me a few extra years?'

Samson stared at her, his mouth dropping open.

'Sorry,' Harrie said. 'That just came out. I shouldn't have said—'

'I would if I could. Believe me.'

Harrie could have sworn there were tears in his eyes as he said this but, if there were, he quickly blinked them away. She'd often had this response – she was the one with the disease and yet she found she spent an awful lot of time comforting others as they cried. Harrie hadn't cried herself for months now. Not what she considered proper crying anyway, other than with Honor, that was. She'd had sympathy crying, like when she'd told Lisa and Audrey. How could one not cry when one's friends were in such pain? But she hadn't really cried for herself for a long time now. She must be getting good at this cancer lark, she thought.

'I'll leave you to it,' she said to him, reaching out to take his mug from him.

'Harrie?' he said, just as she'd turned to leave. 'I'm here. If you need to talk. I might not be much of a talker myself, but I've been told I'm a pretty good listener.'

'Thank you,' she said. 'That means a lot.' She paused. 'And I promise – no more chisel jokes.'

He grinned. 'Okay,' he said.

Audrey stood at the edge of the swimming pool, looking down into its aquamarine depths before diving in. She needed to lose herself in a world without words, without phone calls from husbands or advice from well-meaning friends. So she swam, slicing through the water with grace and precision, her body fully supported and her mind concentrating only on movement.

She wasn't sure how long she spent in the water but, when she got out, she felt both refreshed and relaxed as she grabbed her towel from the sun lounger and dried herself. The sun was warm on her bare skin and she applied some lotion before putting on her hat and glasses and sitting down.

She had to admit that she was hurt by Harrie's words. Well, maybe *hurt* was too strong a word. Surprised. Yes, that was more like it. Harrie had surprised her. Ever ready to fight one another's corner, Audrey had felt almost betrayed that her friend had taken Mike's side so quickly. She'd been so sure that Harrie would be as outraged as she was by Mike's audacity at having an estate agent around and his subsequent proposal to leave London, but Harrie had simply smiled and thought it all a wonderful idea.

But was it wonderful? It was Audrey's instinct to fight for herself and she had to admit that she didn't always see the point of view of others. Now, she tried to imagine how Mike was feeling and how he'd endured all those years in a place he felt no love for. He'd done that for her and he'd never complained. Well, he'd dropped a few hints throughout the years about how much more space and air and sky there was in Norfolk and how much less noise and pollution. She'd always smiled and nodded, but hadn't really paid it much attention.

But maybe you should, a little voice said. Maybe Harrie was onto something and a new adventure, working closely with her husband, might just be worth considering. Oh, but her beloved school. She had such dreams for it and yet, if she was totally honest with herself, it had been a total nightmare from start to finish. She kept telling herself that things would get better, easier, but there was no guarantee, not really.

As she closed her eyes against the sunshine, Audrey began to wonder what it might be like not to have to get up so painfully early each weekday morning and do the commute to a job that was proving punishingly hard and work long into each evening and still not be able to keep on top of things. She'd had a small taste of what it might be like while staying at the priory. Of course, if they were to run a bed and breakfast, that would be hard work too, but it would be a different sort of work and Mike had said that they would own their property outright and so not have a mortgage to worry about anymore. That in itself was a wonderful incentive.

Audrey groaned. What was she thinking of, even considering such a ludicrous idea? She could never walk away from her school and give up her life in London. She'd have to put Mike straight. Norfolk was just a dream. Maybe they could have a holiday there so he could get it out of his system. Yes, that's what they both needed – some time out together, walking along those endless sandy beaches and eating chips sitting on a sea wall. Then, she thought, normality could resume.

'How's Samson getting on?' Honor asked as she and Harrie took an afternoon walk down the lane. They'd all had a marvellous lunch made by Mrs Ryder that had consisted of far too many goodies, and Harrie had felt the need to burn some of it off.

'You should really go and see for yourself,' Harrie said.

'Oh, I did.'

'You did?'

'I sneaked in the other day.'

'Did you say hello?' Harrie asked.

'No, I didn't want to disturb him.'

'He doesn't mind. Well, he says he does, but he's slightly less grouchy if you take him a cup of tea. Maybe you could do that when we get back.' Harrie smiled at her daughter, but noticed a shadow pass across her face. 'What is it?'

'I got a call from Benny.'

They'd reached the end of the track to the priory now and took a footpath which crossed a meadow. Harrie waited for her daughter to continue.

'Are you going back?' They stopped walking.

'Would you mind?' Honor asked, her eyes full of anguish.

'Of course I wouldn't mind! I've been expecting it.'

'But I don't want to leave you, Mum.'

'It won't be for long. I'll see you as soon as I get home.'

Honor sighed. 'I'm not sure yet. I might stay. Benny can do without me for a little longer and I want to spend more time with you.'

Harrie could see the conflicting emotions in her daughter's face and heard the unspoken words. Honor knew all too well that this would be Harrie's last summer and that tore her heart, and so she decided to make things really easy.

'If you want to know the truth,' she began, 'I was going to suggest you go back. I know you've got so much going on and it must be an agony not seeing Benny, and I'll be just fine with Audrey and Lisa to keep me company. And you can come back any time you want,' she added, feeling Honor's indecision like a great weight.

'You're the best!' Honor hugged her mum in the middle of the meadow as the joyous song of a skylark poured down upon them.

Evening was an especially quiet time at the priory. The frantic buzz of the bees and the high-spirited singing of the birds had mellowed. Harrie, Audrey and Lisa were sitting in the courtyard garden, breathing in the heady scent of the lavender in the fading light. It seemed almost luminous at this time of day; its rich purple positively glowed.

It had been deeply relaxing, watching the slow progress of the shadows across the lawn, feeling how the temperature dipped ever so slightly. Harrie loved sitting there and would often do so for hours, the pages of her book turning slowly for she found it hard to concentrate when there was so much beauty around her.

Although she didn't believe in regrets, it had always seemed a great pity to Harrie that she'd never owned a garden, but the properties within her budget had never come with anything more than a simple backyard. She would have loved somewhere with sunny corners and shady nooks – somewhere she could feel protected. Rooms were all very well, but they could never really compare to a garden. What a joy it must be to be able to leave one's house and enter a garden, she thought, and a garden such as the one at the priory would be a daily blessing.

She gazed up at the great tower, her mind drifting towards the past.

'Cistercian, Augustinian, Benedictine – they're wonderful words, aren't they?' she suddenly said. 'Your tongue can cartwheel around them.'

'You've had too much wine,' Audrey said.

'I haven't had a single drop. I'm drinking fruit juice.'

'It's funny without Honor,' Lisa confessed.

'Yes,' Harrie said, 'but it was right for her to go.'

'Missing her chap?' Lisa asked.

'Absolutely.'

'Ah, young love. It's so wonderful,' Audrey said.

'Middle-aged love can be wonderful too,' Harrie told her.

'Oh, don't say that! Don't say *middle-aged*!' Audrey said with a cringe.

'Yes, it sounds awful, especially to someone like me who's still single,' Lisa said.

'Are you still single?' Harrie asked.

'What do you mean?'

'I mean you and that gardener.'

'We're just friends,' Lisa announced. 'Like you and that stone bloke.'

Harrie laughed.

'Aren't you two having a fling?' Lisa asked.

'No, we're not!'

'Why not? He's a good-looking man.'

'I'm not here to have a fling. I'm here to be with my friends and just relax.'

Lisa seemed puzzled by this. 'Really?'

'Yes. Why are you so surprised by that?'

'I don't know. I guess, well, if I was you' – she paused, swallowing hard – 'I think I'd be wanting to do stuff like jetting off around the world and jumping out of planes over the Alps or swimming naked in the Great Barrier Reef.'

Harrie smiled. 'I think that's what people *think* they'd want to do, but I want to sit here and think. I want to watch the clouds in the sky and listen to the doves in the tower or find myself a nice deep window-sill and just stare out at the garden.'

'But isn't that . . .'

'What?'

'Depressing?'

Harrie shook her head. 'I'm not just thinking about the you-know-what. I'm thinking about everything. I'm thinking about when I was a child . . . when I found out I was pregnant after being told I could never have children . . . All sorts of things that normal life doesn't give you time to think about. That's what this disease has given me – the chance to slow down and just think. I don't have to run around anymore like a mad creature. It's so incredibly freeing.'

Lisa still didn't look convinced. 'But aren't there things you want to do? I mean—'

'If you're trying to ask if I have a bucket list, just ask.'

'Okay then – do you?'

Harrie nodded. 'Honor made me write one after the first diagnosis. I didn't want to because I've always thought that, if you really want to do something, you'll just do it. You don't have to write it down first.'

'But lists are good,' Audrey said. 'They help you to focus on what's important.'

'I understand that now,' Harrie said.

'So, what did you do?' Lisa asked.

'Don't get excited, I didn't bungee jump off a bridge or anything. But there were some places I wanted to see so I booked a ticket to Italy and Honor and I spent three weeks over there.' She smiled at the memory. 'It was wonderful. Everything I've ever dreamed of. We drank hot chocolates in San Marco in Venice and had one of those gondola rides where an impossibly good-looking Italian sings to you.'

'Now, that's going straight on *my* bucket list!' Lisa said, and they all laughed.

'We stood on Juliet's balcony in Verona, drove around hairpin bends along the Amalfi Coast, ate ice cream on the Spanish Steps in Rome and too much pizza in Naples. I think I put on at least a stone.'

'But that's good, isn't it?' Lisa said. 'I mean, you lost weight, right?'

'It was all good,' Harrie told her.

'What else?' Lisa asked.

'Well, I'd always wanted to see New York so we went there for Christmas and we bought matching necklaces from Tiffany's and posed like Audrey Hepburn outside the shop. There were lots of little days out too, like a trip to the Cotswolds, where we did a one-day chocolate-making course, and a night in London seeing *Mamma Mia!* But now, I want to be still and just commune.'

'Commune with what?' Lisa asked.

'Please don't tell me you've gone and found Jesus,' Audrey said.

'I haven't found Jesus,' Harrie confirmed, 'and I thought you'd understand, Lisa, what with your meditating. I mean, how many times can you truly be still?'

Lisa nodded. 'Good point. Stillness is good for the mind and the soul.'

The three of them sat for a little longer until the sun slipped slowly over the horizon and a pale moon started its ascent. It soon became too chilly to stay outside and, reluctantly, they went indoors. Harrie hovered for a moment at the front door. Another day had passed. The thought could have brought on a bout of melancholia but, instead, Harrie decided to think about all the wonderful things the day had given her: Samson's kindness, the generosity of Mrs Ryder's lunch, the moment of intimacy with Honor in the meadow, and the shared laughter with her friends in the garden. So many beautiful moments.

'Thank you,' she whispered into the soft cool night.

Chapter 19

'And you're *sure* she's not coming back?' Mrs Ryder asked as she heaped Honor's bedding into her arms.

'I've said she's welcome to, but I don't think she will,' Harrie said.

'And you're *not* expecting any more unannounced guests?'

'No.'

'Right! At least I know where I am.'

Harrie tried to hide her grin at the housekeeper's bossiness.

It was funny just being the three of them again, Harrie thought as she walked into Honor's empty bedroom. She hadn't realised what a difference it would make not having her daughter there, but she'd brought a different dynamic to the group.

Nothing stays the same for long, she mused. That's what she'd learned over the past few years. You could take absolutely nothing for granted. Every single moment had to be recognised and grasped. That's why she had booked the priory. She'd instantly known that one of life's beautiful moments could be shared here.

She'd been thinking about life's special moments a lot lately. Many of them could be planned for, such as birthdays, Christmas, anniversaries, et cetera, but others had to be met halfway – you had to go out and search for them – to make an effort and play your part in realising them because life passed by all too quickly and it was so easy to get swept up in a busy routine with work, paying the bills, cleaning the house and doing all those mind-numbingly dull things which meant that all the good things were postponed until tomorrow. The mythical *tomorrow*. One of the hardest lessons to learn in life was how to turn tomorrow into today. Harrie hoped she'd learned how to do it.

Leaving Mrs Ryder grumbling about the ancient washing machine, Harrie ventured into the garden. She was wearing her broad-rimmed sun hat and its golden straw had bleached wonderfully that summer. They'd been so very lucky with the weather. They'd all practically lived outdoors and it would be a real wrench leaving the place and to be forced to wear shoes once again. Harrie had read somewhere that walking barefoot was good for one's mental health – that the positive connection with the earth was something that humans had long forgotten in their concrete jungles.

Harrie tried to imagine herself walking barefoot down the high street of her small market town. She would be seen as quite mad and would also be too fearful of treading on or in something. But here, she was safe, as long as there wasn't a wayward thistle growing in the lawn. She was free to flex and curl every single toe and what a great pleasure that was. One often forgot how many individual toes there were when one's feet were scrunched up into shoes all day. And what appalling shoes too. Honestly, it was a miracle that evolution hadn't changed the shape of women's feet into arched, pointed weapons by now.

So Harrie walked across the grass with her sun hat on and her shoes off. Audrey was sitting in a sunny corner, one of her books in her hand.

'You've really embraced this doing nothing, haven't you?' Harrie said, sitting down next to her.

'Does it suit me?' Audrey asked.

'Very much.'

Audrey laughed. 'I don't believe you, but it's actually quite nice sitting in the sun just reading. You know, I haven't thought about checking in with work for a few days now.'

'That's good.'

'Or checking my emails. I think a lot of things like that become nervous twitches and you have to step right away from them.'

'Mike would be proud of you.'

'You think so?'

'I *know* so.' Harrie decided to push her luck. 'Have you thought any more about what he said?'

'You mean the Norfolk idea?'

Harrie nodded.

'Yes.'

'And?'

'I think we should go there.'

'Oh, Aud! That's so exciting!'

'For a holiday.'

'Oh.'

'I think we need to spend more time together, for sure, and Norfolk might be just the place to do that. Maybe we could even talk about retiring there one day.'

'You might change your mind when you're there,' she told Audrey.

'I don't think so. I think a breath of sea air will do us both some good and then we can knuckle down and get back to work.'

Harrie sighed inwardly. Poor Mike, she thought. He was certainly going to have to work hard to persuade Audrey to leave her job and London.

'Those two are spending a lot of time together. Are you *sure* they're just doing yoga?' Audrey asked, peering over her sunglasses at Lisa and the gardener.

'I think so.'

'He comes here even on his days off now.'

'Lisa told you that?'

'She didn't need to. He's here practically every day.'

'She must be a good teacher,' Harrie said.

'That's a funny sort of yoga, don't you think? They're writing stuff down.'

Harrie craned her neck to try and see properly, but couldn't make anything out.

'I'm going to find out what's going on,' Audrey said.

'You probably shouldn't,' Harrie said as Audrey stood up and headed over there. Harrie sighed and got up too. After all, she didn't want to miss anything.

Five minutes before Audrey spied Lisa and Alfie with their heads together, they'd just completed a twenty-minute meditation.

'Feel okay?' Lisa asked him.

'Feeling *good*!'

She laughed. 'Brilliant.'

'Hey, I had a chat with my dad last night.'

Lisa's eyes widened. 'About work?'

'Yep.'

'What did you say?'

'I fessed up and told him I didn't want the position he was offering me.'

'Oh, Alfie! I'm so proud of you.'

'Well, I had Mum on my side. She told Dad pretty much what you said – that I had to find something that fulfilled me, and which was *my* dream and not his. I felt a bit sorry for Dad actually.'

'Yes, but you would've been feeling sorry for yourself for the next few decades if you'd taken the job.'

'I know.'

'How did he take it?'

'Pretty good. He didn't swear or turn red or punch me or anything.'

'I should hope not!'

'But he said he was disappointed, but then went on to say that he's got his eye on some graduate who's been working there for the last year. Seems he was made for the role Dad's been keeping for me.'

'Then it's all worked out for the best?'

'Yeah, I guess.'

'So what now?'

'You know the friend I told you about with the outdoor-activity centre? I texted him last night.'

'And?' Lisa said. 'Don't keep me in suspense!'

'He wants me to start next week. Can you believe it?'

'That's great!'

'Yeah, isn't it? I can't wait. He says he's got schools queuing for visits and I've got all sorts of ideas for the kids.'

Lisa smiled. 'And this is what you see yourself doing in five or ten years' time?'

'What?' he cried.

'You said you've got all sorts of ideas.'

'Yes, but that's for the immediate future.'

'So project further.'

'I can't think that far ahead!'

'No? Well, you should. Just imagine it for a minute. Go on!' She gave him a little nudge with her elbow.

'You've slipped into teacher mode again.'

'I know, and you love it.'

He laughed at her as she got up from the yoga mat and went to get the bag she'd brought out with her.

'Somewhere in here is a notebook.'

'What do we need that for?'

'We're going to brainstorm. Ah! Here it is,' she said, returning to the mat with the notebook and a pen. 'Right, let's write down everything you want to be doing in the future, whether that's next week when you start your job or in five, six, seven or even ten years' time.'

'You're crazy!'

Lisa smiled. 'Just a little bit, but crazy sometimes works.'

Alfie was halfway down the page when Audrey and Harrie approached them.

'What are you two up to?' Audrey asked.

'Nothing!' Lisa said, looking up in surprise.

'Doesn't look like nothing. What's that?'

'She's got me writing a list for the future,' Alfie said.

'Can I see?'

Lisa looked at Alfie and he shrugged, handing it to her.

Audrey took her sunglasses off and appraised it. 'Opening your own outdoor-activity centre. Taking a team to the Alps. This sounds impressive.'

'I might not achieve all that,' he said.

'But the will is there,' Lisa said, 'and I find it's easier to make things happen if you write them down first. Like a lesson plan.'

Alfie grinned. 'Can I keep it?'

'Of course,' she told him, neatly tearing the page from her notebook.

'Thanks,' he said, leaning across and kissing her cheek.

Lisa gasped and felt her skin flush. Luckily, he'd got up and had waved goodbye, seeming not to notice her fluster.

'You've got an admirer there for sure,' Harrie said after he was out of earshot.

'I'm just trying to help him.'

'You've done something really wonderful there,' Audrey told her. 'Now, if only you were as good at inspiring yourself.'

'What do you mean?' Lisa said.

'I mean about your career. If you teamed your natural talent for teaching with your love for yoga, I really think you'd be onto something. Give me that notebook.'

'Why?' Lisa asked, flinching as Audrey sat down on the mat beside her.

'Come on – you're going to make a list of your own.'

'Oh, no, no.'

'Why not?'

'I'm just a teacher. I inspire others.'

'Well, it's time to inspire yourself. Let's start with the basics. What do you need to earn a year – roughly?'

'Oh, blimey! I'm hopeless at this sort of thing.'

'Just give me a really rough figure and I'll do the number-crunching.'

Lisa took a deep breath and scribbled something down. 'There.'

'Okay. Good start.'

They then worked everything out in more detail, from what Lisa paid in rent each year to all her outgoings and a little bit extra for luxuries. After all, what was life without a few luxuries? Then they focused on how she could make that money by teaching yoga. They went indoors and got Harrie's laptop out on the kitchen table, did some research about yoga retreats, the price charged for courses, venues you could hire, equipment needed, insurance – everything they could think of.

Finally, Audrey turned to Lisa and nodded, a big smile on her face.

'It's feasible?' Lisa whispered in awe.

'It's *totally* feasible,' Audrey said.

Lisa sat staring at the computer screen for what seemed like an age.

'I don't know why I didn't think of it before,' she said at last.

'I think you'd be a total natural,' Harrie said.

'It would certainly beat waiting around for my agent to call,' Lisa said.

'You could advertise in all sorts of clever ways too with Instagram and Facebook. You could even make your own videos for YouTube.'

'I could have my own channel!' Lisa said.

'Absolutely! You know the popular ones make good money from advertising fees,' Audrey told her.

'Yes, and my agent wouldn't see a single penny!' Lisa declared. 'That'll teach him!'

'And you could always supplement it with supply teaching if it didn't work.'

'It'll work,' Harrie said.

Lisa reached out and wrapped her arms around Audrey. 'I'm going to do this. I'm *really* going to do it!'

Audrey laughed. 'Just let me know when you're up and running and I'll be your first pupil!'

Harrie left them both to it. During their session on the Internet, she'd felt her phone vibrating in her pocket and took a moment to check who it was, expecting it to be Honor. Only it wasn't Honor – it was Charles.

Going up to her bedroom and sitting on the bed, she took a moment to think about whether or not to ring him back. She made a guess at what had happened. As soon as she was back, Honor would have seen her dad, who, naturally, would have asked after Harrie. But had Honor told him the truth? Maybe she was jumping to conclusions and Charles was just reaching out of the blue for a general catch-up. Their calls were becoming rarer now that he was married to Lizzie, but they still managed to keep in touch.

Believing that she would probably regret her decision, she called Charles. He answered his phone immediately.

'Harrie?' He sounded upset and she immediately knew. 'Why didn't you tell me?' He swore and she could hear him crying. She'd never heard him cry before and she felt utterly helpless.

'Charles? Are you okay?'

'No, I'm bloody not okay! Our daughter's just told me that you've got terminal cancer.'

She kept quiet while he ranted some more.

'Why didn't you tell me, Harrie? Honor said this has been going on for years. Why did you keep all this from me?'

'Because we're not married anymore, Charles,' she said simply.

'What's *that* got to do with anything? I still care about you, for god's sake! You're still the mother of my child and you're still my first wife!' He swore again and she couldn't help but feel touched by his passion. 'Harrie?' he said after there was a moment's pause.

'I'm still here,' she told him.

'You should've told me.'

Hearing the pain in his voice, she suddenly realised that she'd made a huge mistake in not telling him. She had tried to protect him from the pain of it all, but she'd probably just made matters worse and caused him more.

'I'm sorry,' she said in a small voice. 'I should have told you.'

They took a moment to calm down and then he apologised.

'And I'm sorry,' he said. 'I didn't mean to shout like that.'

'It was quite impressive!' she told him with a tiny smile, wishing he was in the room with her so she could hug him. They might well be divorced, but she did still love him and he was one of the last people on earth that she'd ever want to hurt.

They talked some more, calmer now. Harrie told him about the priory and what they'd all been doing there. She told him about the special time she'd spent with Honor and the two of them talked about her relationship with Benny.

'She's sounding serious,' Harrie observed.

'You think so?'

'Trust me. I've not seen her like this over a boy before.'

'A boy? He's a man, Harrie, and Honor's a woman.'

Harrie smiled wistfully. 'She'll always be my little girl.'

Harrie heard him mutter something.

'What is it?'

'Nothing.'

'Are you sure?'

There was a pause and an intake of breath. 'You know you'll always be the love of my life, don't you?' Charles told her.

'It's safe for you to say that now that I'm dying, isn't it?'

'That's not why I'm saying it. You know it's true. I'll always regret us breaking up. We should have fought harder to keep things going, Harrie.'

'And how would Lizzie feel, hearing you say that?' she asked with a light laugh.

'Oh, god! Lizzie's great, but she isn't you.'

She took a deep breath. 'I love you to bits, Charles, but we did the right thing breaking up. You know we did.'

'Yeah, well, I can still miss you, can't I?'

'I haven't gone yet.'

There was another pause.

'I wish you'd told me,' he said.

'I'm sorry I didn't,' she said, even though there was a part of her that wasn't sorry really. The more people she could save from the sorrow, the better she felt. She knew they'd find out eventually or she'd be forced to tell them, but every day she saved them from her revelation felt like a little victory to her.

'Can I see you?' he asked.

'What – now?'

'Yes!'

'I'd rather you didn't.'

'Oh, thanks very much.'

'I mean I'll see you when I get home, okay?'

'When's that?'

'Not long.' She waited for his response. 'Okay?'

'I guess,' he said. 'Harrie?'

'Yes?'

'Are you feeling all right?'

'I feel fine. I have pills which I don't really need yet. At least, I'm not taking many.'

He swore again.

'You really have a mouth on you, don't you?' she teased.

'I think it's warranted in the circumstances.'

She heard him sigh and wished she could reach out through the phone and squeeze his hand. 'Listen,' she said at last, 'I've got to go.'

'Just don't forget you've promised to see me.'

'I won't forget.'

'I love you, Harrie. I always have.'

'I know, and I love you, Charlie.'

She hung up and switched off her phone, giving herself a moment to compose herself after the call before walking out onto the landing. She stopped at the top of the spiral stairs as she heard the happy voices of Audrey and Lisa as they made plans for the future. Harrie smiled as she listened, but it was a sad kind of smile and she decided not to join them, but took the back staircase downstairs and walked through the cloisters towards the chapel.

Samson's light chiselling could be heard. It was funny but, when she'd been told that there'd be restoration work being done during their stay at the priory, she'd worried about the level of noise and if it would disturb them, but she'd come to love the strange musicality of Samson's chisel. It was like a stony kind of soundtrack to their summer, she thought. A melody in limestone; a chisel concerto.

'Hello!' she called up to him as she entered. The chiselling stopped.

'Hello!' he called down.

'Can I come up yet?'

'Not yet. I'll come down. Just give me a moment, Harrie.'

She waited, trying to see what he was up to, but the bulk of his body was hiding what he was working on and so she waited patiently until he'd come down to earth.

'How are you?' he asked, his gaze a little more fixed than usual.

'I've just been on the phone with my ex.'

'Oh.'

'I told you about him?'

'No, you didn't.'

'Well, his name is Charles and . . .' She paused and shrugged. 'I didn't tell him about – you know what – but our daughter obviously did when she got home.'

'You didn't tell him?' Samson looked shocked by this confession.

'No.'

'Why not?'

'Lots of reasons, but I guess the biggest one is because he's not really in my life anymore. I know he's the father of my daughter and there's a part of me that will always love him, but he's moved on now. He's married to Lizzie, who has big hair and wears tight tops. So, you see my health isn't his concern anymore.' She looked down at the floor and scuffed her trainers around.

'If I was him, I'd want to know.'

She nodded. 'Well, I apologised to him.'

Samson took a step closer towards her. 'Are you okay?'

'Of course I'm okay. Why shouldn't I be?'

'Because you sound . . .'

'What?'

'Odd.'

'Odd?' She stared up at him.

Samson frowned down at her. 'I don't know. I'm waiting for you to tell me.'

'What do you want me to tell you? That I've just told my ex-husband that I'm dying and that my two best friends are in the kitchen planning their happy futures? Is *that* why I'm sounding odd, do you think?'

'Harrie—' He reached out and gently touched her arm and it was then that something began to creep up on her. She hadn't felt it at the time that they'd been sitting around the kitchen table chatting about all the possibilities open to Lisa, and she hadn't felt it when imagining Audrey's future with Mike in a beautiful little corner of north Norfolk. She hadn't even felt it when Charles had cried on the phone, but she felt it now and she had to get away.

'I've forgotten your tea!' she said, her mind skipping quickly to find a distraction that would mean she could leave the chapel and regain her composure in a private little corner somewhere.

'Never mind about the damned tea,' Samson told her.

'It won't take me long. I'll just go and—'

'You're not going anywhere.'

Suddenly, her breathing had become fast and shallow. She needed to get out of there and back to her bedroom so she could lie down for a bit. Then she would be all right, she was sure of it. But, before she could make a move, her legs buckled.

'Harrie!'

Samson swept forward, catching her in his arms as she fell. She didn't faint, but she did feel horribly light – as if the slightest breath of air would blow her away. Stunned for a moment, she remained absolutely still, her chest rising and falling at an alarming rate. And then the tears started. The strange thing was, Harrie didn't try to stop them. She wasn't sure that she could even if she wanted to and so they fell, large sploshy tears that burned her eyes and blurred her vision. She clasped her hands around Samson's arms as she tried to get her breathing under control.

'Deep, slow breaths,' Samson coaxed. 'That's it. Nice and slow.'

But she couldn't stop crying.

'I'm so scared,' she confessed in a screech of a whisper. 'I've never told anyone that before, but I am. I don't know what to do. What am I meant *to do*?'

Still the tears fell, welling up from a place deep inside her where they'd been suppressed for so long.

'I don't have a future! I don't have a *future*!' she cried, feeling the raw fear and panic as if for the first time. 'There's just this huge full stop waiting for me and I'm scared. I feel so helpless. I don't want to die! I don't want to leave everyone!'

Harrie felt as if she was spinning out of control as that thing inside her – that deep, dark, malignant thing – threatened to engulf her. It was a part of her she'd chosen to ignore, pushing it down and refusing it its rightful place in her life. But, now, it was coming after her, making its presence felt. She couldn't block it out any longer.

She wasn't sure how long she remained in Samson's arms like that but what was so wonderful was that Samson didn't tell her that it was all right and that everything would be okay. She'd never understood those platitudes because they were blatantly false and she knew that he knew that too. Instead, he simply held her in those strong arms of his and repeated the same three words.

'I've got you,' he said. 'I've got you.'

Chapter 20

'I knew it!' Mrs Ryder told them. 'I didn't say anything to anyone. I'm never one to say, *I told you so*, but I knew she was heading for a breakdown. She was just too good at holding it all in and that never bodes well. And she needs more meat in her diet in my opinion.' She slammed the fridge door shut and turned to face Audrey and Lisa.

Audrey felt terrible. She should have seen it coming. What kind of a friend was she not to have noticed? She'd been so wrapped up in her own worries with Mike that she hadn't seen how fragile her friend was. And then they'd been discussing Lisa's new future! How insensitive was that? Oh, she could kick herself, she really could.

Samson had found them both in the garden and had explained that he'd taken Harrie up to her bedroom, given her a glass of water and drawn the curtains. She'd been exhausted, he'd told them, and needed to rest, but it was more than that, Audrey could see that as soon as she'd looked in at her sleeping friend. Her face had been pale and tight and she'd clearly been crying.

'It's my fault,' Lisa said once they were back in the kitchen. 'I should *never* have gone on and on about my future like that.'

'It's not your fault,' Audrey assured her. 'If anything, it's mine. I was the one who pushed you into all that planning. Why didn't I think of the effect it would have on Harrie?'

'It's not so much talk as it is food,' Mrs Ryder said.

'I don't think it's as simple as that, Mrs Ryder,' Audrey said. 'I wish that it was.'

Mrs Ryder shook her head. 'I'll take her up some soup and bread before I go.'

'I think we should just let her sleep,' Audrey told her. 'I'll keep an eye on her and make sure she has something to eat as soon as she wakes up.'

Mrs Ryder pursed her lips, looking proprietary, and then she walked across the room and picked her handbag up from a chair and took out a notebook, ripping out a page a moment later and scribbling something down.

'My number,' she said, handing the piece of paper to Audrey. 'Call me if you need me. Doesn't matter what time it is.'

'Thank you,' Audrey said, genuinely surprised and moved that this irascible housekeeper cared so deeply about Harrie.

After both Mrs Ryder and Samson had left the priory, Audrey and Lisa crept around the place, trying not to make any noise. The atmosphere had changed now. They both felt it. It was as if the summer had come to an abrupt end and reality was creeping in upon them like a cruel and early winter.

'Should we let Honor know?' Lisa asked. 'I think we should call her.'

'No need to worry her. I don't think Harrie would want us to.'

Lisa sighed, looking stressed. 'Should one of us at least sit with her?'

'I don't think she'd want that either,' Audrey said. 'I mean, would you?'

'Probably not.'

'We'll let her rest.'

And so they did, tiptoeing around the priory, checking in on her every couple of hours until it was time for bed.

In the morning, Lisa brought Harrie a glass of water and some orange juice and placed them by her bedside while Audrey opened the window to let some cool air into the room. Still Harrie didn't stir.

'Are you sure she's okay?' Lisa asked. 'Should we call a doctor?'

'Her breathing's regular. I think Samson's right and she's just exhausted.'

It was dinner time before Harrie got up. Audrey and Lisa were in the kitchen warming up some of the soup Mrs Ryder had made when Harrie came into the room.

'Hey!' she said. She was wearing a loose jumper over a long skirt and looked flushed with sleep. 'Is Samson still here?'

Audrey was surprised by the question. 'It's Saturday, Harrie.'

'What?' She looked confused.

'He left yesterday for the weekend.'

She frowned and then her eyes widened in comprehension. 'I've been asleep for – *how* long?'

'A little while,' Audrey told her. 'Not to worry. You look better for it.'

'You should've woken me!'

'No way.'

Harrie walked towards the table with a little wobble and sat down. 'I've really been asleep since yesterday afternoon?' She put her head in her hands.

'Are you okay?' Lisa asked. 'Are you dizzy?'

'I think I—' She stopped.

'What?' Audrey asked.

'Are you going to faint?' Lisa said.

'I think I had an episode,' Harrie finished. 'Oh, *poor* Samson! What must he think of me?'

'He thinks you're exhausted, *that's* what he thinks.' Lisa sat down next to her and placed an arm on her shoulder.

'I'm fine.'

'You still look horribly pale to me. I'll get you some soup and bread,' Audrey said, and Lisa got up to get bowls, cutlery and water.

Then, for a few moments, they all ate their soup in silence with Audrey glancing up at Lisa as they both anxiously watched Harrie's progress.

'Blimey, I've not died yet,' Harrie suddenly said.

'Harrie!' Lisa exclaimed.

'Sorry.' She smiled. 'I find myself increasingly drawn to gallows humour.'

'That's not funny,' Lisa added.

'Well, cheer up then, for goodness' sake, and talk to me.'

Audrey didn't know what to say, but did her best to smile. Harrie put her spoon down.

'I'm sorry,' she said. 'I'm feeling odd.'

'Odd how?' Lisa asked. 'Can we get you something?'

She shook her head. 'Just out of sorts. I'm sorry.'

'Can I get you some of your pills? Or do you want to go back to bed?' Audrey asked.

'No. I don't want to sleep the summer away. I want to spend time with you guys.'

'Please don't exhaust yourself, Harrie,' Lisa told her.

'I won't.'

'You need plenty of rest,' Audrey said.

'And there'll be plenty of time for that soon enough.'

'Oh, Harrie!' Lisa cried. 'I wish you wouldn't talk like that.'

'Sorry. There's that dark humour creeping in again.' Harrie smiled. 'I haven't told you about the guy I met at the treatment centre who used to crack the darkest jokes, have I? At first, I hated it. I wanted to tell him to shut up and keep his grim humour to himself, but I soon realised that it was his way of coping and, before too long, I found myself joking alongside him.'

'I can't imagine what you went through,' Lisa said. 'It must have been so gruelling.'

'It was fine,' Harrie said. 'Horrible, but fine. I got through it. What was really scary, though, was when the treatment stopped.' She slowly swirled her spoon in her bowl, making circles in the soup. 'I went through all sorts of odd emotions then. Relief came first, I suppose – that I didn't have to go through it anymore – but then the fear set in because I realised that I was on my own. You see, when I was having treatment, I had a team fighting the cancer with me. I had somewhere to go where there were others who were going through the same thing. I didn't realise what a lifeline it was at the time.'

'You should have called us,' Audrey said. 'We'd have been there.'

'Absolutely,' Lisa said.

'I know,' Harrie told them, 'and that's so kind, but cancer does something funny to you. I think you need to be around others who are going through the same thing.'

'Are you still in touch with the people you had treatment with?' Audrey asked.

'A couple of them, yes.'

'And the gallows-humour guy?' Lisa dared to ask.

Harrie took a moment before she answered. 'He's not doing so well.'

'Oh, no! I'm sorry.'

Harrie nodded and gave a rueful smile. 'We once had this talk about it all. He told me how he'd slowly come to accept his diagnosis and with that acceptance came a strange sort of calm. It was as if you were acknowledging the inevitable, nodding to it and shaking it by the hand. He said you weren't inviting it in exactly, but you were letting it know that you knew it was there. I liked that.'

'And is that how you feel?' Audrey asked. Lisa glanced across the table at her as if wondering if she should ask such a thing.

'Yes,' Harrie said, seemingly happy to talk about it all now. 'I think it's healthy to face it, but I don't think you should give it free rein. You should still lead your life as well as you can and not give in to it and lock yourself away from the world while you wait for it to come for you. After all, it's a physical illness and I feel strongly that you shouldn't let it infect your spirit too.'

Audrey could see that Lisa's eyes were welling up with tears.

'And you're *not* doing that,' Audrey said, desperate to turn the conversation positive again.

'And you're not alone, Harrie,' Lisa said.

Harrie put her spoon down. 'I know I'm not. But, when you wake up in the middle of the night, it can feel pretty lonely.'

'Then call us,' Lisa insisted. 'Whatever time it is.'

'Yes, we want to be there for you,' Audrey added. 'We need that as much as you do.'

'Promise us,' Lisa said. 'Promise that you'll let us know when you need us.'

Harrie looked from Lisa to Audrey and back again. 'I will,' she said with a smile. 'I promise.'

Their final week at the priory was blessed with glorious sunshine. They read and they walked, they sunbathed and they talked. They meditated together and ate fabulous meals and laughed until they were hoarse. Harrie even went out with Samson to visit two more of his favourite churches.

Then, on their last day, Harrie announced that they should go shopping.

'Oh, can't Mrs Ryder do that?' Lisa asked from her sun lounger.

'Not for what I have planned.'

'And what is that exactly?' Audrey peered over her sunglasses. 'Should we be worried?'

'Well, I think we should do something special for our final night here, don't you?'

'Like what?' Lisa asked.

'Like a party,' Harrie said. 'And, for a party, you need to get dressed up.'

'You want to go shopping for new dresses?' Audrey asked.

'Don't you?' Harrie said.

'I'm afraid my budget doesn't stretch to a new dress,' Lisa said. 'Unless it's in the sale and about twenty quid.'

'Don't worry about that,' Harrie said. 'This is my treat.'

Lisa's mouth dropped open in protest.

'Now, no argument! I want to do this. It's my way of thanking you for being here this summer.'

'Thanking us?' Audrey said. 'But we should be thanking *you*!'

'Rubbish!' Harrie cried. 'I'm just so grateful that you took time to be here for me. You've no idea how much that means to me. Now, there's someone I need to call, but then I think we should go straight into town.'

An hour later, the three women were standing outside a rather beautiful boutique in the backstreets of Wells.

'Isn't this place a bit over the top?' Lisa asked, looking at the gowns in the window.

'Yes, shouldn't we just go to that nice department store on the high street?' Audrey said.

Harrie glared at them both. 'How many times in our lives do we get a chance to dress up? And I don't just mean a pretty day-dress – I mean a proper glamorous red-carpet number. I can't remember the last time I wore a dress like that, unless it was for my own wedding.'

'She's right,' Audrey agreed. 'I can't remember either.'

Lisa nodded. 'I'm always flicking through those celebrity magazines, ogling the acres of satin and lace, but there isn't really the opportunity to wear such things when you're a supply teacher.'

'Exactly!' Harrie said. 'And I want our last night at Melbury to be special and sparkly, and that means looking our best.'

'Hey, isn't that Mrs Ryder?' Audrey said as their housekeeper came stomping towards them, looking perplexed.

'Mrs Ryder!' Lisa said in surprise and then she leaned towards Harrie and whispered in her ear. 'What's she doing here?'

'She's with us.'

'You're buying her a dress too?'

'Of course!'

Mrs Ryder went straight up to Harrie. 'Now, what's all this?' she asked, shoving her handbag further up her arm. 'What might I have forgotten on the menu this time?'

'A dress,' Harrie said, linking her arm through hers. 'Come on, Mrs Ryder, we're going shopping.'

The young sales assistant was a gem, but perhaps she was a little too enthusiastic for she'd managed to pull virtually all the dresses from the rails and had filled the tiny changing rooms with acres of fabric.

'These are much too extravagant, Harrie!' Audrey shouted over the cubicle.

'Nonsense!'

'My arms are stuck!' Mrs Ryder called through.

'I'll be right there,' said the sales assistant.

'I can't get the zip done up on this one!' Lisa cried.

'You want a hand?' Harrie called.

'No, it makes me look like a huge strawberry anyway.'

Forty minutes of huffing and puffing later and the four of them emerged from the changing rooms, laughing and gasping at each other.

Audrey had settled on a cherry-red knee-length dress in a satiny fabric which looked so wonderful with her long dark hair, and Lisa had chosen an emerald-green figure-hugging dress which skimmed her ankles, giving her a sort of femme fatale look when she swept her chestnut hair up. Harrie had picked a sky-blue gown which reminded her of the one she'd always loved in a Grace Kelly movie and was just right for her pale colouring, and Mrs Ryder was absolutely transformed in a midnight-blue dress which did wonders for her hourglass figure, making her look like a cross between Jane Russell and Ma Larkin.

'Well I never!' Mrs Ryder exclaimed. 'Will you look at the three of you!'

'Look at *you*!' Harrie cried. 'You look like a movie star, Mrs Ryder.'

She batted her hand at Harrie, but her cheeks were tickled with pink. 'I think it's about time you called me by my Christian name. After all, I've seen you all in your undies now!'

Harrie grinned. 'Yes, what is your name?'

'Gladys.'

Lisa giggled and Harrie glared at her in warning.

'That's a very charming name.'

'Not many Gladyses around these days, I warrant you,' Mrs Ryder said. 'It's a little old-fashioned, but it was an aunt's name. An aunt that my mother was very fond of and she said she couldn't think of anything better.'

Harrie could see that Lisa was biting her lip in an attempt not to laugh.

'I think it's a beautiful name,' she told her, and then turned to the sales assistant. 'Now, what have you in the way of tiaras?'

'You can't be serious, Harrie,' Audrey said.

'Why not?'

'Because . . .'

'There, you see, you can't think of a single reason!'

'If Harrie's having a tiara then I want one too!' Lisa said.

'Let's all get them, shall we?'

There then followed twenty fun-filled minutes where every single tiara in the shop was tried on every single head. Gold, silver and copper-coloured glories were ogled and cooed over. Even Mrs Ryder got into the spirit of things, settling on a beautiful rose-gold-coloured one decorated with a delicate garland of leaves. Lisa and Harrie chose pretty silver tiaras decorated with diamante and Audrey chose a simple gold design.

Then came shoes. After all, as Harrie pointed out, you couldn't have new dresses without new shoes.

'You look like glorious butterflies!' the shop assistant told them when they had finally finished.

Flushed from the excitement of so much concentrated shopping, the four women left the boutique with bulging bags.

'I can't believe you just did that,' Audrey said.

'I've not finished yet,' Harrie told her. 'I thought we could all get matching necklaces too.'

Lisa sighed. 'What a lovely idea!'

'There's a little jeweller's across the way and we've just enough time, haven't we, Gladys?'

Mrs Ryder checked her watch. 'You'll have to be quick.'

'Why do we have to be quick?'

'Gladys has kindly booked us all in for a wash and blow-dry. A manicure and pedicure too,' Harrie told them in delight.

Audrey shook her head. 'You really are the limit, Harriet Greenleaf!'

Harrie smiled. 'Come on – let's go and get some jewellery! We'll see you back at the priory, Gladys!'

Mrs Ryder waved at them and left.

The jeweller's was a perfect cocoon of a shop and Harrie immediately fell in love with it. Together, they looked at an assortment of chains, pendants and lockets, but Harrie felt drawn to one design in particular. It was a simple gold chain with a pretty round pendant featuring a tree, its delicate leaves so wonderful to touch.

'The tree of life,' the jeweller told them. 'The symbol of harmony, positive energy and eternal life.'

Harrie liked that and asked for three of them.

They then made their way to the hairdresser's, where they were treated to a luxurious wash and blow-dry before enjoying a manicure and pedicure.

'I've never been so spoilt,' Lisa confessed.

'I don't know why I didn't think of it sooner,' Harrie said. 'I mean, I've been organising the food.' She gasped.

'What is it?' Audrey asked.

'That was meant to be a surprise.'

'This is *all* a surprise!' Lisa said.

Harrie smiled. 'Good!'

It was as they were coming out of the hairdresser's, their hair shiny and swishy and their nails perfectly painted, that Harrie spotted the second-hand bookshop.

'Can we?' she asked. 'Just a quick peek?'

They walked across the road and looked in the window. Harrie saw the book straightaway. It was a small hardback with a plain blue cover with gold lettering on the front and sides. *Medieval Buildings of Somerset.*

They went into the shop and she picked it up, flicking through it quickly and soon finding what she'd hoped would be there – Melbury

Priory. There were only two beautiful old black-and-white photographs of the priory, but one of them was of the chapel and Harrie could just make out the little bump of Samson's angel. There was also a whole page dedicated to the little church he'd taken her to visit, giving special mention to his beloved misericords.

She took it to the counter and paid for it. Audrey bought a Penguin classic and Lisa found a book about yogic breathing. All in all, it had been a tremendously successful shopping trip.

Chapter 21

Mrs Ryder had done them proud. When they returned to the priory, the trestle table was laden with enough food to feed the whole of Somerset. How glorious it all looked, set with candles and sparkling glassware, and how incredible Mrs Ryder looked too in her new dress.

'Is this really just for us?' Lisa asked.

'Of course!' Mrs Ryder said.

'You've not invited anyone else, Harrie? Like Honor or that stone man?'

'No!' Harrie laughed. 'This is *our* night. Just for us ladies.'

The three of them embraced right there in the kitchen, their heads pressed together and their arms tight around each other's waists.

'Right!' Harrie said at last. 'Let's get dressed up!'

Squealing with girlish excitement, the three women went to shower and change into their new dresses, returning to the kitchen half an hour later, where they admired each other once again, reaching out to touch one another's dresses and tiaras and sighing with pleasure at their matching necklaces.

Naturally, they all wanted photos taken together and Mrs Ryder did the honours with the cameras, following them around the priory and the garden as they posed in alcoves and under arches, leaned against walls and apple trees.

'We must have one with you, Mrs Ryder!' Audrey cried as they were about to go back inside as the sun was setting.

Mrs Ryder batted them away.

'Yes, come on, Gladys!' Harrie agreed.

'Well, if you insist.'

'We absolutely do!' Lisa told her.

They each took it in turns to take selfies, grinning into their cameras like loons, the majestic backdrop of the priory looming behind them.

It was with some reluctance that they returned indoors, leaving a blush-pink sky. But they had supper to look forward to and Harrie, Audrey and Lisa were soon grabbing plates and stacking them high before filling their glasses with the champagne Harrie had insisted on buying for their special night.

There was salmon and quiche, baguette and cheese, heaps of rocket and watercress, a plate of pasta salad, mini jacket potatoes, a meat pie which Mrs Ryder had made especially for Harrie, sausage rolls, buttered asparagus, roasted Mediterranean vegetables served with quinoa, and an enormous bowl of Eton Mess as well as fresh mango and grapes and a large strawberry cheesecake.

'It's a good job we're eating this *after* buying these dresses,' Lisa said. 'Although you may have to unzip me a bit as I work my way through dessert.'

'Mrs Ryder – *Gladys*,' Audrey said, 'this is really something else!'

'Yes, and I hope you're going to join us,' Harrie said.

Mrs Ryder looked genuinely shocked by this. 'I couldn't!' she said.

'Of course you could!' Harrie told her.

'Yes, we insist!' Lisa added. 'We can't possibly eat it all ourselves.'

Mrs Ryder looked up and down the table, as if eyeing her hard work and wondering if she dared to partake of any of it.

'Come on – grab a plate!' Audrey took charge and handed one to her.

Mrs Ryder glanced up at her and then down at the plate. 'Oh, go on then!'

Everyone laughed and got to work with the very serious business of eating, and what a treat it was. There was only one tiny accident when Lisa dripped butter from her asparagus down the front of her dress, which necessitated an urgent rush to the sink before her emerald gown was stained.

When everybody was fully sated, Harrie made a move to start tidying away. Mrs Ryder slapped her hand.

'Don't you dare!' she said. 'That's my job. You just go and enjoy yourselves. Have some more champagne and I'll soon have this looking shipshape.'

'But it's so late,' Harrie said, glancing at the clock and seeing that it was after ten.

Mrs Ryder put her hands on her hips. 'It's the last evening of your holiday and I *won't* let you spend it in the kitchen!'

'In that case, I'll top up the champers,' Lisa said.

Harrie approached Mrs Ryder and, before she could protest, she'd wrapped her arms around her.

'Thank you!' she said.

'Don't be silly! Now, go and enjoy yourself.'

The three friends left the kitchen and Audrey drew the curtains in the living room as Harrie switched on the lamps, realising that it would be the last time they went through this simple nightly ritual. As she turned on the last one, she let her fingers lightly touch the blue-and-white porcelain of the lamp base, her eyes soft as the warm amber lit the room.

'Come and sit down, Harrie,' Lisa said, and Harrie took her glass from the table and sipped it. She then noticed Audrey.

'You've got a great fat smile on your face,' Harrie told her.

'I was just thinking of Mike.'

'I bet you can't wait to show him your new dress,' Lisa said.

'Yes, but I'm not sure what he'll make of the tiara!'

They laughed.

'Have you heard from Alfie?' Audrey asked Lisa.

'Yes. He texted me yesterday.'

'So he has your number?' Harrie teased.

'Of course. We're good friends. He's started at the outdoor-activity centre.'

'Already?' Audrey said.

'Yes, and he loves it.'

'Where is it?' Harrie asked.

'The Lake District. On the banks of Windermere.'

Audrey gave a knowing look. 'Oh, yes?'

'What's that supposed to mean?'

'I mean that Cumbria isn't that far away from Leeds, is it?' Audrey pointed out.

Lisa gave Audrey a weary sort of look. 'It might be hard for you to believe, but we were only ever friends. That's all. Just a nice easy-going summer friendship. Like Harrie's with that stone guy.'

'Samson! His name's Samson!'

'Yes, tell us what's been going on with him,' Audrey said.

'Nothing's been *going on* with him,' Harrie stated. 'We've just been – I don't know – sharing time together.'

Lisa smiled and her eyes shone in the lamplight. '*Sharing time together*,' she repeated. 'I like that.'

Harrie nodded. 'I do too.'

They sat sipping their champagne for a few moments.

'I can't believe the summer's nearly over,' Lisa said at last.

'What will you do when you get back home, Aud?' Harrie asked.

'I was just wondering that myself,' she said. 'I don't think Mike's going to let me return to the school straightaway.'

'Maybe you can have that Norfolk holiday you were talking about,' Harrie prompted.

'Maybe.'

'What will you do, Harrie?' Lisa asked, her face anxious now.

Harrie took another sip of champagne. The truth was, she hadn't thought much further ahead than the summer holidays. Everything beyond that seemed so vague and tenuous.

'I don't know,' she said honestly with a little laugh. 'There are some things that – you know – need sorting out.' She gave a little shrug and smiled.

'Anything we can help with?' Audrey asked.

Harrie took a deep breath. 'Yes. There probably is.'

'Good,' Audrey said.

'Yes. You mustn't forget to let us help you,' Lisa said.

'I won't. I promise,' Harrie told them, and she really meant it.

It was then that Mrs Ryder came into the room.

'Dishwasher's on and all the leftovers are wrapped up and in the fridge.'

'You've done all that already?' Lisa said in amazement.

'Not much to it, really.'

'Please take some of the leftovers home with you, Gladys,' Harrie said.

'No, no. That's for you girls.' She took off her pinny, revealing the splendour of her midnight-blue gown again.

Harrie stood up. 'Well, we can't thank you enough for tonight and for the whole summer too. It wouldn't have been the same without you. It really wouldn't.' Harrie opened her arms to give her a hug and Mrs Ryder graciously accepted, her face flushing in delight.

'I have to say, this is one of the nicest jobs I've ever had,' she told them. 'It's not every day I get to work in a building like this and for such appreciative people either.'

Audrey and Lisa stood up and joined in with the hugging.

'I wish I could take you home with me,' Audrey told her. 'I'm going to miss having my meals prepared and my bed made for me.'

'Yes, thank you so much,' Lisa said. 'I have to admit that I was a bit scared of you when we first met, but you turned out all right in the end.'

Mrs Ryder's mouth dropped open in surprise. 'Scared – of *me*?'

'I think we all were,' Audrey admitted.

Mrs Ryder tutted and shook her head good-naturedly. 'You young women!'

Harrie laughed. 'Oh, how I love being called a young woman!'

'You take care of yourselves now, won't you?'

'We will!' Lisa said.

'And thank you for your kindness, Harriet,' Mrs Ryder added, her hands stroking the silky blue folds of her dress.

'You're more than welcome.'

They all embraced again and everyone's eyes filled with tears as Mrs Ryder walked into the kitchen and picked her handbag up for the last time and left the priory.

'That's really it, then,' Audrey said. 'That's the end of the holiday.'

Lisa sighed and brushed the tears away from her cheeks. 'Are you sure we can't stay, Harrie? Can we not lock ourselves in and refuse to go?'

'I think there might be somebody else wanting to enjoy a holiday here tomorrow.'

'Yes, but they're not as important as *us*, are they?' Lisa said.

Harrie grinned. 'I don't think they'd see it like that.'

'I thought this summer would last forever,' Lisa said.

'Forever doesn't last as long these days, does it?' Harrie said.

'No,' Audrey agreed. 'Remember when you were a child and the summer holidays seemed to stretch endlessly? I wish we could get that feeling back again, although I have felt it here this summer – that wonderful feeling of everything going on forever.'

'Have you?' Harrie asked, and Audrey nodded.

'I just wish it could last a little bit longer.'

Harrie smiled, doing her very best to hold the tears back. 'Me too.'

Later, in her room, Harrie looked at her reflection in the old mottled mirror. It seemed a shame to have to take her tiara off, but she couldn't very well sleep in it, could she? Slowly, her hands reached up and she gently removed it, holding it in her hands as if it were the most precious thing in the world. Would she ever get a chance to wear it again, she wondered? Possibly not. But it had made her feel positively regal for the space of one evening and that was enough. It was another of those little life moments she'd promised herself. The sort that you had to go out and meet halfway. The summer had been filled with wonderful moments and she remembered some of them now, from her arrival at the priory and walking through the hushed cloisters for the first time to welcoming her friends. She remembered Samson's angel and the misericords he'd shown her. She remembered his big dusty boots, and the way he'd held her in his arms when she'd cried. She remembered Honor's revelation about Benny, and Lisa's meditation session with the candles.

She smiled as her mind leapt from one memory to the next. There'd been the power cut and dancing in the rain. Cake-cutting, tiara-wearing, pool-swimming, meadow-walking, food-sharing and laughing. Lots of laughing.

Such heart-warming, soul-enriching memories.

'And I won't forget a single one,' she told herself.

Chapter 22

The suitcases were packed.

Harrie stood in the middle of the kitchen. Audrey and Lisa had decanted the food from the fridge into cool bags and were now sitting in the garden waiting for Harrie to join them. It was nine thirty, which meant they had just half an hour until they officially had to leave. She took a deep breath, slowly walking through the downstairs rooms in case a stray novel had been left on the arm of a chair or a sun hat left hanging from a peg. But all was tidy. All trace of the three women had been removed, which meant she had one last thing to do.

Picking up her handbag, Harrie made her way through the cool morning cloisters towards the chapel, listening out for the light tap-tap-tap of Samson's chisel. How she would miss coming here, she thought, wondering if the next group of holidaymakers would appreciate Samson as much as she had come to. Or would they see him as an annoyance and something to be endured? She truly hoped not.

'Hello?' she called as she approached the scaffolding.

'Harrie?'

'For the last time, I'm afraid. We're just about ready to leave.'

His sandy head popped over the top and he beckoned to her with a hand.

'I can come up?' she asked.

'Of course you can. I've got something to show you today.'

Putting her handbag down, she grasped the side of the ladder with nervous fingers, wondering what it was Samson wanted to share with her.

'Hey,' she said once she reached the top. 'So, what have you been hiding from me all this time?'

'The angel,' he said.

'Have you finished work on her?'

'Yep. She's all done. Safe now for another few hundred years. But there's something else.'

'What?'

He pointed to a stone just behind the angel's left wing. Harrie peered closely and spotted a mark in the golden limestone. It was an 'H'.

'Oh, how wonderful!' she said. 'Your stonemason's mark?'

Samson glanced at her and shook his head. 'Not exactly.'

Harrie frowned. 'Is that not "H" for *Haverstock*?' she asked.

Samson rubbed his chin. 'No,' he told her. 'It's "H" for *Harriet*.'

'You did this – for *me*?'

'Of course for you! This is your angel, Harrie.'

She looked at the angel once again, at the serene face and the strong wings. '*My* angel?'

'She's looking out for you,' he told her. 'I'm sure of it.'

Harrie reached out, her hand shaking as she sought to touch the beautiful single letter carved deep into the golden stone. *H for Harriet.* She really didn't know what to say and so she did the only thing she could and hugged Samson.

'Thank you,' she whispered. 'You've no idea what this means to me.'

She felt his arms close around her, awkwardly at first as if he hadn't expected such a display of emotion, but then she felt him relax and she heard him sigh. They stood like that for a moment, the silence of the chapel filling their souls.

'I have something for you,' she said at last, pulling away from him. 'But you'll have to come back down to earth to get it.'

'Okay,' he said.

Harrie took one last look at her angel, smiling up at the beautifully carved 'H' above her wing. Would anybody else ever see it, she wondered? Or would it be her and Samson's secret forever? Perhaps a future stonemason would find it and speculate on the identity of the mysterious 'H'.

Quickly, quietly, she got her phone out of her jacket pocket and took a photo.

'I want to take her with me,' she told Samson, and he nodded in understanding before the two of them climbed down the ladder to the chapel floor.

Harrie walked across to the chair where she'd left her handbag, opening it up to retrieve the little blue hardback book she'd placed inside.

'It's not much but I wanted to give you something to remember me by,' she said as she handed the book to Samson. 'It's got some pictures of the priory and the first church you took me to see.'

'Has it?'

'Yes. There's a whole page about the misericords there.'

He opened the book.

'I've written in the front so you can't resell it now,' she said with a little laugh.

She watched as he read her inscription.

To Samson. Thank you for making my summer so special. With love, Harriet. x

He looked up at her. 'Thank you.'

'You're welcome.'

They stood looking at each other for what seemed like an age and then he moved forward an inch, his hand reaching out to touch her cheek in a gentle caress.

'You're special, Harrie.'

She shook her head.

'Yes, you are. And I won't ever forget you.'

Somewhere high above them came the feathery sound of a dove in flight. Harrie was going to miss the jackdaws and the doves that lived amongst the ruins, filling the air alternately with raucous calls then soft ones. She'd miss the brilliant pink valerian growing out of the stonework at bold angles. She'd miss the gentle sound of the trees that cushioned the priory from the outside world, and she'd miss the cool stone floors and the shadows in the cloisters.

But, most of all, she'd miss Samson.

Reaching out, she took his left hand in her right one and held it for a moment.

'I'm going to go now,' she told him. 'My friends are waiting outside and my daughter's come down to drive me home.'

'Shall I—'

'Stay here. Please,' she said quickly. 'Don't come with me and don't let's say goodbye.'

Samson nodded, his bright eyes watching her attentively.

She smiled, trying to capture the beauty of his face in her memory because she knew that she'd need it in the weeks to come. Then she leaned forward and kissed his rough cheek.

'Harrie . . .'

She felt him squeeze her hand and then she slowly removed her own, turning around and quickly leaving the chapel.

Once outside, she looked up into a sky the colour of forget-me-nots. The sun was climbing and the day was already warm and filled with the scent of lavender.

Audrey and Lisa were sitting on the bench in the courtyard next to Honor. Harrie was glad to see her daughter. She was feeling tired all of a sudden, as if the whole of the summer was just catching up with her.

'There you are!' Lisa called, waving to her.

Harrie approached them, hugging her daughter close to her before taking one last glance back at the priory.

'Ready?' Audrey asked.

Harrie turned to face them and nodded. 'Yes,' she said. 'I'm ready.'

The Next Summer

There were three women sitting in the courtyard garden of Melbury Priory and each was wearing a gold tree-of-life necklace.

'I'm really glad we booked this place again even if it is just for three nights,' Lisa said.

'Me too,' Audrey agreed. 'Harrie would approve, wouldn't she?'

Honor nodded. 'I'm so glad I came back.'

'You should have brought Benny with you,' Lisa said.

'No, he wanted to stay in Rome. I'm going to join him there next week. Then we'll be going on to Sicily.'

'Oh, to be young and travelling the world!' Audrey said with a sigh.

'What are you complaining about?' Lisa said. 'You've got the whole of Norfolk to enjoy and explore!'

'Yes, but only between guests,' Audrey said. 'I had no idea running a bed and breakfast would be so full-on!'

'Surely not as full-on as running your school?' Lisa asked.

'Oh, no! Nothing could ever compete with that.' Audrey grinned. 'You know, I never thought I'd say this, but Mike was right. I don't really miss London at all.'

Lisa did a double-take. 'Really?'

'I thought I might pine a bit, but I honestly haven't. I think we made a really good decision selling up in the suburbs.'

'And your business? Do you miss that?' Honor asked.

Audrey took a moment before answering. 'There's something about being close to the sea,' she said at last.

Lisa laughed. 'What kind of an answer is that?'

'It means, no – I don't miss it.'

'No? Do you think she's telling the truth, Honor, because I'm not convinced?'

'I think she is,' Honor said.

Audrey laughed at their confusion. 'I must admit that I rang the office a few times after handing everything over to my replacement. But, after that, Mike and I were so involved with getting our new home sorted and planning the bed and breakfast that I really didn't give it another thought.'

'Good old Mike,' Lisa said.

'Yes,' Audrey agreed. 'I'm a very lucky woman.'

A few moments passed.

'Are you still in touch with Alfie?' Audrey asked Lisa.

'We've exchanged a few texts,' Lisa told her. 'I got a postcard from him last week. He's taking a group of students to the Swiss Alps next month.'

'He'll be climbing Everest before you know it,' Audrey said.

'I wouldn't be at all surprised.'

'And how's the yoga?' Honor asked.

'Fantastic! I've got three venues fully booked for residential courses later this summer and the weekly classes are going well too.'

'Oh, that's great, Lisa! I'm so proud of you,' Audrey said.

Lisa beamed at her friend's approval. 'It was such a relief to give up all that commercial work.'

'So you haven't missed being an actress?' Honor asked.

'Not a bit!' Lisa told her, sighing in satisfaction.

It had been a beautiful day. The three women had walked out to the coast, wending their way back through the fields and the orchard and, every step of the way, they'd talked about or thought about Harrie. When they'd got back to the priory, they'd looked through the photo album Honor had made up of all the pictures they'd taken during that special summer holiday.

It had been seven months since that cold December day when they'd attended her funeral. The pain of losing her had been almost unbearable and the only reason they'd got through it was each other.

Audrey looked at Honor now as she gazed up at the clear summer sky. Harrie's beautiful daughter. A living legacy and a constant reminder of her mother's precious presence in their lives. Audrey smiled and then got up from her chair.

'Where are you going?' Lisa asked.

'Just for a walk.'

'Well, don't be too long,' Lisa told her. 'I'm going to make us cocktails for sundown.'

Audrey nodded and made her way across the grass. She wasn't quite sure where she was going, but something drew her towards the cloisters and, from there, to the chapel, her light summer shoes almost silent on the stone floor.

The scaffolding had long gone and it was hard to see what exactly Samson had been working on all those weeks. Harrie had known more about it than Audrey had. The work had fascinated her friend.

Audrey walked into the centre of the room, listening to the doves and looking up to admire the fan-vaulted ceiling, and that's when she saw it. At first, she couldn't quite make out what it was because it was so high up but, as she let her eyes focus, she could clearly see a beautiful angel carved in stone. It seemed strange that she hadn't noticed it last summer, but perhaps it had been obscured by the scaffolding.

She stood there for a few minutes, taking in the beauty of the place, the silence and the solitude, and then she turned to look at the angel again. There was something about it that made her smile, but she wasn't quite sure what. Maybe it was the gentle expression on its face or the way it seemed to be waving to her with those wonderful golden wings.

Audrey gazed at it for a little while longer, and then it came to her. She was quite certain about it and yet a part of her knew that she was being fanciful. All the same, as she slowly walked away from the chapel, she couldn't help feeling that their dear friend Harrie was watching over them all.

AUTHOR'S NOTE

When writing this novel, I was inspired by a wonderful post Leah Bracknell wrote on her Facebook page. Known for her role in *Emmerdale*, Leah was diagnosed with stage 4 lung cancer in 2016. I hope I managed to capture some of her spirit and joy for life in my character, Harrie.

With her kind permission, here is Leah's post:

Dearest friends,

Thank you so much from the bottom of my heart for your continued love and support. I truly feel it envelop me, and feel humbled, and so blessed, and grateful. It is magic and divine medicine, and its power is profound and deeply healing, and I wish I could share more of it around.

I am not frail, nor victim, nor sufferer, tragic, stricken, battling, dying. Labels not of my choosing. I choose — warrior, spirit, invincible, joy, love, grace, beauty, empowered, journey, adventure, growth, healing, laughter. I choose that having cancer makes me bigger, not smaller. I choose to celebrate LIFE. Come with me. Dance with me. Walk with me. Let us celebrate life together.

ACKNOWLEDGMENTS

To my wonderful friends Linda Gillard and Ellie Mead, who let me ask so many questions about their cancer and were so open and giving in their answers. You are two of the strongest and bravest women I know.

To my yogini, Sophia – thank you for teaching me how to stretch . . . and breathe!

To the publishing team at Lake Union, especially Sammia, Victoria and Bekah. It's a pleasure working with you all.

And to my husband, Roy – remembering that wonderful holiday at Woodspring Priory.

ABOUT THE AUTHOR

Photo © 2016 Roy Connelly

Victoria Connelly studied English Literature at Worcester University, got married in a medieval castle in the Yorkshire Dales and now lives in rural Suffolk with her artist husband, a young springer spaniel and a flock of ex-battery hens.

She is the author of two bestselling series, Austen Addicts and The Book Lovers, as well as many other novels and novellas. Her first published novel, *Flights of Angels*, was made into a film in 2008 by Ziegler Films in Germany. *The Runaway Actress* was shortlisted for the Romantic Novelists' Association's Romantic Comedy Novel award.

Ms Connelly loves books, films, walking, historic buildings and animals. If she isn't at her keyboard writing, she can usually be found in her garden either with a trowel in her hand or a hen on her lap.

Her website is www.victoriaconnelly.com and readers can follow her on Twitter @VictoriaDarcy and on Instagram @VictoriaConnellyAuthor.